THROUGH WATERFALLS

A Story of Love, Adventure, and Change

HEIDI MIRSHAH

THROUGH WATERFALLS. Copyright © 2025 Heidi Mirshah. All rights reserved.

ISBN: 9798306281117

Imprint: Independently Published

Chapter One

Laura happily put her bar exam results on the kitchen counter and was relieved she would not need to take that monstrous test again. She spent many nights up until three in the morning reading books so heavy her wrist hurt when she picked them up. There was a summer ahead of her, and she wanted to enjoy that instead of being her regular self always focusing on what needed to be done or worrying about everyone else. She had tired herself out by always giving and not thinking about whether people deserved it.

It was in her quiet moments alone when all of her deepest thoughts came to the surface about ways she wanted to improve her life and herself. It was lightly raining outside and with each patter that fell, Laura went through her memories, especially ones of past relationships. Laura often thought about relationships when she had a spare moment. She felt that in relationships, people saw the best and the worst parts of life. The phone rang, and it was her friend, Chloe.

"Hey! What are you up to these days? I can't believe you're going into family law. I'm glad I decided to go on and get a business degree after school," said Chloe.

"Ya, well you were always a non-confrontational person. It makes sense," said Laura.

"Ya, who knows. Who the heck knows what they are doing when they are young?"

"That's the problem. Most people don't. There should be some training class in school that teaches people about that stuff. Too many people just get sidetracked and lost," said Laura. The two finished their conversation, and Laura went back to doing the dishes and thinking of the past. She thought of the intelligent and attractive guy, Andy, she used to know. She would run and make him chicken soup when he caught a cold and call him whenever he asked her to, but he would freely ignore her messages when they were not convenient for him. It was good that she left him, but looking back, it had taken her too long to leave. She couldn't help but wonder what had changed that she paid attention to these things now and didn't before. She could not pinpoint any reason for it, but she also tried to remember the good things about Andy. She had probably stayed for a while because of his good traits.

Duck, North Carolina was quiet, full of flowers, and ocean air. It had a fair share of summer visitors for the beach, but that was fun as the small town would come alive. She would see all the visitors, mostly families, come into town with wide-eyed kids and tons of beach balls. People were always joking and anticipating all of the things they would do on their one week off that year. Laura could enjoy the beach surroundings and be by the water daily if she wanted. She would take long walks on the beach to clear her thoughts and watch the seagulls. Those simple moments meant a lot. She would get in touch with herself and her emotions during those solitary walks. That morning, she decided to go out onto the porch with her morning coffee. She had bought a new brand at the grocery store last week that was called Coffee of Passion which was an odd name, but somehow the very light tropical scent worked even in a coffee.

Laura's neighbor, Grace, walked up. Grace was sixty-four and lived alone next door. Her husband passed away two years ago, and she spent most of her time gardening and making pottery that she sold in a store in town. Her vases were beautiful, and Laura bought a couple of them and displayed them in her dining room. She must have been a talented person in art, but she had never used it in her career as a physical therapist. The two vases she bought from Grace had copper and gold stripes going all around them and when the sunlight hit them, they would brighten up the space around them. It seemed like the light would carry all the way across the room sometimes, but Laura wasn't sure if it really did.

"Hi, Laura. Out enjoying the morning?" asked Grace.

"Well, hi, yes. Thank goodness it's Saturday. The past week has been exhausting."

"Why, were you busy with a new man? You know how demanding that can be!" Grace said with a smile.

"Oh no. I have no time for that. Relationships take time and right now that is not for me!"

"So, what are your plans for today? Want to come over for lunch?" asked Grace.

"Thanks, not today. I'll call you about coming over soon though." Laura knew she needed alone time that day. She was proud of herself that she had finally learned to pay attention to her needs instead of saying yes to everything people asked of her.

"Ok, then, I'm going to go for a walk. I'll see you soon," said Grace.

Grace walked away around the circular road and into the distance, not in any rush to get to where she was going.

Grace had a peaceful energy about her and was not one of these people who got old and became bitter. Laura wondered how things would be when she was Grace's age. Grace's husband's passing had taken a toll on her, and she did not have very many friends to distract her. It seemed that she knew how to be happy alone though, and that was a skill Laura wanted to learn. She was already pretty good at it and had never been the clingy type; most men she dated before really did not like that although they somehow liked her anyway. It seemed to Laura based on her experience that many men wanted a woman to keep chasing them and to need them. Laura did not really have that aspect to her. She would spend time with men when she respected them and liked talking to them, and she did not have many other reasons for that.

So far in life, Laura was either planning tasks, doing work, or usually helping others with their problems. She only recently started thinking about her own emotions and intuitions. She liked living next door to Grace not only because Grace was a nice person, but they learned from each other. Grace loved to hear about all of the interesting academic theories Laura was always talking about from the meaning of life to how to negotiate a divorce agreement. Laura liked to hear Grace talk of her many years of married life and the different adventures she and her husband went on in the past. It was a great relationship, and Laura was grateful that she lived next door to Grace. An orange and black butterfly landed on Laura's white, wicker table. The life of a butterfly - just flitting around from one flower to another – not sitting in traffic, having the flu, or wearing tight shoes. She enjoyed being outside in the fresh air with her tropical coffee and the butterfly for a few minutes longer and then went inside to get ready for Rebecca to arrive later that day.

    Her closest friend, Rebecca, was coming over for dinner, and Laura was almost done preparing the meal and the house. She had light pink peonies on the dining table; she loved how scrumptious those flowers were. She had fluffed up all the pillows on the couch including the one with Venetian gondolas all over it. When she had someone over for dinner, she always wanted the entire space to be perfect. Dinner parties were never just about the food for Laura. She was ready for some time with Rebecca just talking and figuring out their summer plans. There was piano music playing in the background while Laura finished throwing some chopped parsley on the salad. Cooking and music were always a good combination and a combination that helped get all of the day's stress out of her. She opened the oven door to take out the baked squash side dish. The house smelled sweet like a historic cottage in France where the owner liked to cook a lot. The main dish was baked cod in a white saffron sauce, Rebecca's favorite dish. The cod smelled more like butter and saffron than fish which was a good thing.

"Hi there!" Rebecca said as she bounced into Laura's house. Laura always loved time with Rebecca because Rebecca had such good energy. She was a genuinely loving person deep from the inside and everyone could tell. Laura felt lucky to have had her as a friend for so many years.

"Hey! You are right on time as usual! Come have a seat while I finish getting dinner ready."

"Ok, can I help you with anything?" asked Rebecca.

"Nope, I'm fine you know how I am in the kitchen. I have to do everything alone or else I get confused and start putting salt on the cheesecake." Laura just wanted Rebecca to sit and relax with her glass of wine and be served by her best friend. A little steam was rising from the cod, and it smelled like saffron, butter, and lemon. Too bad saffron was so expensive, and she could not use it more often.

As smart as Rebecca was, she never went to college - not that everyone who went to college was smart. She was always one that knew what she wanted and did not want in life. Laura could not say the same about herself. Her indecisiveness had cost her, and she had finally realized that. She was not sure exactly what it had cost her but she just knew it had. If she had to guess she'd say it had cost her adventure, and it had cost her time. Rebecca was twenty-six and felt like she was at a crossroads in her life. It was a good thing she was at Laura's house because the women always could help each other figure things out. The table was set and looked beautiful with light, orange wispy napkins tied loosely with straw for each place setting.

"So, this summer I want to go to Italy and meet a good man," Rebecca said with a glimmer in her eyes. Rebecca had started to think that it was time to be responsible and think of things like the future, and when she thought of the future, she also pictured a husband. As independent as she was, she still thought about this. Sometimes she wondered if it was a waste of time to think about marriage in modern times. Was that something for the 1800's?

"Are you kidding me? Why would you go there? Are you planning to leave me here in North Carolina while you prance around Italy? I thought we were going to do something together this summer," said Laura.

"It's just something I want to do and you know me when I get an idea in my head, I tend to follow it! Why don't you come with me?" asked Rebecca.

"Yeah, that's true you've always been that way." Laura remembered how things were when she would just go more with her heart in a free-flowing way the way Rebecca lived her life. These days that just was not true for Laura, and she noticed that it had made her feel more stuck in life. So much planning, just doing duties, and much less living. Then again, a true accomplishment in life was to be happy with just doing tasks and looking at them in a more meditative way. There had to be some balance between these two points.

"So, are you going to come with me?" asked Rebecca interrupting Laura's thoughts.

"I don't know. This summer I was planning to just prepare for my start at the Baker law firm in September. I mean I thought we would come up with some ideas of things to do together during the summer, but I'm not sure I'm ready for a big trip."

"Oh, come on Laura, you've become way too responsible the past several years. You never think of doing things just for fun anymore."

"Maybe my definition of fun has changed that's all." Laura said that and believed it, but she also felt that some of what Rebecca was saying was true.

"Who knows, let me think about it, Rebecca, maybe you're right." Rebecca wished that Laura would decide to come with her because it would make the trip a lot more fun; at the same time, if Laura did not come Rebecca was prepared to go alone. She would sit in restaurants alone, walk around town alone, all of it. She wanted to expand and explore. Time was going by so quickly. They decided to sit on the porch at the end of the meal and just continue talking. The ladies did not need too much to entertain them when they were together. Laura needed these conversations with Rebecca to center herself and to remind herself that there were always good people around and fun times to be had. Rebecca enjoyed talking to Laura because she was so smart and could always help her problem-solve like when Rebecca did not know how to solve a fight between herself and her last boyfriend. He wanted her to dress differently, and she didn't think how she dressed had anything to do with him. Laura came over to her house and talked to both of them, and by the end of that, they were no longer fighting, and Rebecca was dressing just a tiny bit more like what her boyfriend wanted. The ladies were so open with each other that they would tell each other at least a few times a year how much the other meant to them. That kind of open communication seemed to be of a bygone era but not for them.

Rebecca left at eleven o'clock, and Laura thought a little more about possible trips she could take during the summer. She was not planning to take a trip until Rebecca put the idea into her head. This evening for some reason, Laura had an urge to take a trip alone. Italy was a wonderful place to visit, but Laura thought it was just too tried-and-true. She started to do research about New Zealand. The country was not Morocco or Belize or some remote unheard-of island in the middle of nowhere, but it seemed more unique than a trip to Italy. She wasn't the type to enjoy a hut in the woods of Belize anyway. Would it make sense to go to New Zealand especially on her own? Would she get bored and not know what to do with herself? Rebecca was going to Italy so there was no point in asking her about a trip to New Zealand. Besides, going alone would give Laura the extra challenge she wanted at this point in her life. She had recently realized that she had too strong of a desire to play everything safe. It had held her back in life to some extent.

Laura's house was a little crème one-story with lots of windows. She enjoyed it, but the problem was homes always needed a little fixing. Her kitchen sink had started to leak, and there was water inside the cabinet so the plumber would be showing up later that day. Good to be getting things done, but yet another day of just responsibility. Too many of Laura's recent years had been like that – leaking kitchen sinks and stubbed toes. Somehow though, she had a feeling that was going to change.

Chapter Two

At 10 am, the doorbell rang and a tall, blond man who looked like he had not eaten for days was standing in her doorway.

"Hi there, are you Randy?"

"Well, yes ma'am. I'm here for your 10:00 sink appointment."

"Great, follow me." Laura took him through the house which was immaculate and well-organized. No need for

Randy to have to step over anything or brush anything aside to get to the kitchen. Laura felt better when everything in her life was organized.

"Well, here it is," said Laura. She opened the kitchen sink cabinet and showed him the leak.

"Oh, I see. It looks worse than it is ma'am. I think I'll be done fixing this in about twenty minutes."

"Great, that's a relief, "said Laura. Randy started to get his tools out and started to work on the plumbing under the sink. He seemed like quite a peaceful man. Laura could not figure out why she thought that, but he just had that kind of air about him. Laura had noticed over the years that her intuitions were often correct. She wished that she had followed them more often in her life and nixed the bad habit she had of second guessing herself too often.

"So do you live here all alone?" asked Randy. If some creepy man had asked her that, Laura would have been a little concerned but with Randy it just did not seem like a strange question.

"Yes, I do. I've finished law school and am going to be starting a new job in the Fall."

"Oh, well congratulations. It's nice to see a person who's not a computer programmer these days! It seems like everyone works in computing!"

"Thanks! I know what you mean! The world has definitely taken some sort of turn. I'm not sure if it's all good," said Laura.

"Ya, people don't talk to each other enough anymore and are getting more disconnected," said Randy.

"I agree completely. Too many screens and not enough people anymore. Well, let me know if you need anything. I'm going to do some work," said Laura.

"Sure, thanks Ms. Townsend." Randy thought that Laura looked too mature for her age and that she was taking life a little too seriously. She was always hurrying and looked like she could not really relax. Randy wondered why a person as young as her would act that way. When he was her age, he walked slowly, talked slowly, and didn't have a care in the world.

After a few minutes, Laura decided to start researching the trip idea. The first thing she saw about New Zealand mentioned volcanoes and glaciation as well as busy harbors and adventure sports. A country that she imagined was very green with water everywhere. She wanted to be away from everything she had ever known and see if that helped give her different perspectives. She remembered a philosophy class she was in during college when the professor had them change their spot in the room and look at a plant that was sitting at the front of the room. It was amazing how the same plant looked completely different when looked at from a different location in the room. Maybe all of life was that way.

In those philosophy classes they talked about things like the meaning of life, beauty, war, and almost anything else a person could think of. She always had a broad perspective because of those classes. Even as she looked at pictures of New Zealand, she found herself thinking about what the trip could mean. She was not the type of person to view the trip as a simple trip. She felt there was a reason she had this desire at this point in her life and that she was somehow drawn to New Zealand. She wondered whether it was the need to challenge herself or whether she was just bored with the regular routines of life. Law school had been very challenging, and it was full of very serious people. Despite her love of reading and writing, Laura was a bit more lighthearted than most of the other students at law school. She didn't think life should be taken quite as seriously as they seemed to take it.

Something welled up in Laura as she scrolled through the New Zealand pictures showing boats and people smiling. She really wanted to go to a beautiful place and be alone for a while. It was amazing how people lost touch with the things they wanted until they suddenly welled up inside. The conversation with Rebecca had gotten her thinking and trying to look beyond her duties at least for a few minutes.

Chapter Three

Randy sounded like he was almost done with the kitchen sink. Laura heard the clatter of tools being put back into their places. As she headed downstairs, she saw an old picture of herself on a boat in the Chesapeake Bay that her dad took when she was fifteen. Her blond hair was blowing in the breeze, and she had a smile on her face that showed the last remnants of a blue icee eaten earlier. Her mother was standing next to her looking tired as mothers often do. Her mom was a great mom, but she never spent much time developing herself outside of her role as a mother. That was okay because being a mom was the most important job in the world, but Laura wondered whether she ever regretted that. Most moms gave so much, and unfortunately many times people did not appreciate it. She had seen that in her mom's friends and even in her own friends' parents. Laura got to the bottom step and saw Randy packing his tools.

"Well, ma'am, it's all taken care of. We will put our bill in the mail if that works for you."

"Sure, thank you so much. Would you like to sit down and have a cup of coffee before you leave?" Randy looked like his back hurt, and Laura wanted him to have a break.

"Well, I only have about ten minutes before I have to get to my next job, but that's very kind of you. Sure." Laura went into the kitchen and started making Randy's coffee.

"Please have a seat while I get the coffee," said Laura.

"Oh sure, thanks." Randy was not used to a customer ever offering him a cup of coffee, but it felt good that someone seemed to care to do that. Most days after work, his back and legs hurt a lot, and it felt good to be able to properly sit down for a moment during the day. Randy sat down on Laura's soft couch and started looking at her coffee table book. It was a book about art and poetry. He slowly turned the pages and thought about how he never looked at books like this. Laura was nearby in the kitchen getting the coffee ready.

"You know, there are so many sophisticated people out there that create these things. Sometimes I feel bad that I never had a passion like that. I just never really knew what I wanted to do. Then I fell into this type of work," said Randy. He looked down at the book, and Laura sensed sadness on his face.

"If you ask me, work is work! We all end up doing something and no one should really feel superior to anyone else," said Laura.

"I remember being twenty years old and telling my mom that I really didn't know what I wanted to do with my life. It did not seem like such a big question at the time. Everything is so carefree when you are twenty. Even when it's not," said Randy. The coffee was ready, so Laura started pouring it into her nice, light blue mugs that she only used when people came over. Laura wondered whether having to kneel under sinks and having to contort the body that way all day gave him sore muscles at the end of the day. She appreciated the fact that there were people with these skills. She brought the coffee to the living room and sat down on the chair opposite Randy.

"So do you do a lot of plumbing jobs per day?" asked Laura.

"I do. For our company to stay in business, I need to do at least ten per day," said Randy.

"Well, I hope that you aren't too tired by the end of every day."

"Thanks. It really depends on the day and sometimes which customers I have to deal with. I have a daughter who is ready to hang out as soon as I get home. She is really a great girl. Unfortunately, her mom and I got divorced two years ago, but she has adjusted to that now. When things seem tough, I think of her and just keep going," said Randy. Laura started to wonder how old Randy was. He looked older than her, but she really could not tell. His hair was blond and straight, and he looked like if you put him in a suit he would look like a certified public accountant. He just had this settled kind of sadness in him. It was the type of sadness that seemed it may never leave. Laura often picked up on people's energies, which was a blessing and a curse.

"I'm sorry about your divorce. I hope that you have been able to get through that transition ok," said Laura.

"It's much tougher than you think it's going to be, but yes, that part of my life is definitely over now." He felt that it would not be something he would ever be completely over though since he had a child with his ex-wife. Laura found herself wanting to talk to Randy more. There was something about him that just seemed intriguing in some way that Laura could not put her finger on. He seemed like he hid a big part of his mind from people. She generally didn't like people like that; people that were like fortresses no matter how close you were to them. She thought that Randy was probably limiting himself a lot by being like that. What was the point of being on this planet with billions of other people if each person just stayed locked in their own mind? As hurtful as relationships could end up, they also could bring the most joy in the world if someone was open to it. Well, maybe she only thought that way because she was mildly extroverted. Regardless of that, she believed strongly in her heart that people should share themselves with each other. Laura could not imagine life any other way.

"Well, thanks so much for the coffee, ma'am. It was really a pleasure to meet you," said Randy.

"Not a problem at all!" said Laura. Laura was stumbling to think of something to say to leave the door open on them talking again in the future. She did not know why she had an interest in talking in the future, but she felt it inside.

"Um, by any chance, would you like to stay in touch Randy? I don't mean to be too forward, but you seem like a nice guy, and it may be nice to stay connected," said Laura as her face flushed with blood, and she felt heat surge into her head. She was surprised that her body had such a reaction to asking Randy a simple question. She figured it wasn't something she did often.

"That sounds great! I wanted to ask you the same thing but wasn't sure how to do it." Randy was excited and relieved that Laura had asked the question that he was thinking of. Randy took his business card out of his back pocket and handed it to Laura and with that started to walk out the front door. Laura was glad that she mustered up the nerve to ask Randy if he wanted to stay in touch. There were so many situations like this where she just let them pass by. As she had gotten older, she realized that many times in life there was only one chance to do something.

That evening, Laura decided to lie down and watch a movie. She promised herself that sometimes, no matter what was calling for her attention, she would just STOP. Her body was giving her a signal to stop, and she had finally started noticing those signals instead of ignoring them. She lied down on her bed and started looking at what movie options there were. As she clicked through the channels, a picture of a lady running through snowy mountains caught her attention. As she watched, it became clear that the woman was being chased by something or someone. The phone started to ring. It was her mom.

"Hi, mom. How are you?"

"Good, Laura dear. What are you up to tonight?"

"I'm watching a movie right now."

"Laura, when are you going to find yourself a boyfriend? You know, if you ever want to have kids, you are starting to get old!" Candace wanted to get straight to the point. Candace had been worried about the decisions her daughter was making for several years now; perhaps she was overreacting, but she knew she had to say something at least. Obviously, she had been really responsible and gone to law school, but Candace was worried about her personal life – the family, the marriage, and the kids.

"Mom, not everyone has to have kids, right? I'm not sure what I want to do in that department yet. Can we just not talk about this?" Laura got annoyed by this kind of badgering from her mother. Many women no longer even got married, yet her mother seemed to think that she should.

"Ok, well, enjoy the movie then." The ladies said their goodbyes, and Candace hung up the phone and hoped she wouldn't spend the whole night worrying about Laura and her seeming lack of interest in truly settling down in the way Candace expected it. After they hung up the phone, Laura continued to watch the movie. The woman in the movie was wearing pink from head to toe and continued to run through the mountains. It looked like it was almost dusk and she just kept running. Suddenly, the woman entered what looked like an abandoned cottage at the foot of a large mountain. She opened the deep brown, creaky door and inside there were people drinking and laughing. From the outside, it looked like there would be no one in the cottage, but it was full to capacity. There seemed to be too many people for the size of the main room.

The sounds of violin music and comradery permeated the cottage as the woman entered looking tired and distraught. She kept turning her head from left to right as if she was looking for just the right person that could help her. The contrast between the fear on the woman's face and the happiness of all of the people around her was odd. Laura decided to turn the movie off. The woman just looked too distraught, and right now Laura wanted a movie to take her away to an island or a party not to fear or negative anticipation.

Chapter Four

The next day, Laura threw some white shorts on and a bright yellow top and headed outdoors to do some weeding in her yard. The back yard was shaped in a strange almost triangular way, but Laura liked having a little back yard. When she looked out at this triangular yard, she felt like she had her own little corner on Earth where she could feel free and tend her plants. She found that when she was watering her plants or digging soil to plant something, her mind was calm, and she thought of pleasant things.

Laura bent down and smelled something like lavender or rosemary or something very much herbal. She knew some things about plants but did not know enough about them to know what that was coming from. The fragrance was very calming though, and she felt like she was in a remote village in Scotland that had magical flowers in it as the fragrance wafted through her nose. As she started to pull weeds out, she looked around the yard a bit. Copper colored bushes and some straggly yellow bushes, no flowers, and a big maple tree. Rebecca had got her thinking a bit about how responsible she had become. Soon the summer would be over, and she would have to start a demanding job at the Baker law firm. Instead of being on a trip, at a concert, or hanging out with friends, she was here spending the day weeding her yard. She very much enjoyed the time alone and the time in nature, but at the same time she realized that she had become almost robotic in the way she lived her life. Laura decided right there and then while pulling a particularly tough weed, she was leaving for New Zealand within two weeks. She did not care how much extra her ticket would cost because it was so late nor any of the other details. She would just need to get a visitor's visa if they required that for American travelers and do whatever paperwork was necessary to go.

Two weeks later, Laura got out of the cab and just completely stopped moving finding herself in New Zealand. The beauty around her was mesmerizing. There was a cool breeze wafting over her face and the fragrance of what smelled like honeysuckle plant or something similar to that. When she arrived in New Zealand, it was not a fully sunny day, but there were rays of sun coming down in angles onto the pavement in front of her. The light looked a bit different than in North Carolina. She wasn't sure why. Maybe there was some meteorological difference here. This was actually New Zealand! What a long flight she had just endured, and she still could not believe she was here. What the hell had she done just showing up here? Was this even safe to do alone?

She approached her hotel with her bags and looked at the glass doors and the beautiful potted plants outside of the building - greens, reds, and whites. She always liked the hospitality industry because they paid so much attention to creating beauty for people to enjoy. Some of people's best lifetime memories were created in hotels. She took a moment to appreciate being able to stay at this hotel since it looked so inviting and upscale. There was a good crowd of people milling about inside the front hall, and at every turn, a hotel employee asked her if she needed help with her bags or whether she would like a Lemon & Paeora drink. Apparently, that was a special drink made in New Zealand with lemon and water. She accepted one from the staff. It was cold and tasted like a grown-up version of the lemonade she grew up drinking.

Her mom, Candace, was a bit worried about this solo trip, but she always encouraged her daughter to do these things while she was young because as her mother said, time goes faster and faster with each year. Her mother would have liked this hotel. It was decorated in a classy and sophisticated way with gold, geometric vases and exotic plants all around. There was gentle music playing in the background as well. Laura walked through the lobby and was surprised when she saw a fountain that looked to be seventy feet tall pouring down different colored water onto a makeshift boat that was floating backwards and forwards in the waves. There were multi-colored fish swimming around the boat, and they had even created a gentle sound like a ship makes running over water. If it weren't for creative people designing such things, the world would be a much less interesting place. She slowly walked and made her way to her room. Upon entering her room, she resisted the urge to immediately start reading about places she should go and things she should do. Unpacking, though, made sense to do right away. Then she would feel all at home. A few minutes later, someone knocked on her door.

"Yes, who is it?" Laura asked without opening the door.

"Yes, ma'am it's just the hotel staff. I want to drop off some extra blankets and a bottle of champagne for you." This hotel really seemed to want to take care of its guests. She felt so pampered already. Laura opened the door and saw a young man standing there in a formal navy and white work uniform with the most luxurious beige blankets Laura had ever seen and a large bottle of champagne in the other hand. Looking at him standing there with those items in his hands felt like a deep tissue massage that had all of the stress out of the body in forty-five minutes.

"Thank you, sir, what a pleasant surprise." Well, she was here alone so she was not sure if she needed the champagne, but then again, who did not need champagne? Laura closed the door and set the items down. She was starting to feel the stress melt out of her body. How little it took sometimes to turn anything from bad to good. If only people were better at recognizing that. She felt so happy to be in this hotel room with not a care in the world and only the anticipation of exploring New Zealand starting the next day.

She opened her eyes to sunshine rushing in through the windows of her hotel room. It was 7 am, and Laura had the entire day to explore Wellington. She had to keep reminding herself not to rush. It was just her habit to run even when it was possible to slow down. She had become automated and non-thinking in that way. She gently reminded herself that she wasn't rushing to an appointment and that she needed to slow down and take the sights in. Laura stepped out of the hotel at nine-thirty without a map or an idea of where she was going. Most people she traveled with in the past always wanted to know what time they were going to do what, but Laura wanted to change all of that here.

One time, she remembered going on a trip with her good friend Sara, and all Sara could do on the trip was run. There was no sitting and having gelato. No sitting and watching the birds in the courtyard. It was all about getting to the next destination. This was part of the pleasure of being on this trip by herself. She would not need to chase after anyone. She left that trip with Sara more exhausted and negative than before she went. Sara was chaotic in her mind and never satisfied with where she was. Laura had tried talking to her about that and tried to explain to her why it was important to be content with little things and not to always look for the next big thing, but none of it seemed to get through Sara's brain. She would be running so fast that she could barely even hear what Laura was saying and viewed most of it as garbage. Laura knew that Sara was just a very unhappy person deep inside, but unfortunately some people didn't care to improve.

The street outside of the hotel was made from red cobblestone, and it felt good to walk on that instead of always concrete or asphalt. Not everything should be about functionality after all. All around there was grass and little bushes she had never seen before that overflowed with different shapes of flowers. She almost felt as if she was in some sort of magical jungle. Although Wellington was a bustling city with a waterfront, there was a lot of greenery around her. She remembered reading once that being in nature had healing properties. She had definitely noticed on her walks by the beach in North Carolina that her blood pressure seemed to drop, and her mind was clearer. It never took exotic locations though. She would make sure to include time in nature on this trip; it felt like all parts of New Zealand were nature anyway.

She walked down the street, and it had just the right number of people in it. The street wasn't too deserted where she felt frightened nor so busy that she felt stressed. She slowly walked around and took the time to look at what was around her. There was a boutique with big gold bows in the window, a wood-paneled coffee shop, and a small art gallery. She wandered into what looked like a traditional pub. Once inside, it was dark, and there were a lot of candles everywhere. She usually did not go sit at a bar but decided that this trip was about doing new things. She took a seat at the bar and ordered a bloody mary with extra olives and celery. She loved the saltiness of olives and their texture. This was always her favorite drink – the saltiness, the crunch, and the smooth olives. She could probably drink three of them, but she wasn't going to. A guy next to her kept looking over which made her a bit uncomfortable. He was cute, and it may have been fun to talk to him but for once she wanted to be anonymous while out enjoying things. The pressure of having to make conversation was not something she was really interested in doing right then. She wanted to have time to have a slow and almost empty mind. A mind that was focused on nothing but the next olive she was about to eat.

    Thomas tried to look at Laura without making it too obvious and making her uncomfortable. Who was this girl? He came to this bar regularly and he had never seen her there before. Should he say something to her? He had no interest in picking up a girl, but something was drawing him to her. She was pretty but in an unassuming way, and she looked smart. The main reason he came to this bar was to sit and talk with his friend, Larry, the bartender. It was just some time with Larry and time to watch some sports – not a time to overdrink. Larry loved the environment of the pub and even though he had a degree in sociology, he had been working there as a bartender for ten years. He knew most of the customers and had learned so much about people in that job. After thinking about it for a few minutes, the guy looking at Laura decided to just say hello. It could not be that hard.

"Hi, there. My name is Thomas. I've never seen you here before and just wanted to say hi." Laura jumped in her seat not expecting to have to talk to someone.

"Oh, well, hello. I'm Laura. I'm American, and this is my first time here." She didn't know why she blurted all of that out but he had taken her by surprise, and she felt like she had to fill the space with some words.

"So, just visiting our little country, huh?" smiled Thomas.

"Yes, I've always wanted to come to New Zealand."

"That's great! What are you going to do while you're here?"

"You know, I've decided not to know. Why does everything in life have to be pre-decided?" asked Laura with a smile, surprised that she said that. Maybe her mom was right, she did sometimes talk too much. If he did care to listen, she could talk to him for a long time about her thoughts and feelings on having everything pre-decided in life whether that was a life plan or the day. She decided to be kind of quiet though.

"I think I'm gonna take it easy. I don't even care if I don't see everything. I would rather linger longer in one spot and really take that in," said Laura.

"Well, I don't mean to impose, but if you want a local to hang out with sometime, I'm available!" said Thomas. Thomas was proud of himself for being so direct. It was not easy to do that with pretty women.

"That's nice of you, thanks. I'll give you my cell number and maybe we can connect," said Laura. It just seemed like the natural thing to do, and she did it without overthinking. The guy just looked very sweet, and maybe it would be fun to spend some time with him while she was here. Laura handed Thomas a card she had with her cell phone number on it.

"Great! Well, I don't want to bother you, and I do need to head out now. It was a real pleasure meeting you," said Thomas. Thomas had started getting nervous while talking to her and felt like he just needed to end it right there. He didn't usually get nervous talking with new women, but Laura intrigued him in a way he couldn't quite put his finger on. He didn't want to say something stupid and ruin the possibility of their connection so quickly.

Thomas walked out of the pub, and Laura immediately started to question herself. Had she just done that - given her phone number to some stranger in New Zealand while she was here all alone? A mixture of fear and absolute excitement came over her. Well, she had only one life. Why not. She wondered why the guy bothered to approach her though. Probably just a typical guy and not something to think too much about. He would probably just end up wasting her time.

Chapter Five

It was morning, and Laura was walking out of the hotel after eating a delicious eggs benedict and having the best coffee she ever had. She wasn't sure if they put cinnamon in the coffee, but there was some sort of delicious spice in it. Just that one change from her regular morning coffee was nice and signaled to her that she was on vacation, and it was time to think new thoughts and relax. That day, the streets were busier with people in business suits and as well as tourists all frolicking and happy, even the ones in business suits. The culture down here seemed different. People were very friendly and seemed to have made their peace with things in life. She did not know how else to think of it. It didn't feel like a bunch of people running around chasing happiness; it felt like they had already found it. Maybe part of it was that they had a slower pace and were surrounded by so much natural and created beauty.

She remembered to wear tennis shoes because she would be walking a lot that day. Laura was not one to always remember things like that. She was often so deep in thought that little things like wearing the right shoes for certain days might be forgotten, and as a result, she had lived through many welted feet. She wanted to get a little away from the busy city and touristy spots and just look around. As she continued walking down the street, she came open a residential neighborhood. There was a kid trying to pull an ice cream cone away from another kid while the other stomped his feet. There were older people planting flowers in their yards and government workers trimming trees. Was this the "real" Wellington? Were there any bad neighborhoods? Were there any parks that were decrepit and strip malls with boarded up shops? She didn't know why she thought of that, but maybe it was because she had gotten old enough that she knew not everything was picture perfect all of the time.

She saw a bench and sat down. An older lady started to approach the area where Laura was sitting. It looked like she had her granddaughter with her. The ladies smiled at each other as the lady helped the girl get on the swing set. After a few minutes, the lady seemed to want to sit down; Laura could tell that because she looked tired. Since there was only one bench there, she came over towards Laura.

"May I sit here? My legs are killing me," said the lady.

"Well, of course," said Laura. The lady slowly sat down looking as if her hips, legs, and back all hurt. Old age. The lady looked both happy and sad at the same time. Her face was thin and wrinkled and her clothes thrown on. Laura saw a few stains on her shirt as well.

"So, are you from this area? You certainly don't have the accent," the lady said interjecting upon Laura's thoughts.

"No, just visiting from the United States," said Laura.

"Oh wow, my cousin lives in New Hampshire. I'm Edith," said the lady.

"I've never actually been there. I'm Laura." Laura loved talking to new people anywhere. It was one of her favorite things to do. Each person seemed to have a different frequency. Edith looked at Laura and wished she could be her age just one more time. Laura looked healthy, vibrant, and smart. She had a glean in her eye that reflected an active mind. It seemed like just the other day that Edith was about that age. She did not know where the years had gone and was not particularly enjoying older age.

"So, I don't mean to be rude, but can I ask how old you are?" asked Edith.

"I'm twenty-six," said Laura.

"Well, I'll tell you why I ask. This neighborhood doesn't have too many young people in it so it's odd to see you here today. Seeing you here just made me think of my younger days," said Edith.

"Oh, I see. Yeah, I was just walking through town and wanted to get away from the resort areas for a bit," said Laura.

"Did you come to New Zealand alone?" asked Edith.

"Yes, I did."

"Well, that's brave of you! It's good to see women doing things that are braver these days. Back in my day, we were always discouraged from taking too many risks and were expected just to support our husbands while they were busy taking risks and making marks on the world. We were supposed to have a supporting role. My life withered in that role," said Edith.

"I know what you mean. My mom has complained about similar things at times," said Laura. Laura was surprised how talkative Edith was being with her. She didn't expect to get into a deep conversation with her, but at the same time was intrigued by it. She could tell that Edith was not one to just talk to everyone; Laura could see that on her face.

"Well, if you feel comfortable, please feel free to come with Stacey and I back to the house for a cup of tea," said Edith. Edith thought it would be nice to show this

American girl some New Zealand hospitality. She remembered being on a trip to France when she was young and running into local people that invited her to dinner. She wanted to return the favor to Laura.

"Sure, thank you!" said Laura. Thirty minutes passed and the girl, Stacey, just ran through the playground and chatted with other kids like a social butterfly. She did not seem to have any trouble making friends. She took off her tennis shoe and repeatedly threw it up towards a tree branch. Laura overheard her telling another kid that she wanted the shoe to get stuck up there. She wanted to know whether it could stay there forever. She thought her time with that shoe was over anyway. Edith and Laura continued to talk about their lives and enjoy the fresh air and sunshine. After a while, Edith walked towards Stacey and tried to explain to her that it was time to go. Stacey did not want to have anything to do with that and just kept running away.

"Stacey, please listen to your grandmother. I'm tired and just can't chase you today. Finish things up and let's go," said Edith. Eventually, Stacey was ok with leaving, and the three started walking away from the park area. They approached a stone house with a pale blue oversized door. This certainly was no cookie cutter house like the kind they had in the US, efficient, but sometimes boring. It was shaped in an angled way and was covered in grey stones. Inside, there were pillows all over the couches, too many pillows, but they beckoned you to stop moving and sit down. That was nice and one of the main reasons Laura wanted to be away on a trip.

"Do you have a favorite tea?" asked Edith.

"Oh, I don't want to impose. I like all tea really, but I had an orange herbal tea once that I really liked," said Laura.

"That's great, I have that right here." Edith began brewing the tea, and the fragrance quickly took over the kitchen. Edith added some cinnamon sticks to the teapot as well as some things that looked like little rose buds. Stacey had already left and gone upstairs to her room, so it was just Laura and Edith standing in the kitchen. Suddenly, as Edith began pouring hot tea into the teacups, she began to cry. She got embarrassed and started frantically trying to wipe the tears off her face.

"It's ok, please don't worry, we all cry sometimes," said Laura. She was taken aback by Edith crying but did not want her to feel embarrassed.

"No, I'm so sorry I brought you here to have a nice cup of tea and enjoy your time while you are here in New Zealand. This is no way to treat a guest on vacation. I'm so sorry."

"Please don't think of that. Sometimes our emotions just get the better of us," said Laura.

"Oh, Laura, it's such a long story. I'm afraid I will upset you or bore you to tears with it."

"It's good for all of us to be able to get our emotions out. If we leave them stuck inside, they only make things worse," said Laura. For the next hour and a half, while the ladies drank tea, Edith told Laura the story of her daughter. Her daughter, Emily, went to college on an extremely competitive scholarship that only highly intelligent students received. She was studying to be an astronaut and was ready to work hard and start her life. She met a handsome and loving man that was in the same program, and they started dating very seriously. Edith was concerned that Emily would lose focus on her studies, and Edith was right because Emily ended up becoming pregnant with Stacey while in the program. At first, this was a real concern, and everyone thought she had single-handedly ruined her future. Stacey was born, and they all loved Stacey more than anything in the world; they found a way to make everything work. One night, Emily asked her mother to watch Stacey so that she and her boyfriend could go to a local concert. They did not show up when they were supposed to pick Stacey up. It turned out, they never returned to pick her up.

"I didn't know how she could do this. I later found out that Emily and Robert wanted a complete change of life and moved to Brazil. I couldn't believe my good and responsible daughter would do such a thing. She wrote me a letter and said how much Stacey loved me and what a good mother I was. She knew I was capable of raising Stacey well," said Edith.

"Wow, this must have been truly shocking. Are you still in touch with Emily?" asked Laura.

"A year after that letter, Emily wrote me another letter. She said that she had two months to live, and that the whole reason she and Robert moved was because they knew that Emily was dying. She did not want to stress everyone out then and thought the earlier she left, the easier it would be for Stacey to accept me as her parent. It was a completely selfless act," said Edith. Stacey ran down the stairs and asked her grandmother for lunch. She had her purple bear tucked in her arm and was running towards the television. She looked like the happiest girl in the world.

"I don't know what to say, I'm sorry I burdened you with my story," said Edith.

"Oh, please don't say that. How are you handling this type of life? Do you feel you are up to this?" asked Laura.

"Yes. All is working out well, and Stacey is growing into such a great girl. Sometimes I miss Emily though, and that makes me cry. I wish she allowed me to be part of her life even when she was sick." Laura had never heard a story like this before. She was young enough that she had not endured too much in life yet. She was sure that would change over the years as she aged, but that was where she was at that moment. Laura was glad she met Edith and heard her story; she was impressed with Edith's friendliness and hospitality and was sure she would always remember her.

Chapter Six

After tea, Edith and Laura sat in the garden. Edith showed Laura all of the things she planted there and told her about how she would sit there every morning and meditate. Those few moments of stilling her mind and not thinking about anything helped her for the rest of the day. It was late afternoon, and Laura needed to head back to her hotel. She thanked Edith for a wonderful day, hugged her, and they exchanged phone numbers and email addresses. She walked out of Edith's house full of thoughts about what Edith had been through. Her cell phone rang, and it was Thomas, the guy she met at the tavern.

"Hi Laura?"

"Yes, Hi Thomas. How are you?"

"Doing well. Wanted to see what you were up to and if you felt like meeting me out for dinner tonight." Thomas had barely had a moment without thinking of Laura since he met her, and he knew he had to ask her out. Actually, doing it was much harder than he expected though.

"Actually, I was just starting to think I'm getting hungry. That would be great. Where should be meet?"

"How about I pick you up at your hotel?"

"Ok. It's the Faneygo on Eva Street. How is 6:30?" asked Laura.

"That's great, I'll see you then," said Thomas. Laura started going through the images in her mind to see what she remembered about Thomas. He was athletic looking, had light brown hair, and green eyes. He was attractive, but more than just that he had a good energy about him. One thing Laura was not looking forward to was figuring out what to wear and doing all the jazz that comes with going on a date. She was a more casual girl normally except of course for when she needed to dress up. Laura had never reveled in that fancying up process as much as many women seemed to. Maybe they didn't either, but they just thought they needed to do that if they were ever to get anywhere in life. Laura headed back to her hotel to start getting ready for her date.

She decided instead of wasting so much time looking through her clothes and setting up a blow dry appointment for her hair, she would just put on whatever seemed natural and do her simple best. If that was not enough, so be it. Men seemed to expect more, but this way she would find out who Thomas truly was. She had never been the type to want to present a perfect picture of herself; she believed in authenticity, and if someone didn't like it that was fine.

She was all ready and waiting to be picked up for her date with Thomas. As she waited, she started to think of Brian, a guy she liked a long time ago. He was such a fresh-faced guy, a great student, and he would bring her flowers a lot. He would clearly and openly express to her how much he liked her. She loved that about him; he was not afraid to express his feelings. Those days were so carefree. Back then, she cared more about getting ready perfectly for her time with Brian because she was younger, and things were different then. She remembered the day when Brian surprised her with a trip to her house to present her with a brand-new music player. It was a top-of-the-line product back then, and Laura could not believe he cared enough about her to give her that. Those were days filled with pools, pizza parties, movies with friends, and long summer days. They were one big blur of fun and freedom. Brian went on to get a PhD in astrophysics, and she still sometimes heard from him now and then. She learned that not all relationships last, but she still watched lots of romantic movies. Back in the days with Brian, love really did seem to make the world go around.

Laura sat on the silver bench outside of her hotel and waited for Thomas to arrive. It was not long before he drove up in a yellow sports car. She didn't know anything about cars and had no idea what kind of car it was, but it was clear that it was a fancy car. She wondered whether he was a jerk that always wanted to show off nice cars and expensive things. She had never liked people like that but didn't want to be judgmental. Laura got up and opened the door to his car as Thomas was walking around the car to open the door for her. She did not know men tried to do that anymore. Maybe it was different in New Zealand. It made her feel very special, and she smiled from the inside when she saw an attractive and kind man walking to open a door for her. Such a simple gesture, but it had a lot of impact.

"Well, hi, Laura, you look great," said Thomas.

"Thanks so do you." The two got into their seats and stopped a moment and smiled at each other.

"So, what kind of food do you like? I should have asked you this earlier, but I didn't think of it until now. Sometimes it's fun to decide things at the last minute," said Thomas.

"Well, it's your lucky day because I am pretty flexible. It's really more who you are with that determines the quality of a dinner for me," said Laura.

"That's true. Ok how about we go to the seafood place by the harbor?"

"Sure, that sounds great," said Laura. The two arrived at Michael's restaurant and got a table quickly. Laura started to get a little nervous. What if they could not find anything to talk about? Laura never really liked the formality of dates but knew it was something you had to go through to get to know someone.

"So, how are you enjoying your trip so far?" asked Thomas.

"It's really been great. You have a beautiful country, and it just feels so good to decide to do something and then actually do it – especially something adventurous," said Laura.

"That's true. We don't always get the chance." The waiter came and Laura ordered scallops with roasted potatoes and spinach, and Thomas ordered lobster.

"So, I've gotta say, I've never been one to love dates. I just cut right to the chase when I want to get to know someone. So let me just ask you - why did you want to meet me for dinner?" asked Laura.

"Well, that's funny! You know that's a good habit. The reason I wanted to meet you for dinner was because you are cute, and you seemed open and fun. I go to that pub regularly, and I had never seen you there before, so I was also curious about you," said Thomas.

"Ok. So, have you been married before? How's your dating life been?" Laura felt like just digging deep quickly and not having boring and formal conversation. She knew this was a chance and likely temporary meeting but still.

"Never been married, and I'm not sure I want to be married. Most of the married couples I know are not happy, and it seems soon after the marriage people aren't happy together anymore. They have the kids, the busy jobs, and then everything falls apart. I don't mean to sound negative, but it's rare to see a happy married couple anymore." Thomas was surprised but found it refreshing that she was asking these questions. Most people were so superficial. He wanted her to know how he felt about marriage and relationships honestly.

"You know I've never really looked at that so deeply. I guess I'm still young and just finished school so never really had time yet to think about all of that. I guess that could be true, but at this point I would have to say I am still kind of a romantic girl," said Laura. Laura was kind of disappointed that Thomas had such a negative view of marriage.

"Nothing wrong with that! It's probably a good thing in a way," said Thomas. Laura and Thomas finished off their dinner in the restaurant and decided to take a walk outside by the harbor. They stepped out into the night, and Laura wrapped her turquoise shawl around her neck since there was a slight chill in the air. Somehow, she felt safe walking around in the dark, in New Zealand, with Thomas. He gently picked up her hand and held it as they walked along the sidewalk. He had to psyche himself up to do that but was glad she didn't move her hand away. He seemed so gentle and calm and that was Laura's favorite quality in men. Being around him felt like being around a sturdy, wide width, maple tree that produced a lot of shade.

There was a lady on the sidewalk walking quickly toward a young, good-looking man in a suit who was holding what looked like two dozen white roses. She smiled and almost ran towards him as he waited for her to get close. She bounced into his arms and had not let go as Laura and Thomas passed them by. They must have been walking in a romantic place. There was no one else in sight, and the moon was shining down on the water next to them.

"So do you like adventure sports?" asked Thomas.

"To be honest, not really. I don't seem to need an adrenaline rush much. Why? Were you thinking of doing something?" asked Laura.

"Well, while you are here you may as well try some of the adventure sports we offer down here in New Zealand," said Thomas.

"I'll think about it. When I was researching coming here, I saw that you offer a lot of that, but to be honest, now that I'm here I feel like just wandering slowly and not having to do too many new things. Is that bad?"

"Of course not! You gotta do what your body and mind are telling you to do. Too many people do things just to say they did or to show off. That really doesn't make much sense if you ask me," said Thomas.

"I don't want to bore you with just a simple dinner out though. There are sports activities we can even do in the evening," Thomas continued.

"Oh, you have no idea. It is ridiculously hard for me to get bored. I can find interesting things in a bowl of cherries. I think most of the people in my family are like that. So much seems to be genetic don't you think?" asked Laura.

"Never really thought about it." All Thomas knew was that he wanted Laura to remember this date no matter what he had to do. They got near the parking lot where they had parked Thomas' car.

"So, what made you pick a yellow sportscar?" asked Laura.

"Oh, just get tired of the same old things. Bright colors make me happy," said Thomas. They got in and started heading back to Laura's hotel. She told Thomas that she wanted to go to sleep early so that she would not waste the next day feeling sluggish even if all she ended up doing was wandering around as she had hoped. As they drove, they kept the windows slightly open and the fresh night air engulfed them. She started wondering what the point was of going out to dinner with Thomas. She would never seem him again since he lived in New Zealand. Why did they bother with this? She certainly was not going to sleep with the guy if that is what he thought.

"Well, I had a wonderful time with you, Laura," said Thomas.

"Yes, me too, thanks so much for taking me out. I think I will remember this night. "

"When do you leave?" asked Thomas.

"I still have six days left here," said Laura.

"Well, without getting into a sad goodbye, let's just say maybe see you again before you leave," said Thomas.

"Yes." With that, Laura stepped out of Thomas' car after his peck on the cheek and started to walk back into her hotel. Back in her room, Laura decided to read some of her book of poetry before dozing off. The first poem she saw was about a windmill and a cat.

Chapter Seven

Before long, it was morning again and the sunlight fell upon Laura's eyelids and started to tickle her awake. At first, she forgot she was in New Zealand and started to think about the pile of bills she needed to pay and the trip to the grocery store to buy laundry detergent. Then she realized she was far away from all of that. It felt so good to be somewhere alone. As much as Laura loved people, she realized that she needed to be comfortable spending time alone to figure out who she was and what she wanted in life. It was not until she picked up a book arbitrarily in the book store one day that she started to think about that. She started to implement it into her daily life to see if the things you read in books really do make a difference.

Laura never considered herself too adventurous of a person, but today she was going to do something very adventurous. Last night when Thomas mentioned it to her, she just didn't feel it in her bones, but she woke up feeling differently about adventure. She was a little scared but there was no turning back. It was called canyoning. A bus would pick her up and take her to a different town for it. She did not even bother remembering the name of the town. The bus driver would handle that. She was scared since she had never done anything like this before and didn't know why she was going to do it. She understood canyoning to mean a combination of rock climbing, falling down waterfalls, diving into water, and swimming as well as walking through bush. She could not believe she had decided to go through with this. Was this something she would come to regret?

The bus would arrive in one hour. With the time she had, Laura decided to lie on the floor and let the hard ground straighten her spine. She usually only thought about doing this, but it was something she always felt better after doing. If only she could do more of the things that always made her feel good like playing the piano, baking cookies, making flower arrangements, having wine with a best friend, and so many other things. As she lied on the ground in her hotel room, she took the time to notice the throw rug next to her feet. It had spirals of different shades of blue going through it from the top to the bottom. Laura's favorite color was blue because it always made her feel like she was floating in a place where everything was calm and smooth.

Laura was ready when the bus arrived. It was a dark mauve colored bus which was unusual. They did not have many of those in the States. Laura felt her heart skip a beat as she started to walk. She made her feet move forward by sheer will and stepped onto the bus. There was not anyone else on it yet. Hopefully, she was not the only person crazy enough to do this, and they would be picking up other people along the way. The bus driver was a matronly looking woman with severely curled blonde hair that bounced up as if she had hit her head on one of the rocks during canyoning! Laura decided to lay her head back on the seat and just close her eyes. They stopped a few minutes after Laura got onto the bus, and yes, it looked like it was a bus stop of sorts. A man that looked to be in his twenties got onto the bus with his backpack and came and sat right next to Laura. Laura guessed this made sense since this was kind of a social event.

"Hi, I'm Ethan," he said.

"Hi, I'm Laura how are you?" Laura hoped this wouldn't be a complicated conversation because that would increase her nervousness right now.

"Oh well, judging by your accent you aren't from around here," said Ethan.

"Ya, I'm from the U.S. Just here to visit and want to be adventurous today but to be honest with you right now I'm scared to death and second guessing my decision," said Laura.

"Don't worry! I do this all the time. It's the most fun you will ever have!" The bus pulled through some long flowing leaves that surrounded it on all sides and by then there were six other people on the bus not including Ethan. Laura wondered whether the eight of them would be together at all times during this canyoning process or whether it was more of a solo process. Their guide quickly appeared and explained to them that they would need to listen to an hour-long class on what would be involved with this and how to be safe and all those types of things. Laura never really liked having to listen to information like this for very long. That was the funny thing about her, even though she was not adventurous when she finally decided to do something she was perfectly willing to just do it with no instruction. She thought of the time she went skiing for the first time, and she decided she did not have the patience to do a class and just literally went straight down the hill. It was the bunny hill but not the wisest decision. To her credit, she did not fall except right at the beginning when she jumped off the ski lift. The rest of the way was a straight slide to the bottom. After the canyoning instruction, Laura decided she would try to follow what they said but just not worry about it too much. They all got off the bus and slowly walked up through a dark, brushy area. Greens and grays everywhere even the water in sight was dark green. Laura felt wrapped inside this grayish, green blanket. Right now, her house did not exist. The Baker law firm did not exist. Nothing existed except this grayish, green blanket and the sounds of rustling water, her heavy trembling feet, and the feeling of anticipation in her gut.

    A streak of sunlight was cutting through the bush and created dancing spots on the water. It was time to dive into that water, and Laura jumped without thinking; she realized that if she thought too much about it, she would get stuck. She found herself underneath the water being buoyed back up to the top. She could not believe she did that with no traceable fear. Ethan was behind her and soon in the water too. He swam around a little, but Laura preferred to float on her back and analyze the clouds. Soon, they were approaching a strong waterfall that looked a bit like it was angry. It was not one of those slowly moving peaceful type of waterfalls. It looked like it was attacking everything surrounding it. Some of the others were sliding down it and falling into the water below. Laura thought this thing looked dangerous, and she was not sure if she should do it. She reminded herself that she was going to do things, and she was not going to overthink and psyche herself out of doing things. She crawled forward with her legs in front of her and pushed herself down. Something seemed to grab her leg, and her head went backwards and forwards. She felt a slight clicking sound in her arm, and the next thing she felt was excruciating pain.

Chapter Eight

"Laura, you're ok. Just open your eyes." Laura started to think that she must have been hurt in the waterfall. She looked out the sunshine filled window to just try and forget.

She opened her eyes and saw Dr. Wallace's face peering down at her. They explained what had happened to her when she pushed herself down the waterfall; she did it at a spot on the rocks which was not ideal and had slammed her body into a sharp-edged stone. She went under the water and did not come up fast enough. She was going to be ok the doctor said but she would need some recovery time. Laura could not believe an adventurous trip to New Zealand had led to this. All her life she had been careful, and finally the one time she decided to be different she hurt herself – just her luck. She felt like a sunburned person who did not want to move or even look at the burns. Her body was achy, and she felt very tired like someone who had not slept in weeks. She had never felt this way in her body before. It felt like the body of a ninety-year-old woman with arthritis.

"You are ready to be released. We are going to call a cab to come pick you up and take you back to your hotel. Don't worry about it buddy, you'll recover pretty soon," said Dr. Wallace.

"Ok, thank you. Am I fine now? Is there anything I need to be careful about?" asked Laura.

"You just need some rest, and your cuts and bruises will heal up. You will be sore for a while, but you were lucky and nothing major happened to you," said Dr. Wallace. Laura breathed a sigh of relief. Her mother was going to go crazy when she heard about this. In a moment of second-guessing, she started to think that maybe she wasn't made to take too many risks.

The cab pulled up in front of Laura's hotel. She went in and lied down on the bed and started to think about Thomas. She had a sudden urge to tell him about what happened. She was alone in a foreign country and had injured herself and somehow needed a familiar face or someone to talk to about it. She picked up the phone and called him.

"Hi, Thomas, it's Laura."

"Well, hi there, my friend. How are you? Been thinking about you lately," said Thomas.

"I'm okay, ya. I had an accident during canyoning, but everything is ok now."

"Wow, what happened?" asked Thomas.

"Don't worry, I'm ok now but just wanted to talk to you a bit."

"So, if you're not busy, I can come over and visit you now," said Thomas. Thomas got instantly worried and wanted to see her.

"Ok, come on over." Thomas walked in wearing faded blue jeans and an over-sized white T-shirt. He looked so fresh and alive. His light brown hair and green eyes were so attractive.

"Hey, you're pretty beat up. What happened?" asked Thomas as he gently touched Laura's bruised arms.

"I just don't want to worry about it. Let's just say I fell and got beat up a bit during the canyoning trip," said Laura. She did not have the energy to go into all the details and did not really care that it had happened anymore. Some things were best ignored.

"Ok, that's fine. I understand. So, you want to order some room service and just hang out?" asked Thomas. Thomas was not one to pry if the other person looked like they did not want to talk.

"Sure, let's do that." The two perused the menu for a while. So many good choices from beef tenderloins, grilled salmon, omelets, and sushi. After talking about how good everything looked, they decided to just get some veggie pizza and beer to keep things simple and casual while they spent time together.

"So, what made you call me? I thought you would forget all about me and go back to the States to be honest with you," said Thomas.

"You know, I'm not sure. Guess I remembered you and just wanted to see you again before I left," said Laura.

"When do you leave?"

"Two days from now," said Laura. The two both got sad at that point, realizing that their connection would be lost in just two days.

"So, tell me a little bit more about yourself, Thomas. The first and second times we saw each other we never really had time to get too much into that," said Laura.

"Well, what do you want to know?"

"Whatever you want to tell me."

"Well, I grew up in Wellington and have always loved living here. Nature is around you all the time in a very tangible way whether you like it or not. People here tend to be nice, and we have a surprisingly good culture down here. I think I've had a rather good life so far."

"That sounds great, and yes, I've found the people in New Zealand to be pretty interesting. Would you ever leave New Zealand? What do you think your future will look like Thomas?" Laura wanted to have yet another meaningful conversation with him.

"How do you mean? I mean I'm not that old yet I'm not sure I think too much about the future at this point," said Thomas.

"I mean what are your goals? What do you want out of life?" Laura kept pushing.

"That must be the lawyer in you talking Ms. Laura! I don't think everyone thinks of life as analytically as you seem to, my friend!" joked Thomas. Thomas wondered why Laura was trying to ask so many questions. He was intrigued by her and trying to get to know her, but he felt that women often ruined good moments by asking too many questions.

"Really? You think so?" asked Laura.

"Definitely!"

"Well, I wonder if that's bad. If you ask me, if more people looked at things a little bit more deeply, some of our problems would be better solved and more quickly solved," said Laura.

"Problems like what?" asked Thomas.

"You know, hunger, crime, so many things like that," said Laura.

"Ya, I see your point. The other side of it though is life should be enjoyed and doesn't always have to be so heavy if you ask me," said Thomas. The two turned on a movie that was showing a cute couple ice skating outside during Christmas season and started to munch on their pizza. They sat in silence for a while, each lost in their own thoughts. Thomas scrunched closer to her on the sofa and looked at her for a second closely in the eyes. Laura felt herself flush and was not expecting that. Laura looked away and waited to see what would happen next. Thomas resumed eating his pizza and did not say a word.

"So, how come they never show people in movies falling while ice skating? I would like it more. People fall in real life," said Laura. She had certainly been an example of that during her risk-taking adventure of canyoning.

"Ya, good point. I don't know, Laura. Yet another thing you thought of that I have not," said Thomas with a smile.

"It's kind of nice having someone like you around. You make me stop thinking," said Laura.

"Well, I hope that's good," said Thomas with a smile. The two finished the entire pizza and decided to watch the rest of the movie.

When Laura opened her eyes, she was lying on the couch with the tv still on and Thomas by her side. The pizza box was open with crumbs on the floor and the shades were never closed the night before. It must have been early morning; Laura looked over at Thomas and thought that he surprisingly still looked handsome even this early in the morning with a little pizza sauce left on his cheek. She felt an interesting sense of attachment to Thomas but wondered how that could be. She barely knew him. She was going to be flying back to the States the next morning after all. Thomas opened his eyes and chuckled.

"What are you doing waking up before me?" joked Thomas. He wondered whether he looked like crap and felt insecure for a second.

"Oh, I don't know how that happened!" said Laura. She felt a little bit awkward waking up next to a man even though they were both fully dressed and half upright on the sofa.

"So, what do you have going for today?" asked Thomas.

"Well, I want to take it easy and just pack and relax today. The night before a long flight it's good to get to bed early. Plus, my body definitely can't take much more at this point," said Laura.

"Ya, that's understandable." Laura thought she saw a trace of a tear in Thomas' eye but started to think that she did not really see that in this man. If she was right about seeing that, it would mean she could have even more respect for him.

"Laura, I don't know how to say this, but I can't really envision not seeing you again," said Thomas.

"Ya, I know what you mean," Laura tried her hardest not to get emotional because that would be embarrassing even though Thomas was showing some emotion. They both sat up on the sofa and stared straight ahead.

"Why do you feel any connection with me?" asked Laura not being one to shy away from a deep question.

"I don't know. Let's not sugar it up and just say sweet things. I really don't know, Laura." Thomas knew it was important to be expressive in relationships, but he was not one to just say things to make the other person feel good, and he wasn't sure himself why he felt the way he did.

"Let's just not think about it, ok? There's no point, right Thomas? There is nothing we can do. People just must be in the moment and enjoy things as they happen but never expect things with anything or anyone. That's my belief," said Laura matter-of factly. Thomas sat and did not say anything for a few minutes. He was surprised that Laura did not seem to care about what he was saying. He truly felt that she felt something for him too, but right now she was acting like none of it meant anything.

"Laura, stay here. Do you really need to go back? We are both young and at the beginning of our lives. We met in some coincidental way here in New Zealand which maybe wasn't coincidence. You decided to come to New Zealand of all places. You decided to come to that pub at the same time I did. We have fun together, but it seems to be more than that, too. Laura, is there any way you could stay?" asked Thomas with a trace of fear and bewilderment in his eyes.

"Thomas. That's sweet, but what are you talking about? You barely know me. I'm only twenty-six. I'm starting a tough job in the Fall. I just came here for some fun and adventure. There is no way I can stay in New Zealand. I'm surprised you would even mention that, but thanks, it's so sweet," said Laura.

Laura was not sure what to say to him. She felt uncomfortable and as much as she believed people should be expressive with each other, many times in life it was hard. Maybe he had not woken up fully yet and just did not know what he was saying. She had never been spoken to this openly by any man. Usually, men were quiet and did not want to say too much or show their emotions. All of this had taken her aback a bit but in a wonderful way.

"Laura, I will come to the States with you. I'll just come back to New Zealand if things don't work out. Who cares. I'm young, and I have time to make mistakes," said Thomas. For a moment, Laura thought what Thomas was saying was pretty strange. She felt judgmental for a minute, but then her emotion over-rode that. She did feel a connection with Thomas and did not want to just let him go. At the same time, what he was saying was so impractical.

"I don't even know what I'm saying right now, but okay. Come with me. Let's go back to North Carolina together," said Laura. She was not sure why she said that, but she felt excited. It was probably just talk and emotion. With that, Thomas moved toward Laura's face and gently brushed his lips against hers the way a feather brushes the wind as it is falling.

Chapter Nine

As the cab pulled towards the airport, Laura looked outside of her window. People milling about pulling suitcases, in a mad dash to make their flight. It was such organized chaos, like much of life. Thomas had a faint smile on his lips and was looking out the window too. They were holding hands and not saying a word, but there was an energy of positive excitement between them. Their cab driver looked like a forty-year-old man, and he told them that his wife had just been accepted to medical school. They had one child named Jasmin, but his wife decided that she was going to pursue her dream of becoming a surgeon. It was something she thought about all the time and at a recent barbecue they went to, his wife would not stop talking about it. The cab driver told Thomas and Laura that after the barbecue, he decided to encourage his wife to apply to medical school and pursue her dreams. He was a bit afraid of losing having her around, but he did not want her to lose out on one of her life's dreams because of him. He joked that he accepted the risk of her becoming a doctor and then dumping him.

The cab driver liked to talk to his passengers it seemed. Laura didn't mind it; she thought it was fun and interesting to hear different people's life stories. He said that his life took a bad turn while he was in college. He was studying to become an engineering professor, but then his mother got ill very quickly. His emotions took over, and he dropped out of school to care for his mother. He thought he would go back, but he never got the chance. He regretted that all his life and with each passing year, time went faster, and he had more complications in his life. Neither Laura nor Thomas could relate to those circumstances, but they were both sure that was only because of their relatively young age. They pulled up to the section for their airline and said goodbye to the cab driver. He was an interesting guy, and Laura did a little prayer for him as she stepped out of the cab. Laura was not religious, but she believed in good energy. He was another example of the unpredictability of life. Thomas helped Laura carry all her bags out, and they walked into the airport to head to North Carolina.

On the flight, Laura thought about how amazing this whole trip to New Zealand had been. She left on a whim and came back with Thomas. Just when she thought life was completely routine and nothing new happened anymore, it did. Life was always one step ahead. Thomas spent the time on the plane reading a book about landscaping. He had ideas about what they could do to the yard back at Laura's house. She had told him about her little house in Duck, and he said that if she wanted, he would immediately start fixing up the yard. He grew up without a yard and was always envious of the other kids in school that had the space to run around and have friends over playing soccer in the backyard. He obviously didn't need that anymore, but a pretty space with a good book was appealing. Laura was more than happy that Thomas had an interest in gardening. She had always liked the concept of English gardens and other regular gardens that were taken care of because they created an oasis to go to right at home. Laura loved to sit outside and flip through an artistic magazine with a cup of coffee – having a beautiful garden there would make that even better.

On the other side of the aisle on the airplane, there was a young mom trying to calm her very fussy baby. Laura was annoyed by all the coyote like screaming. The mom looked exhausted and at a loss for what else she could do. She looked like she was about Laura's age, but wow what different lives they had. The pilot announced that they would be landing in thirty minutes. Laura would be landing in North Carolina as a different woman. One with a boyfriend from New Zealand who had left his country to be with her. She got a little nervous when she thought about that because there was always the chance Thomas would not like the United States and decide to leave. She did not want to think about that, but she guessed anything could happen. The plane landed and the pair gathered their things to leave.

They got to the house, and Laura started getting things out of the cab. Laura wondered why Thomas felt so comfortable just going inside the house and sitting down on the couch while she continued to bring things inside from the cab. This was the first time she recalled having any negative feelings towards him. Was it a bad sign that it was so quick upon arrival at home? She brushed the thought away and continued carrying in the bags and jackets.

"Hang on a minute, I'm just gonna have some water and then I'll bring everything in. You don't need to do that. Please go sit down," said Thomas. He had not had much water on the flight because he did not like airplane bathrooms so he really could not wait to have water once they arrived at home. Laura was relieved that he wasn't so oblivious as to think she should carry everything inside alone. That would have been a very bad start for them.

"That's ok, I've almost got everything inside." Laura felt funny when she was honest with herself about having Thomas back in her home with her. Would he cramp her style? Would he become a jerk the minute things got comfortable? Laura had heard a lot of bad tales about relationships and how they corrode over time but had also heard that it wasn't good to think of negative possibilities because that could bring those situations about.

"So how do you want to spend the rest of the summer?" asked Laura.

"I don't know, sweetie, do we have to figure it all out right now?" asked Thomas. Thomas remembered about how when they met at the pub in New Zealand, Laura had said she didn't want to always know everything ahead. Laura realized that no, she didn't need to jump ahead to that right this very minute. Her house felt like it had been abandoned just with the brief time she had been away. She opened the windows and sprayed some lemon room spray around.

"You know, I've gotta start looking for a job soon. I'm not gonna just be sitting around here while you get ready for your job. I guess the best thing for me is to look for an entry-level engineering position since I have the degree. I wonder if it will be hard to find something," said Thomas.

"You have some time for that honey, don't worry, for now if I were you, I would just get acquainted with the town and spend what time you have with me." Laura could always put herself in someone else's shoes and could imagine Thomas' situation would need some adjusting to. She slumped down on the couch next to Thomas, and they both sat quietly there together for a few minutes. It was nice to be able to do that with someone and not feel the need to always talk. The phone rang. It was her mom. Candace knew Thomas was coming back with her since they had texted throughout her trip to New Zealand. Her mom was excited to meet Thomas and wanted to know if they could schedule when to come visit. Laura really was not in the mood to figure that out right then and let her mom know that she would get back to her. She was proud of herself for being more assertive with people, including her mom. Her mom was wonderful but had a way of being pushy at times.

There was always a part of Laura that thought in terms beyond her age. Even though she was only twenty-six, she started to think about how temporary this time in her life probably was. Here she was at the beginning of her life, about to start a new job, and now with a new man. Everything was ahead of her. Things must feel so different in the fifties of life. So much behind you and so much less ahead of you. She wondered why she bothered thinking of these things. Wouldn't life be easier if she just thought about what meal she was going to cook and what shoes she was going to buy? Her mom always used to say to keep life as simple as possible. When Laura used to have her head buried in philosophy books during college, her mom used to say, oh those books do not help anyone. Laura never agreed with that, but when she caught herself overthinking, she would try to balance that out and remember her mom's words. The two agreed on where Thomas would put his sparse belongings and decided to go to bed.

Chapter Ten

Laura would start her new job on the 15th of September. She and Thomas had fallen into a nice couples' routine of calling each other before they got home and each making a meal for the other if they were home first. Thomas bought a Toyota so that he could get around and not have to rely on Laura's car. Each morning, they would wake up early and take a walk in the neighborhood together. That helped keep them emotionally close. They never wanted to lose the emotional connection they had with each other. They got a chance to breathe fresh air on those walks, get their circulation going, look at nature, and talk about things that were on their minds. They both looked forward to that time every morning. These little rituals they had together kept their relationship alive and fresh.

 Laura sensed some sadness in Thomas that she did not feel when they were in New Zealand together. She decided to ask him if anything was wrong, and his response was just that he missed his home culture sometimes. He thought people in Duck were a little more judgmental and did not have that open attitude towards life that he was used to. Laura was not sure what she could do about that. Was he going to leave and go back? She really did not want him to and had gotten very used to his bear hugs and their deep conversations. She felt that if he decided to leave, she would become totally lost in life. Thomas said he had not been feeling well for the past week and went to the doctor. After some lab tests, he was diagnosed with diabetes.

"So, are you going to ship me back to New Zealand now that I am a sick person?" joked Thomas.

"Well, let me see!" Laura joked. She didn't care what Thomas had. She would take care of him. Laura knew before then and especially in that moment, that no matter what happened she wanted Thomas by her side. She felt such a strong bond with him and did not know how she lived her life before meeting him. Having him there to take walks with and talk about life just that even if there was nothing else had given her life a joy and a meaning that it didn't have before. The two decided to have a healthy lunch at the new salad place down the street. Customers picked their own ingredients, and they had all kinds of interesting vegetables, toppings, and lettuces. That was the best food for a person with blood sugar problems. The line inside the restaurant was long, and Laura found herself feeling impatient.

"Do you think we should just go home and make a couple of eggs?" asked Laura.

"Ya, let's go." Laura loved how she and Thomas always seemed to easily think the same things. That was really hard to find in any relationship. Things between them were smooth with very little disagreement.

It was the night before Laura had to start her new job at Baker law firm. She had organized her briefcase, suit, and lunch bag and was ready to go to sleep. She felt herself getting nervous and wondered whether she remembered anything from law school or whether clients would take her seriously given her young appearance and lack of experience. She could not sleep a wink that night and just kept wondering what was going to happen the next day. She read that most lawyers were introverts which she thought was unusual since they were in a talking profession; on other hand, it made sense because lawyers spent so much time alone just reading, analyzing, and writing. She wanted to have that quiet time in her office too but hoped that at least a few of the other associates would want to be a little social as well. She hated situations where there was no friendliness or interaction. Before she knew it, it was morning, and she was off to the car to head to work. One of the wonderful things about a town like Duck, North Carolina was that it was not Los Angeles or Washington, D.C. with lots of traffic going to work and people everywhere. She would have a short ten-minute drive to her office. She got there and was greeted by a young girl with long blond hair and sparkling blue eyes.

"You must be Laura. I'm Amanda. Nice to meet you."

"Hi, yes. Nice to meet you too." Laura felt nervous in the law firm since it looked like a very serious place, and it was really quiet. Amanda did not look like a particularly happy person despite how strikingly beautiful her blue eyes were. She looked like she was overworked and had bags under her eyes. She seemed to be in perpetual motion with not enough time to stop to really hold a conversation with anyone.

"Ok, let's go. I'll take you to your new office." The two walked through long hallways bordered by dark wood and heavy looking pictures of serious things like the scales of justice and something that looked like a Greek God. There were not any pictures of flowers or sunshine on the walls. Laura loved the law, but she always felt that it was too serious of a profession for her when she checked in with her emotions. Laura was more light-hearted about life. She felt this inner conflict as she walked around the hallways. She was here now though and had to make the best of it. She reminded herself that she would be able to help people with her education from law school.

They entered an office that had huge windows on one side and a bookcase on the other. There were geometric patterned colorful pictures on the walls and a beautiful potted plant on a side table in a beige wicker type pot. Someone had spent time making this office look attractive for her. She liked the lighter and more modern décor in her office much more than the rest of the place. Laura appreciated the nice surroundings because she always felt that a nice environment helped productivity. She put her briefcase and coat down, and Amanda quickly shuffled away.

There was a pile of case files on her desk already. This is what she had been worrying about all summer. What if she was not up to the task? She secretly hoped the clients would not be too demanding and nasty. She had heard that some clients were difficult to have a good relationship with and working as a lawyer meant your clients controlled most things. She decided to relax a bit and have a positive attitude as she started the process of looking at the first case. The lady in that matter wanted to have her marriage annulled as if it had never occurred. Laura wondered what it was emotionally or otherwise that would make a person want that. How did things change so quickly from love to hate or complete indifference? She spent the rest of her first day meeting some staff and continued to look at her files.

Her first day of work was officially done, and it had gone well overall. She was allowed the time to get used to her new surroundings and meet the other attorneys and partners. As she suspected, most of them were quiet and very much into their quiet office environments, but everyone seemed nice enough. Thomas was waiting at home for her with a beautifully cooked salmon and potato dish. It was nice to come home to that. She took her shoes off and sat on the couch rubbing her feet. She started to think about her first day of soccer practice in fourth grade. It was a sweltering day and all around her were kids screaming and running. She was not too much for all the noise, but it was a good, grounding feeling to be out there running around like that. Well, her feet hurt the same way as they did that day after soccer practice in 4th grade. Why did women have to wear such cute but extremely uncomfortable shoes? The shoes men wore looked so comfortable and big. She would look silly wearing that to work, but she would not have minded doing it at all.

After dinner, Thomas was upstairs reading in the bedroom. He had this habit of having certain activities planned for certain times of the day. He took good care of himself that way. He had his television time, his meal time, his relaxation time, and a time for every other thing it seemed. It made Laura wonder why she always felt the need to do all her tasks and help everyone and everything before even thinking about taking a moment for herself. In fact, every woman she had ever known or been close to was the same way. Maybe it had something to do with the caretaking role and the fact that one day the women might become a mother? Whatever it was, it did not ever seem to leave much time for her. One of the cases she looked at earlier that day involved a woman who wanted a divorce at the age of thirty-six. She had two children, and the soon to be ex-husband was trying to make the divorce as difficult as possible on the woman. He was a Senior Vice-President in a major corporation, and he thought everything should go his way and was going to try to force that by throwing his weight around. He seemed to have a huge ego and a horrible personality based on what Laura read in the case file. Laura started to see how sometimes the fairest results would not occur if one side was substantially more powerful than the other. Laura hoped she would never have to be involved in something as difficult and life-altering as a divorce. She stopped thinking so that she could relax and go to bed to prepare for her court case in the morning.

As they stepped out of the courtroom, Laura noticed how serious and sad everyone looked. It made her have a pang inside wondering whether she had chosen the right profession. She loved the logical part of law, the writing, the helping people, but the very somber parts of the profession sometimes bothered her. People just lost all sense of the frivolity of life once they were in a courthouse or even in a law office for that matter. She finished attending a divorce hearing with her boss who showed her more about how to run those hearings. This one was a simple case – no major witnesses, evidence, or testimony. The husband had been the one to file for an uncontested divorce from his wife so he was the one that had to go on the stand and answer a few questions. He was all confusion and sadness as he sat on that stand answering basic questions about himself. Maybe it would be better to never get married in the first place - no chance of divorce then. As Laura sat and watched the divorce hearing, she wondered whether she would ever have kids. With so much divorce around, she just wasn't sure. She thought that sociologists or psychologists or someone like that should study the phenomena of divorce and figure out what caused it. Happy marriages were a good thing.

When she entered the office again, Amanda was at the front desk talking to a client on the phone. She kept nodding her head and agreeing, and it sounded like she was trying hard to make the person on the other end of the line feel secure. These clients were going through some of the worst times of their life, and they often needed emotional support from their attorneys as well as legal advice. The attorneys involved were in the middle of many different battlefields. Laura got back to her desk and sat down for a minute and decided to just breathe. The pace of legal work would get to her if she was not careful about taking little breathing breaks here and there. She started to implement some of the things she read about in her favorite books about closing her eyes a few minutes and just grounding herself in the moment. After a few minutes, someone knocked on her door.

"Oh, hey Brad, how's everything going?" asked Laura.

"Pretty good, thanks. Just wondering how your case went today." Brad was an associate down the hall who started with the firm about the same time Laura did. He was a scrawny kind of guy, the bookworm looking type.

"Pretty good, thanks. I didn't do much but observe today but it was fun, and I understood the process," said Laura.

"That's great! Ya, I did that last week with Matthew. It was interesting. Courtrooms definitely have their own specific feel." Laura was not sure she loved that specific feel, but at this point, it was what it was. Brad sat down opposite Laura's desk and put his feet up on the ottoman. It was good that he was willing to come in and chat sometimes because the other associates mostly kept to themselves.

"So, how's your mom?" asked Laura. Brad's mom had been diagnosed with COPD and was having a hard time walking around much due to breathing trouble.

"She's doing ok. She's accepted the diagnosis now and realizes the best thing to do is to get back on with life and not dwell on it. My dad is a great support for my mom too. He's with her at every appointment, cooks her favorite dishes, and constantly plans fun trips for them to go on."

"Well, if I ever get married, I would hope it would be to a man like that," said Laura. Brad was not married and did not have a girlfriend. He was twenty-eight, so he did not need to rush into any of that. It was unfair that men had a lot of time for things like that while women were often thinking about their biological clock in the backs of their minds. Laura thought about how Brad seemed to listen to her a little bit better than Thomas did. Thomas was more active in his statements and a little less of a listener. At some point, she would talk to Thomas about that because she did not want to end up feeling resentful about it. Brad got up to leave her office and said goodbye. Laura felt refreshed after talking to him for a few minutes. She turned to her files and opened the next one. The wife needed Laura to file for an emergency hearing because the husband had cut her off completely from all access to funds. The negative emotion between most divorcing couples was something off-the-charts. Another crazy day!

Chapter Eleven

"So, honey, are we going to get married?" asked Thomas after dinner that night. Laura was shocked and not expecting such a question. She liked his direct approach, but she just wasn't ready for the conversation. She saw all of these divorcing couples, and it had affected her.

"Why do you ask me that now sweetie?" asked Laura. At first Thomas wasn't sure if things would work out and whether he would stay in the United States, but he had gotten over his homesickness and would talk to his friends and family every week. He was also going to start a routine where he would go to New Zealand once a year and have some of his relatives come to the States sometimes too. More important than all of that, he loved Laura with all of his heart, and he could no longer imagine his life without her.

"I don't know, I was just thinking about it today," said Thomas. He was at a loss for words to explain it on the spot.

"Isn't there supposed to be a proposal or formal thing involved with a question like this?" said Laura smiling.

"Well, I'm not proposing right now, but I just want to know your thoughts."

"I'm not going to lie, honey. I don't know what we should do yet. I love you, and you know that, but marriage is huge and has so many consequences. I see them falling apart every day. Don't you think we should wait for a while then decide?" asked Laura.

"I have to tell you one time I heard about a woman who was in love with some guy back in the sixties. He asked her to marry him, but she gave an answer like the one you just gave me. Many years passed and the two never got together. Somehow, they got back in touch after many years and then finally at that time, the lady was ready to get married. So, they did. They were blissful in their marriage. They always wanted to be together when they were not at work. Sometimes they would just sit and stare at each other and hold hands. They talked about their deepest, innermost feelings every week. About four years into the marriage, her husband had a heart attack and died. The lady talked about how she was never able to forgive herself for having wasted all that time in between when he asked her to get married the first time and when they did get married. She said that the four years she had with him were the best thing about her entire life and that had she just done it earlier, she could have extended that happiness to so many more years. She never could forgive herself for that," said Thomas.

"Not trying to be cold, but the lady should just be happy that she had those blissful four years. Most people don't ever have that, right?" asked Laura. Laura was trying to look at the story with a logical mind, but inside she also felt the sorrow Thomas was describing.

"I don't know, honey, I kind of see her point," said Thomas.

Laura thought about what Thomas said but just didn't feel ready for marriage yet. It would seem so impulsive.

Maybe they would talk about it again later. Cautious Laura had come out when the topic was marriage. She gave Thomas a hug and set off to go upstairs. She was looking forward to watching a movie. There were always things to get done and work to do, and they did not even have kids! She looked forward to a night when her mind would slow down, and she could just enter another world. She lied down on the bed thinking she really needed to buy a new duvet cover, preferably a nice fluffy, lavender one and settled into her movie.

Chapter Twelve

"So, tell me a little bit more about your husband please," said Laura to her client.

"Well, he really started off as a great guy and father but somewhere in the marriage he changed. He didn't want to spend time with us anymore and only cared about his vacation time and his fun. I felt like I had Jessica totally alone, as if a woman can just pop out a child totally alone," said her client.

"Do you think he was having an affair?"

"I don't. Maybe he was, but my mind never went there."

"So why are you here now asking for a divorce?" asked Laura.

"My best friend passed away recently, and it got me thinking about my life and how quickly time passes. I saw myself constantly working outside the home, for our daughter, and in the home, and it never was enough for my husband. It was really unfair, and I started to ask myself what the purpose of such a marriage was," said her client.

"Well, that makes sense. I'm sorry to hear you went through all of that. We all go into marriage with the best of intentions," said Laura.

"Yeah, that's true. I don't know when it happened or where, but things just went downhill."

"Well, you are on your way to a new life. You've moved out and now that I'm representing you, you will be fine. You have a chance to start over and create a life for you and your daughter that you will be much happier with. No one is saying it will be easy because it's not, but you should be proud of yourself for having the courage to pursue what you really want or at least for standing up to a man who showed you no respect. A lot of people just let their lives go down the drain in situations that are really bad for them," said Laura.

"Thanks, Mrs. Townsend. I appreciate having you on my side." The lady felt much better after speaking to Laura and felt like she would be well-represented in court. With that, Laura's client left her office, and Laura was left alone with her files and thoughts.

Laura's boss, William, was the one to bring in the balloons. Laura had not slept very well the night before, but she knew the office was having a party for her since she had recently won an extremely hard case. They had chosen all silver balloons so it wouldn't look like a kid's birthday party. Laura was flattered that the firm had decided to throw a party for her. Law firms were serious places most of the time, so this felt even more special. Everyone was gathered in the break room which was stocked with nice comfortable chairs as well as hi-tech gadgets and televisions. It was a fancy break room, and a wonderful place for any party. They talked about what an excellent job she was doing and how happy they were to have her at the firm. When the young intern brought in a huge chocolate cake with the words *Congratulations, Laura!* on it, Laura felt really happy and proud to be working at the firm. They could have just ignored her recent win, but instead they wanted her to feel appreciated. It was these little things in life that improved everything. She blew out the candle on the cake, and they all sat and had cake with coffee. The case she had won was very hard because neither side was willing to compromise at all.

On her drive home that night, Laura started to think about work-life balance. She worked a lot, seventy hours a week to be exact, which did not often leave enough time for her to spend with Thomas. He was okay with it since he was busy trying to get his business off the ground. He decided against getting an engineering position but instead opened a small café in the touristy area of Duck. He figured during the summer and high seasons if he made the place nice, he would be able to have a sizable number of customers. It was slow going, but he seemed to be on his way. Laura wondered whether this meant that he was just throwing his engineering degree away. Then again, decisions about what to study are made when people are young and often don't know themselves or anything else well enough. As long as Thomas was happy with his choice that was all that mattered.

Laura started to wonder whether she should consider marriage. She was worried that marriage would ruin their relationship, maybe unreasonably worried but worried, nonetheless. Did she want to have kids? Her neighbors who had kids were always trailing after them in driveways while they screamed. Would she be able to go through her life without ever experiencing the joy of being a mom and holding her newborn baby? She felt some angst in her heart as she continued to drive home with these thoughts. Sometimes it was so much better to be a man. They could decide to have a kid at fifty for all anyone cared. She just wanted to try to make good decisions, and this seemed like a big one. She saw so many lives go wrong with one simple decision. Thomas was watering the grass when Laura pulled up into the driveway. She got home a little earlier than normal because she worked a lot of hours the Saturday before. He was hunched over a bit and looked tired from the day. It was sweet that he bothered to do these things. She always had to do these things alone before. She decided she would talk to him about some of the things she was thinking about on her drive home from work. She got inside the house and changed into her favorite butterfly pajamas.

"So, honey, how was your day?" asked Laura.

"Pretty good! We got a new cappuccino machine in the café, and the customers really like it. I can operate it from my iPhone which is interesting to say the least!"

"That's great. Ya, technology has certainly taken over everywhere. Soon we may be eating steel or something! Honey, I wanted to talk to you about something. On the drive home today, I started to think about our futures and what we want. Now that I'm no longer worried about starting at the firm and having to learn all the things a new attorney needs to learn, do you want to start thinking about what path we might want to take in the future? I know you wanted to talk about marriage recently," said Laura.

"Sure! I've been waiting for you to say this. I mean most women definitely want to start considering babies and other things if they don't have them already."

"Yeah, I bet that's true, but I was never in any real rush. I think it's important to get your education and stabilize your career first. You know that about me, Thomas." Thomas nodded in peaceful agreement. Laura loved how sensible Thomas was. She once dated a guy that was just impulsive and never reflected about anything, and he was so difficult to get along with. The things he said never made sense and no matter what Laura said he would tell her that she was uptight. It was not a loving and complementary relationship. Thomas was so laid-back and understanding and often deferred to Laura in terms of timing for things and what they should do. He really respected Laura's opinions and loved her with all his heart.

Thomas looked at Laura standing in the kitchen and doing the dishes and felt lucky to have a person like that traveling through life with him. He knew it would not be easy to replace someone as thoughtful, loving, and hard-working as Laura. He respected her opinions and was not going to push her for marriage or having kids. As far as Thomas was concerned, all of that would be Laura's decision. It was just good that Laura had brought up the conversation with him, and they would go into the details later.

Chapter Thirteen

Laura sat in her squishy, beige chair that she finally found the time to buy with her big mug of coffee. This was time to just be present and alone with her thoughts and feelings. As good as technology was, it caused people to be distracted all the time and on edge. Laura thought back about when she was ten years old, and there were no smartphones and all everyone would do is watch family comedy shows and peel oranges it seemed like. It was a much simpler time. Her friends who had kids constantly complained about how their kids were always on devices.

The house was quiet, which gave her a chance to meditate a bit. Thomas had gone on his morning run around the neighborhood.

Laura thought about her life in North Carolina. She was so focused on her work and was not sure she should even get married. She loved Thomas, but she couldn't ignore the fact that everywhere she looked, it seemed after women got married, their lives became overwhelmed with responsibilities and taking care of people. It would be fine if it was reciprocal, but often it was not. It was like a personal secret that all women kept from themselves and each other and just painted on a smile when it was time to have guests over. They cooked beautiful dishes and wore the right shoes meanwhile inside they felt desperate about how stressful their life was. Why were women so afraid to change this? What was at stake? Well, upon thinking about all of it, Laura knew that societal structures had been set up this way for many years. She talked about it with Thomas a bit, and he said that women were trained to behave that way from a young age. He thought in some ways it wasn't a bad thing because sometimes it led to great family relationships when the woman tried to be attractive for her man, but at the same time, he understood what Laura meant about women trying too hard to please everyone. Thomas said that as long as the man did the same thing for the woman, perhaps it was just love. After their discussion, Thomas decided to go to bed knowing he had to be at Natalia's house in the morning.

Thomas felt guilty the minute he drove up to his colleague's four-million-dollar house. He couldn't believe he came out there. She mentioned a few times at work how it would be great for him to come over one day for tea, but he did not think he would ever do it. Natalia was a very wealthy lady who did not need to work but chose to help Thomas run the business side of his café. She used to own several restaurants and knew quite a lot about that type of paperwork. She had been a great help to Thomas, and they had become good friends. Her ex-husband was a real estate developer, and they lived an idyllic life before the divorce. Natalia said that her ex-husband did the typical thing which was to trade her in for a newer model as she got a bit older.

Thomas had not mentioned to Laura that he was going to be having tea with Natalia. He felt guilty about it in the pit of his stomach because he was slightly attracted to Natalia. All of this would have been so much easier if he felt no attraction toward Natalia, but all they had was a business relationship so maybe there was nothing to worry about. The weird thing was he did not know why Natalia wanted to have tea with him. One day at work she just mentioned that it would be nice to have him over for tea so here he had gone and showed up at her house. He felt that it would have been rude to decline her invitation considering what a nice person she was and how much she had helped him with the cafe. The iron gate in front of her house opened after the camera took his picture. He drove up her ivory driveway and parked near the white, palatial door. He rang the doorbell and could tell that Natalia ran to the door because her heels were making fast and loud sounds as she approached the door. She flung the door open and started to laugh hysterically.

"Hey, what's so funny? I took a shower for you! Do I look funny?" joked Thomas.

"Oh, come in Thomas. Glad you're here. I was watching an old comedian from my college days. I guess I hadn't finished laughing before opening the door. There was a time I thought I may turn into a comedian myself," said Natalia.

"We certainly need more of them in life!"

"Come in, have a seat. I made you three different kinds of tea. I hope you like at least one or all of them. Normally

I get all the fancy saucers out, but I know you, so we are having a simple set-up today if that's ok," said Natalia. Thomas found it interesting that she was trying to be somewhat formal about this tea. Perhaps that's what her old fancy lifestyle was like. Thomas looked around a bit and took a seat. The house was impeccably decorated with ivory and pastel colors. There were exotic potted plants in just the right spot, and it felt a little bit like an Italian village type of set up. He started to feel nervous because now that he was inside her house it really occurred to him that he did not know why he was there. Natalia looked at Thomas and started to think about how attractive he was. She knew he was married, and she had never thought about him in that way before but at work Thomas always made her laugh. She loved his sense of humor and sometimes on days she did not work, she missed interacting with Thomas. She was not sure why she invited him over, but thought it would be nice to have a friendly tea together and just chat because work was always so busy and pressured.

"Your house is beautiful, Natalia."

"Oh, thanks! It sure is a lot of work to keep it clean and maintained, and I like to do that myself. I'm not sure I need it anymore actually, but it will be hard to leave the place you know as home," said Natalia.

"Ya, I could see that being true. Do you think about your marriage and past a lot?" asked Thomas.

"Well, you sort of can't help it I guess after a divorce. It's really like falling off Earth and landing on Mercury. It's that much change in your life and very disconcerting. I don't think about him that much because by the end of it, I was so over him. I guess what I think about are dashed hopes and beliefs."

"I get that." Thomas saw a purple and blue vase with these luminescent black dots flowing throughout it on the other side of the room. It was beautiful, and Natalia's house was filled with these awfully expensive looking and delicate looking pieces of art. Obviously not everyone could afford such expensive artwork, but Thomas thought about how anything that was beautiful was nice to have around. It changed the energy of spaces.

"So, how are things going with you and Laura? Are you guys thinking about getting married and having kids soon?" asked Natalia.

"I'm not sure. Laura is starting to think about that, but I'm not sure if she is ready for that yet. I would like to have kids and to have someone to throw a baseball with," said Thomas.

"Ya, it's a lot of work though so better to be ready." There started to be an awkward silence where it seemed the two had nothing to say anymore. Natalia looked at Thomas in a way he was not used to being looked at by her, like she wanted to sit closer to him on the couch or something.

"Um, well, how are things with you?" asked Thomas nervously.

"Well, like I said, it's kind of difficult to get past a divorce but overall, I'm doing ok. I enjoy coming to the cafe to help out with things for you, and I'm looking forward to planning some trips to go on," said Natalia.

"Oh, that sounds really nice. If I were you, I would do the same thing because just being in a different location really helps you get some perspective sometimes." Thomas started to feel nervous as if he should not be in Natalia's house. He was not sure if it would look bad if he abruptly left, but he knew he needed to do something because it seemed to him that Natalia wanted to have him over for a reason that was different than what he thought. He started to squirm in his seat a bit and started to feel warm because he was just uncomfortable with the situation. Natalia noticed this and asked him if he wanted a glass of water.

"No, thanks. I'm fine. Just a little tired. I guess I should start getting ready to go home soon," said Thomas.

"Oh, no you just got here! Please don't leave so soon," said Natalia.

"I'm sorry Natalia, I just have to be honest with you and tell you that while I appreciate you very much in life at work, I am very committed to Laura and have no desire to get close with anyone else." Thomas blurted it out and immediately felt better after saying that. Natalia looked a bit confused that Thomas interpreted her hospitality in that way. Natalia was Eastern European and in her part of the world it was normal to be friendly with people. It looked like she should have toned it down a bit with Thomas.

"I totally understand, and I'm sorry you interpreted my kindness in that way." She felt a slight attraction towards Thomas, but that was not why she invited him over. She just wanted them to have some time to talk and relax together since they were always so busy with work things. She felt embarrassed that she made Thomas uncomfortable. They decided it was best to end the visit, and Thomas walked to the door, thanked her, and left. Natalia looked at him as he was walking away and respected his commitment to Laura even if he had misinterpreted her gesture.

Thomas got back into his car and looked at the hundreds of red tulips along Natalia's gorgeous ivory driveway; this place looked like a resort. As beautiful as it was though, he believed that a person could make any place a beautiful sanctuary with some creative thinking and attention. Thomas hoped he had not overreacted to Natalia's behavior, but he was happy to be out of there. He imagined being by Laura's side for the rest of his life and being there for her always. He hoped this exchange at Natalia's house would not hurt their work relationship.

Chapter Fourteen

"Honey, this weekend they have the apple festival going on in town. Do you want to go?" asked Laura.

"Of course. What time should we leave? asked Thomas.

"Let's leave at eleven." Thomas and Laura pulled up into the parking area for the festival and most of Duck was already there. Gentle music engulfed them along with the fragrances of apple cider and cinnamon buns. They needed a few hours to relax together as a couple. Laura loved when people decorated festivals with pumpkins, straw, and colorful leaves everywhere. It just soothed her deep in her soul and reminded her how beautiful nature was. The two walked around and met up with some neighbors that were there then found the funnel cake station. Laura didn't need too much stimulation when she was with Thomas. Something about his presence just made her feel safe and at peace. As they were walking, Laura's cell phone rang. It was her mother calling from DC.

"Laura, hi, how are you darling?" asked her mom.

"We're doing well, mom. We are at a festival in town. How are you and dad?"

"We're doing okay honey; we've decided to take a Mediterranean cruise in a few weeks and just wanted to let you know we would be away."

"That sounds great mom. It sounds like a great time. Stay in touch with me though. I better get text messages from you!"

"Of course, honey. How's Thomas? How are things at the cafe?"

"Great, thanks mom. I'll tell him you said hello." Her mother called her almost every day. It was nice to have that close relationship. With that, Laura hung up her phone and walked through the fields with Thomas. She hoped that one day she and Thomas would have the lifelong relationship that her parents did. Her parents, Candace and Everett, were still so active and happy. They always brought good energy when they were around, and they set a good example of how to live life well. Sometimes Laura thought people just needed more education on how to sustain good, loving relationships. If people were able to do that, they would be happier; if they were happier in their personal lives then their work would be better, and then the world would be better. So many big things could be traced back to little things. The rest of the day was spent arm in arm walking in the sunshine sipping apple cider and breathing fresh air.

A few days later, when Laura got home from work, Thomas was in the kitchen finishing cooking mushroom risotto. The house smelled like fields of mushrooms and rosemary. The couple gave each other a hug, and Laura went to change into her favorite pajamas. She loved how she could just be herself around Thomas and did not need to wear the best clothes or be fancy. He loved everything about her the way it was. The two sat together at the table and enjoyed their meal while talking about a movie they recently saw. Thomas had put regular button mushrooms, shitake mushrooms, portobello mushrooms, and one other mushroom that Laura did not recognize into the risotto. On top of everything else, Thomas was a great cook!

"Honey, I want to talk to you about our future," said Laura. "I've been thinking that I'm not sure there is much reason to wait on figuring out marriage plans. I love you with all my heart, and I know you wanted to talk about this before. What are you thinking about it?" asked Laura.

"You are the person I want to be with forever. I've never had any doubt about that. It was not just coincidence that you came to New Zealand, and you walked into that pub. This was meant to be, and I wouldn't want to waste one day not being married to you. The earlier the better, honey," said Thomas. Laura felt her heart fly up when she heard those words. What had she done so right in life to deserve this man entering her life? She always had a companion by her side and someone who loved her with all his heart. He worked hard every day to make her life better. He was there for her every day in ways she could not even anticipate herself. She felt so at peace in the universe sitting there at that dinner table with Thomas. For a moment she felt confused because recently she had thought that she may never want to get married to anyone.

"Thomas, where should we get married?" she blurted it out before even really thinking about it. It made perfect sense to go back to New Zealand for the wedding. They both knew it and almost said it at the same time. Now, to plan the wedding.

In New Zealand, summer was from December to February, opposite of the Northern Hemisphere. Summer had the best weather, so they decided to have the wedding during that time. It was already late November in North Carolina so they would not have much time to plan the wedding if they wanted to do it within the year, but they weren't concerned about that. They wanted to do the wedding right away, and they wanted to do it in New Zealand. They had no doubt about either of those two things so they would just hurry and figure it all out. How good it was to have no doubt. Laura decided she would ask for a few days off work to fully focus on planning the wedding. Her mom would come from DC, and they would plan the wedding together. Laura did not have any siblings, so she was used to doing everything just with her mom. Her friend, Rebecca would get a little involved too. Laura was starting to feel so excited she could barely think straight. She wanted to daydream about the wedding day she would create for them to mark the official beginning of their life together. The days when young women would daydream about a big wedding seemed to be over, but at the same time, when there was true love, creating a beautiful wedding to represent that love made perfect sense.

She wanted to bring art to life at her wedding. For a moment, Laura wondered whether they should wait a year before having the wedding and started doubting their decision to do it in the next few months. It didn't take long for her to realize that she was overthinking it and needed to put an end to that. She remembered that in high school, her math teacher told the class, if you are in doubt go with the first answer that comes into your mind. That was what she was going to do here. Thank you, Mr. Boxom.

Chapter Fifteen

The judge slammed her client with huge legal bills, and Laura could barely walk straight as she walked out of the courtroom with her client. This judge had a tendency to impose legal bills, and Laura had warned her client of that. Her client was almost in tears as they left the courtroom, but really it was the client's fault for not listening when Laura encouraged her to compromise more. Outside, the regular courtroom staff were doing their duties and checking people in through security and into the courthouse. The halls were a little less full that day, which was nice because Laura was so used to having to bend her way through the crowded courtroom halls. It felt so much more freeing to have space around. She said goodbye to her client, who was still in tears, and walked to her car.

Going through that experience would take her a couple of hours to get over. She felt bad for her client, but she had done all she could for her. It was not all in her hands. Normally Laura brought her lunch, but sometimes it was nice to go sit somewhere and eat and not have to worry about packing things. She was going to treat herself to a nice lunch at Saffron Cafe. When she arrived there, the host sat her at a beautiful table by a sunny window. Laura would have a relaxing lunch instead of wolfing down a sandwich at her desk. She was learning how to be nicer to herself and give herself unexpected, good moments sometimes. Whether that was a lunch hour, a nap, or time with a friend. She spent most of her life just taking care of other people, whether family or friends, and unfortunately many of them had disappointed her or taken advantage of her kindness. She wasn't bitter because that wouldn't help anything, but she was definitely much more aware now.

She slowly looked over the menu and decided on the Croque Monsieur sandwich. It was a classic French favorite that she loved. She wondered whether they would be incorporating saffron into that dish given the name of the restaurant. She was not sure how they could. Maybe saffron would just be in the tea she would order later. She had seen tea with saffron rock candy in an ethnic store before.

"Hello, ma'am, what can I bring for you today?" asked the server.

Laura woke up from her thoughts and said, "Oh, I'd like the Croque Monsieur please."

"Certainly." The server thought that Laura looked too lost in thought and not really in the moment. Laura sipped on her ice water and stared out the window. She read somewhere that a good practice to incorporate into life was to sometimes just stare out of the window instead of focusing on to-do lists and life concerns. This was the perfect time to do that. Outside of the restaurant, she saw a fountain with red birds swimming in it. She let her thoughts wander away as she just focused on that fountain and those birds. Just two minutes of staring out the window and emptying her mind made her feel better. It didn't always take a big vacation to relax. It was quiet in the restaurant, and there was a slight aroma of butter and tea all around. Laura needed this after the day she had in court. The place had the fragrance of what she imagined a café in the south of France would have – a place surrounded by hibiscus flowers and generations of bakers lined up inside.

A few days later, Laura's mother, Candace, and Rebecca were going to meet her at the local tavern in Duck. Laura was only working until lunchtime that day because they needed to work on the wedding plans. She had taken three days off of work, and they were going to focus on this exclusively. Her mother arrived, wearing a white sweater set and beige pants with her blond hair looking beautifully wind-blown. She was staying at the hotel down the street not wanting to impose on Laura and Thomas in their home. Laura had always been proud to introduce her mother to her friends when she was younger because everyone loved her mother's personality. She was a "people person" and genuinely cared about what was going on in people's lives. She was always very put together and well-dressed as well.

"Honey, it's great to see you," said Candace while giving Laura a big bear hug. Rebecca joined in and the three stood in the front of the tavern in a big bear hug. These were the moments Laura looked forward to. Moments that were all about joy, love, and supporting one another. They went inside the tavern, and it was decorated in light purple everywhere. The flowers and paintings all had a lot of purple in them, and there were little purple lights on each table. They sat at a table, ordered their food, and burst into conversation. Rebecca said how much she loved the idea of going back to New Zealand for the wedding. Candace worried that some of the family might not be able to make it that far. Laura just knew it was the right place for the wedding. The beautiful panoramas there, the fresh sea air, the flowers, and the friendly people. Everything was coming full circle and so fast. She met Thomas there, and now they were getting married and starting a whole life together! Laura felt like she had fallen into some magical situation and did not know how it had happened. Her mother had always said to believe in the good energy of the universe. Laura, being more of a logical person than her mother, was not always sure she believed in the mysterious energies of the universe as much as her mom did, but at this beautiful moment it seemed her mom was right.

Laura told them how she read that they could do a guided nature walk as part of the wedding. Her mom looked perplexed and seemed to be expecting a wedding in a church and a reception in a hotel, but Laura's gut was telling her she wanted something different. She wanted to share vows under the sun and take a walk with all her guests through a forest - anyone who wanted to come. She knew there would be people that would want to stay back and then just go to the reception, but she wanted to offer this to her guests. At first, Candace thought her daughter's idea was ridiculous and that people would not want to be outside in nice clothes getting dirty and walking. Laura explained to her that it could be worked out so that everyone would be happy. Candace was never the type of mother that forced her will upon anyone else, including her daughter, so she quickly acquiesced, and the decision was made. Laura was grateful for that because she had seen so many mothers who pushed their will on everyone.

The other thing Laura found out is that there were beautiful caves in New Zealand. Laura knew she wanted the reception to be in a cave. Thomas had agreed to this when they talked about it the night before. She would tell all her guests that the attire for this wedding would be nice, but much more casual than a regular wedding. She never believed in too much formality, and she wanted her wedding to reflect that. What would she wear for the exchange of vows? It would still be a dress, but like the flower-filled white and red sundresses she used to wear as a young girl, a flowy hat, and a pair of white gloves. For the walk and reception in the cave, Laura wanted to wear a white dress preferably with blue streaks in it and silver sandals. She would add a turquoise necklace and some pale pink lipstick. She would leave her hair down because she was lucky with the flowy and beautiful hair she inherited from her mother. She wanted everything to feel free and was hoping there would be a beautiful breeze that day to keep everyone feeling awake and in the moment.

They picked the date - the wedding would be on January 10th. On other January 10ths in her life, she was in DC sitting around a Christmas tree with her parents or ice skating in downtown DC. This January 10th would top them all. That night, Thomas and Laura decided to go for a walk and stop by their neighbor, Grace's house. Grace had started babysitting for Randy, the man who fixed Laura's sink before, and Randy's daughter was going to be there that night. Laura had not seen Grace in a while so she told her that after their walk, she and Thomas would stop by for a visit. As they walked through the neighborhood, Thomas and Laura chatted about everything that was going on. The wedding, the new customers Thomas was getting in the cafe, how much he loved his work and felt that he was providing a comforting place for his customers to go to during their day, and Laura's legal cases. Thomas was always a great listener as Laura told him about her days in court. He was so proud of his wife and knew how hard it was to be a trial attorney.

When they approached Grace's house, they looked at her beautiful potted flowers on her porch. It looked as if she had spent hours plucking away any dead leaves or stems and had given them the perfect amount of water and sun. Grace had a way of making everything comfortable and beautiful. Grace opened the door and looked very happy to see them there. She set out freshly made lemonade on the kitchen table, and the four of them, including Randy's daughter, Sara, sat to chat.

"Grace, I'm sorry I haven't seen you lately. You know it's been busy though. I hope you forgive me!" said Laura.

"Oh honey, please don't apologize. At my age, you realize that younger people are busy with a million things they need to do, and I've learned how to keep myself busy so that I don't feel lonely."

"It's great to be self-sufficient like that," said Laura.

"Well, I love to see you, anytime you have time," said Grace. She was making a grilled cheese for Sara, who was eagerly anticipating eating her favorite sandwich. After Grace found out that Randy was divorced, she offered to watch Sara as Randy needed it. Grace was truly an example of the kindness of strangers, which was something very much needed in the world. Sara was watching the latest kid's comedy on tv and waiting to get a call from the cute boy at school she had a crush on. Randy was uncomfortable with this at first but realized he needed to be realistic about Sara growing up. This was all part of the parenting process – change, change, change.

Chapter Sixteen

As time seemed to do, it had flown by and suddenly it was the wedding day. It seemed like there were millions of lavender Ageratum flowers streaming alongside the pillars between which Laura walked to the altar. Thomas waited there looking like he was going to tear up. Laura loved that

Thomas was not afraid to show emotion, even if one-hundred-fifty people were watching. There was the fragrance of water nearby and white birds flying above the grounds. She walked slowly down the aisle in her slightly fancy red and white sundress with her white sunhat flipped to the right. She did not want to rush; she wanted to take all of the sights and feelings in.

Her mother sat in the front aisle with tears streaming down her face, and the rest of the guests were fully focused on Laura walking down the aisle with genuine smiles on their faces. Thomas looked at her, and he could see the next seventy years in his mind's eye. He pictured them cooking together, shopping together, and traveling all over the world together. She looked just like herself without too much makeup and was the Laura that he loved walking down the aisle. For a moment, he remembered her sitting in the pub in New Zealand the day he met her. Tears welled up in his eyes as he watched her continue to walk down the aisle. He had never felt so happy in his life, and he could not wait for her to stand by him at the altar. After they exchanged their vows, it was time for them and any of the guests that desired it to go on a nature walk together through the Wainui Falls Track. They would be walking through native bush, going through lush forests, and then arriving at the beautiful waterfalls. Laura could not wait to do this with Thomas and any guests that were willing to come. The guests who decided not to come on the walk would be lavishly taken care of in the resort.

Laura and Thomas set off, arm in arm, with a trail of guests following their tracks. You could hear nothing but happy conversation and laughter in the air as the crowd slowly walked through the first set of stones. The nature walk was exactly how Laura imagined it would be. The reception was held in a beautifully lit cave, and they ate lobster, fish, and vegetables while gentle tropical music played in the background. Everett could not believe he had given his little girl away. He still remembered teaching her how to ride a bike as if it was yesterday. He liked Thomas and was glad that Laura had found a good person to spend the rest of her life with. The wedding events flew by, and everyone was pleased with how it turned out. The guests all appeared to have had a great time, and the energy all around was electric. Laura knew she would remember her wedding for the rest of her life.

Back in North Carolina, they felt like they had stepped off twelve beautiful clouds that flew high in a sunny sky. It was time to get back into the routine of work and things at home. Laura's work was keeping her busy, and she started to think about starting a side business as well. She knew that being able to be self-employed would be a wonderful experience if she could make it work. She wondered whether she could start something on the side of her law practice like a hobby business. One of her clients from the week before was a real estate agent. It was not the most creative of jobs, but Laura liked interior design, architecture, and talking to people so maybe it was something worth trying. Plus, her legal background would help a lot with dealing with the contractual aspects of it. Laura started to think about that and started to research what it would take. She was never one to shy away from a new challenge. After some time looking into it, she consulted her intuition and decided that she was not feeling a strong enough pull towards real estate. Plus, it seemed to be a career that was phasing out with the advent of technology. Instead of doubting her decision or second-guessing it, she just threw that idea out.

Thomas recently felt like Laura's mind was somewhere else. Normally she would let him know how she was doing, but recently she was keeping to herself. As Laura and Thomas sat at the dinner table munching on baked sweet potatoes and roasted chicken, Thomas was ready to bring up the conversation. He felt a little nervous, but he was not going to let that stop him. Too much was on the line.

"Laura, how are you honey? I feel like lately you haven't been talking to me as much. Have I done something wrong? Is everything ok?" asked Thomas.

"I can see why you might feel that. I gotta be honest and tell you that yes, I am tired these days. I love you, and I think everything will be okay," said Laura. She didn't feel like going into a lot of detail right then.

"I'm glad to hear that. I was getting worried honey." Thomas wasn't going to push the topic further. Laura left the dinner table and thought that she should have said more to Thomas, but she just did not have the energy to delve into it further at that moment. She did not want to make him anxious, but she knew they were having layoffs at her law firm. Since she made more money than Thomas if she were laid off, they would have trouble keeping up with the mortgage and other bills. Thomas' cafe was doing well, but it could not cover all their expenses. Laura started to feel bad that she did not say anything else to Thomas, but she knew that Thomas was a more nervous person than she was. It was best to wait and see what happened.

Laura sat down in her comfortable chair and started to read a book about supply side economics and drank some hazelnut coffee. Thomas walked in dropping grocery bags all throughout the hallway as he huffed and puffed. It was a balmy, hot day outside and not one to run around outside.

"Honey, we need a change," said Laura. She wondered whether she was being too abrupt, but she wanted to use time efficiently to get things done. Sometimes this showed in the way she spoke.

"Ok, what do you mean? Let me put the groceries away." Thomas was not in the mood to hear anything shocking. As Thomas continued to move bags around and put things into the refrigerator, Laura started telling him what was on her mind.

"You know we are still young, but we won't be young forever. Don't you see all the people around us how quickly their lives and youth went by? People get stuck in routines and trapped with responsibilities that they think must be for eternity. We only get one life, honey!"

"Well, are you unhappy?" asked Thomas.

"No, we have a good life, but we aren't doing everything we could be doing. We are just doing the same routines and trying to pay down our mortgage and all of that. All good things, but there has to be more to life than that."

"Ok, so what are your ideas?" asked Thomas with some fear.

"I don't know yet. I have not thought too much about it yet. I just want to do something different. Something without fear and overthinking."

"Let's go to Thailand." Thomas was not sure why that popped out of his mouth.

"Ok, sweetie, let's go," said Laura. That was it. They did not talk about it anymore or think about any of the details. The couple just continued with their Sunday tasks and went to bed that night with a sense of relief. Laura took Monday off work to go to the doctor, and it gave her time to think a little about the Thailand idea. When she woke up, Laura started thinking about it and knew what she wanted to do once in Thailand. She wanted to volunteer time to help with different problems the Thai people had. Many Thai people wanted to learn English, and she thought one good thing they could do is teach English to people in rural Thailand. Besides that, there were lots of programs involving stray pets and lots of other social issues they could help with. How long could they go for though? What about her legal job? Thomas' cafe?

She started to research where they could stay and started to think about what to tell her boss. Should she quit the job completely or just ask for some time off? She decided she would not let all these thoughts dissuade her or make her nervous. With that type of thinking, she would never be able to make any changes in her life. She looked into it a bit and was inspired by the town of Kanchanaburi, Thailand. She thought about how lucky she was to have Thomas in her life. This was something the two of them could do together. She was not sure if she would want to do something like this completely alone. She could go to New Zealand alone, but they spoke English there and the area was more like what she was used to. Going to Kanchanaburi alone would be a different matter! Thomas was at the cafe so Laura would have the day to think about things, and they could talk about it later at dinner.

She and Thomas often made dinner together which gave them time to talk and just relax while enjoying the process of cooking. She picked up some zucchini, cilantro, lemons, and chicken from the store, so she was thinking just a simple chicken dish with a side of vegetables and a salad.

She would wait for Thomas to get home so they could have a glass of wine together and start cooking. Her mother used to always say when she was growing up that it was good to respect the ingredients of your food. Her mother used to love just washing cilantro and making something beautiful out of it; her mother used to say that people were on the planet to enjoy little things and to make things more beautiful. Thomas walked in the door with a big smile on his face.

"I couldn't wait to get home today and see you!" he said as he grabbed Laura and gave her a big hug.

"Well, hello! I'm glad you're here."

"How was your day at the cafe?" asked Laura.

"It was good! A lot of good girlfriends were there today just chatting away and all looked so happy to have a little time away from their schedules to see each other. It was nice to see people so happy being together. We all mainly see people rushing around these days and only looking at their phones," said Thomas.

"Oh, that's nice. Was business good?" Laura asked this while thinking about her potential job layoff that had been worrying her a bit. Well, if they were going to go to

Thailand then who knew what was going to be happening next anyway.

"Ya, it was a busy day at the cafe. I'm pretty tired actually now."

"Ok, well if you don't feel like cooking, I can do it or we can just order something tonight," said Laura.

"No, it will be refreshing to cook dinner with you, honey." They started washing and chopping the vegetables and soon a fresh, herbal fragrance was whirling around the kitchen.

"So, what do you think about the Thailand trip we talked about?" asked Laura.

"I think we should go."

"But how? Don't we need to figure out what we are doing and why we are doing that and what will happen with all our responsibilities here?"

"If you think like that all the time, you'll never do anything. There will always be things like that in life. How badly do we want to go?" asked Thomas.

"Well, I'm wondering about my job and your cafe. How would we handle that?" Laura had started second-guessing everything. Thomas stopped what he was doing and peered into Laura's eyes.

"Honey, let's just sell everything and leave," he said.

Chapter Seventeen

It was not long before the two were landing in Thailand. Laura liked how these days she was making things happen in her life. It was always a balance between thinking and not being too impulsive and just getting things done. Laura knew risks did not always work out though and could really ruin a life as well as bring good things. She read a lot about having clarity of purpose in life and how doing that would help everything else in life. She achieved becoming a lawyer; she had a wonderful husband; she went on the trip to New Zealand alone as a challenge to herself. Was this decision about Thailand the same thing? How did it relate to her purpose? Laura wondered whether it was possible to continue to live a passionate life even as a person got older. She did not see too many people who had succeeded in doing that. She had seen a lot of older people that only complained of aches and pains and how life had not gone as they thought it would. So many people were filled with regrets and bitterness over all kinds of things.

In the blink of an eye, the couple exited the airport in Thailand. Thomas hailed a cab, and the two got in and drove away from the airport. The cab driver had a name plate on his dashboard that said Aroon. He turned and smiled at them while drinking something that looked like iced tea with cream in it.

"I speak English, don't worry," he said with an accent Laura found pleasing.

"Oh, great! We are excited to be here," said Laura.

Upon leaving the airport, things mostly looked westernized. Laura was looking forward to getting nearer to Kanchanaburi. She read that they had floating markets there, and she was really excited to see one. They would be in the cab for a while before reaching their destination. Thomas had not eaten in a while and since he had diabetes, he started fumbling around in his bag for a granola bar. He wasn't overweight; he probably got diabetes from having some sort of gene. He approached the problem with the same perseverance that he had about most things in life. He just did what he had to do to deal with it the best way he could. It was hot in the cab, and Laura unbuttoned a few of the buttons on her white, linen shirt. It was a good, flowy shirt that would allow air to circulate. After some time on the road, Laura looked out of the window and saw lots of street vendors selling colorful objects and a lot of people milling about without the rushed pace that Laura was used to seeing.

"Hey, it looks like people are having a lot of fun here," said Thomas.

"Very true. Just what I was thinking. Wonder why?" The cab ride continued mostly in silence as both Laura and Thomas were tired. The cab driver also was a quiet person and did not seem to want to make idle chatter. Finally, the couple arrived at their hotel in Kanchanaburi. It looked more like a hut with vegetation climbing over it and the smell of coconutty spicy food seeping outside its windows. It was a warm evening with a light breeze, and the hotel windows were open. After doing registration at the front desk, Laura and Thomas entered their room. Everything was light blue! Well, not absolutely everything, but there was a blue theme going on inside the hotel room. The orchids, blankets, and champagne bottle were all blue. It was not a fancy hotel, but they clearly wanted their guests to feel comfortable and be amused. There was a poem written in English directly on the wall. It said *don't think twice because it will be too late... it will be too late.*

"Wow, honey we are in Thailand!" said Thomas.

"Yeah! I'm tired though. Let's go to sleep and figure things out in the morning." The couple got under the blue, warm blankets and fell asleep to the sound of some animal or insect that made a beautiful whirring sound. With the windows cracked open, the sound and the warm night air engulfed them. They suddenly awoke to the sounds of loud, frantic knocking. Laura stumbled out of bed and opened the door.

"Ma'am, you must leave the hotel now!" screamed the hotel worker. Laura felt her pulse start to race, and she suddenly felt like she could not think. The man looked so distraught and spoke in a way as if something was terribly wrong. Before she had a chance to ask him any questions, he shoved her out of the door and yelled at Thomas to get up and leave too. They saw others doing the same thing in the hallway. People were rushing out of their hotel room doors. Once outside, there was a group of hotel guests and two people from the hotel began to address the group.

"Many years ago, there was terrible civil strife in this town, and some of the people from the past came here tonight to start a fight again. These people are very dangerous. We need all of you to leave for your own safety.

Call us in two days to see if it's safe for you to come back. Now go!" Thomas and Laura looked at each other in total disbelief wondering what was going on and where they were going to go. Laura's heart started racing, and she felt short of breath for a moment. They decided to just walk and see if they could find a place that would be safe to sit down or better yet find a person that would allow them to stay there for the next two days. They grabbed onto each other's hand and started to walk forward with trepidation. Luckily, it was daytime which helped matters a bit. The roads were empty aside from the other people that were walking away from the hotel. There was a lot of mud and some paved roads but mostly mud around them. Something that smelled a bit like honeysuckle plant wafted by them; it helped to release some of their tension for a moment. There seemed to be nothing around this windy path they were walking on except green leaves and vegetation. For a moment, the couple stopped and looked at each other.

"Honey, we have a decision to make. We can either be scared and horrified about this situation or we can view this as an adventure. This is certainly not what we were looking for when we decided to come to Thailand, but how many things in life turn out as expected? Let's try to approach this in the right way. We are in Thailand. It's supposed to be a beautiful country. We are doing something very adventurous. It's really a once in a lifetime opportunity. Let's not let this glitch mess everything up. Who knows what we will discover on this detour." Thomas was nervous and talking fast, but he was right. Laura thought about what Thomas was saying. She did not agree in her heart quite yet. She was trying to get to that point, but she just was not there yet. She was annoyed that they woke up in this way and was worried about where they were going. She started to think that she just was not having any luck because for a moment her canyoning accident came to mind and wondered why the universe was putting her through all of this. She could not approach this problem the way Thomas was approaching it. Well, not yet anyway. Hopefully, she would get there because there was no alternative but to keep walking.

Peering behind a bunch of what looked to be ivy, they saw a house on a hill with lights on and cars outside. They decided to go knock and see what they found. It was a very unassuming and small house that looked like an olive-green box. It had large windows though which made the place feel like it might be nice inside. Thomas and Laura tentatively walked towards it wondering who lived inside.

They were far enough from their hotel now that they felt safer. After knocking, a lady with long, red hair opened the door with a big smile. She did not look Thai at all.

"Hello, our names are Thomas and Laura, and we are from the US and just visiting," said Thomas. He waited to see if the lady understood English. She may have since she looked very Western.

"I speak English, and my name is Elizabeth. I'm British, and I own this house. I come every few months for a change," she said. Thomas and Laura were relieved when they heard this. They could tell by Elizabeth's expression that she wanted to know why they were on her doorstep.

"Well, you won't believe what happened, but we were forced to leave our hotel due to some disturbance there. We have nowhere to go," said Laura. Laura's voice was shaking as she said this, and she realized as she spoke how uncomfortable she was with the situation they were in.

"Wow, that sort of thing doesn't happen in Thailand very often. I'm sorry to hear you're going through that. You are more than welcome to stay here for a couple of days. I don't have much room, but we can figure something out," said Elizabeth.

"We can't thank you enough!" said Thomas. People really were kinder than it appeared sometimes. This lady was allowing complete strangers to stay in her house. Elizabeth led them into the home and gave them a little tour. The house was beautifully maintained, and there wasn't a thing out of place. Laura noticed a big mural on the main wall of Egyptian pyramids. Elizabeth had decorated everything with modern furnishings and art, and no one would have guessed how nice the inside of the house was by looking at the boxy outside of it. That was a testament to what creativity could do. There was a huge, white carpet shaped like a heart in the center of the entranceway. It was a nice touch and looked like it had been put there by someone who knew how to decorate. Laura also thought it was a nice touch to have a symbol of love at the main entrance to a house. They took their shoes off at the door, and Laura felt the comforting softness of the carpet under her feet.

"The two of you can stay in the guest room, here," said Elizabeth. The room was small but looked comfortable with a big bed covered in a blanket with blue dolphins all over it.

"If you'd like to have some tea, meet me downstairs in ten minutes. I understand if you're tired," said Elizabeth.

"Absolutely, we will come down soon," said Laura. When they came downstairs, Elizabeth had cups of steaming peppermint tea on a tray in the center of the coffee table with a plate of very ripe dates. The dates looked like they were about to burst of ripeness. Laura was hungry and could imagine those dates would be deliciously sweet and exceptionally good with the tea. They started to drink their tea in silence feeling relieved to have found a place to stay.

"Try not to let this mishap ruin your trip to Thailand. Things seem to happen in life all the time, don't they?" asked Elizabeth. Elizabeth was always good at picking up on people's emotions and could tell how distraught the two were even though they were being pleasant.

"Yes, thanks. You're right. I'm just worried about this situation," said Laura.

"Why? You'll be fine. You can stay here, and then your hotel will be ready for you again. So, where in America do you live?" asked Elizabeth.

"We lived in Duck, North Carolina. It's a great place. It's a beach town so we enjoy the water all throughout the year in one form or another, and it has a good, slow pace. It seems so many of us are beyond stressed with the fast pace of life these days. Our town is better in that way. We've sold everything though, so we are no longer anchored anywhere," said Thomas.

"I've been to America a few times but never to Duck. I've been to New York and Philadelphia. I have a cousin in Philadelphia, and I just wanted to see New York," said Elizabeth.

"I hope you enjoyed those cities! We are looking forward to seeing things here. I've heard about Hellfire Pass. Can you tell me a little about it?" asked Laura, wanting to get back to positive thinking about this trip.

"Well, I don't know too much about it myself, but it was a railway where there was forced labor, I think. The railway was constructed during a war I believe, and many people died during the construction. There are people in Thailand who now believe that going there and making a wish is a sacred thing to do," said Elizabeth.

"Well, what a name it has. It kind of doesn't seem to go with making positive wishes!" said Laura.

"I know what you mean, but there are people who believe in it 100% and have stories about how it's worked for them," said Elizabeth.

"Is it an eerie place?" asked Laura.

"No, I don't think so. You'll have to go and look and let me know what you think." Laura and Thomas got into bed that night and were both a little disgruntled. They had sold everything they owned in the United States, including Thomas' cafe to start a new life in Thailand. As they laid in bed that night in a stranger's home, they were deeply doubting the intelligence of that decision. On the positive side, they were in a comfortable bed, and Elizabeth was a nice lady. There was nothing bad going on right then, and they decided that the moment was good enough. There was no reason to worry right then so they closed their eyes and went to sleep. When they awoke, Elizabeth was in the kitchen making pancakes for everyone. She had a yellow and orange parrot that was flying around the kitchen making little sounds. It was cute and not bothersome.

"My brother, Edward is going to stop by today. He's in Thailand for a business trip. I hope we can all have a nice breakfast together," said Elizabeth.

"Oh, that sounds nice." Laura hoped they wouldn't be more of an imposition now that Elizabeth would be having a guest.

Edward arrived wearing flowy, beige, khaki type clothes. The top and bottom matched and looked to be made of the same material. He said he wanted to feel cool in the warmer climate and liked to dress differently when in Thailand. He owned a shoe store in London and typically had to dress very fashionably. He looked to be in his mid-thirties and had a sophisticated air to him.

"Edward, meet Laura and Thomas. They are staying with me for a couple of days," said Elizabeth.

"Well, hello! Nice to meet you," said Edward in his adorable British accent. It didn't seem they needed more introduction than that. The four sat down to breakfast and enjoyed pancakes, strawberries, and coffee. Edward told them about his life in London. It was a busy lifestyle but one that he enjoyed overall. He said he had thought many times about selling the store and permanently moving to another country but never got up the nerve to do it yet. Elizabeth started cleaning up the kitchen and making more coffee so they could all sit and chat longer. Edward told them about his ex-girlfriend who was a nice lady but a little too serious about everything. Even though they loved each other, it was not going to work out for them, and they decided early on to end the relationship. Having seen all her law firm clients, Laura knew how hard any breakup was, so it was good that Edward decided to go through it early in the relationship. Laura liked how open and talkative Edward was. He acted like he had known them forever. After breakfast, Thomas decided to go on a walk and tied up his shoelaces and left. Elizabeth had an appointment at the nail salon, so she went to take a shower and get ready for that.

"Well, what do you want to do while these guys are gone?" asked Edward.

"I don't know! It's a bit hot out for me to go hiking or anything like that."

"Well, we can just putter about I guess," said Edward.

Elizabeth and Thomas left, and Edward and Laura went to the back patio just to talk. The patio was covered in flowers and bushes and was a very tranquil place to be. There were pretty wind chimes that were not too noisy and the fragrances of different plants. There were no houses nearby, so it felt like a very secluded spot. The two continued talking about all aspects of their lives. Edward knew a lot about a lot of different subjects from history to art. Laura did not remember ever being able to have conversations like that with anyone before. Thomas was great to talk to but being an engineer by background, he did not really care too much about history or art. Laura felt slightly embarrassed that she was enjoying talking to Edward as much as she did. Laura told Edward more about their lives in North Carolina and how they decided to sell their house and leave their jobs to come to Thailand without any real concrete plan. She told Edward about how she met Thomas in a pub in New Zealand. Edward liked hearing about her life, and the way she told the stories was fascinating; she seemed like a very passionate and intelligent person as he listened to her talk. Edward asked Laura if she would like to go walk by the river Kwai. He said they had floating hotels there, and it was beautiful. Laura was interested despite the heat and the two set out to get there. When they got there, Laura was astounded! The hotels were little cottage looking things with triangular tops and something that looked like straw on the top. Set behind them was a lot of foliage and the river slowly drifting by in the front. She had never seen something so exotic. Duck, North Carolina compared to this was like Earth compared to Mars. Laura thought about one of her literature professors in college reciting a quote. *Life is short, but art is long.* This experience reminded her of that because there was so much to see in the world but not enough time it seemed. There were probably so many different perspectives and landscapes in the world. She was so happy to be at the river Kwai. Edward kept telling her about the different things she was seeing in the area, and she loved learning about that. While listening to Edward, she forgot about everything else.

They spent some time just walking and talking and then decided to stop and get a Thai iced tea. They already felt like they had known each other a long time after discussing everything about their lives and then going on this walk together. Laura could not remember ever having more fun except for when she first got to know Thomas. The two started to return to Elizabeth's house continuing to giggle all the way back. When they arrived home, Elizabeth and Thomas were both already there.

"Well, hello! Where have you guys been?" asked Thomas.

"We didn't have anything to do so we went to the river and looked around," said Laura. Thomas looked at her a little quizzically. Nothing like this had ever occurred in their relationship before. He felt a pang of jealousy as he looked at them and felt uncomfortable inside. His wife looked a bit too happy standing there next to Edward. They were standing close to each other and acting as if they had known each other for years. Thomas felt strange about it but decided to let it go and not worry about it.

Chapter Eighteen

A couple of days passed, and Thomas decided it was time to see if they could go back to their hotel. Inside he wanted to get his wife away from Edward as well. He found himself staying up at night and thinking about how happy Laura looked after the walk to the river with Edward. He trusted Laura completely, but it just felt weird to see that.

"Honey, let's get ready to go back to the hotel today," said Thomas.

"Sure, that sounds good. I'm going to take a quick walk and after tea, let's go." Laura left for her walk and came back energized.

"I saw the prettiest cat ever in the alleyway in town. One eye was green and the other blue. He looked abandoned. It was sad, but at the same time it looked like the neighborhood people were taking care of him. His home was everywhere," said Laura. The couple said their goodbyes to Elizabeth and Edward and thanked them for the help and the stay. It felt like they would all remain friends but who knew. As Laura was getting older, she realized that people were not as reliable as she once thought. She was getting tired of always being nice and often being taken advantage of.

When they got back to the hotel, everything looked completely normal. People were sitting in the lobby drinking tea which was the preferred drink in Thailand. There were kids playing by a fountain outside, and it was as if all the strife that occurred there a few days ago never happened. They settled into their room, and Laura started thinking about their visit to Thailand. What would they do now? What kind of life could they create having sold everything in the States?

Laura had always taken the traditional paths in life, and she was not sure what it was that made her suddenly change. Everything was a blank canvas now. Laura started thinking about the conversations she had with Edward on their walk. He had such a good spirit about him. He had the kind of intelligence that gave a deeper meaning to everything. Edward made it seem like the world really was a magical place that everyone was lucky to be in. She realized that she did not feel the same way when she and Thomas had conversations. She loved talking to Thomas, but he was more run-of-the-mill when it came to conversations. He didn't think too much about the deeper things in life, and he was not particularly funny. Edward made her laugh a big part of the time they were walking around town. Suddenly, she realized that she missed him. She wondered how a married woman who was in love with her husband could miss a man she randomly met recently. *Wow.* Thomas had gone to the market to buy some water and snacks. She impulsively decided to call Edward. With some trepidation, she picked up her phone and dialed his number.

"Hello? Hi Edward. It's Laura. Just calling to say hi. How are you?"

"Hey Laura! I've been thinking about you. How's everything at the hotel?"

"All is back to normal, thanks! So, when are you heading back to London?"

"You know I'm not sure yet. I don't get a chance to see my sister often so I'm considering staying a bit longer than normal."

"Oh, that sounds nice. Maybe we can see each other one more time before you leave." Laura said that before realizing those words were going to come out of her mouth.

"Sure, I would love to!" They hung up the phone, and a few minutes later, Thomas walked in. It looked like his wife was deep in thought. He decided to dismiss it and not think about it anymore. Maybe he was just being insecure or maybe he was just nervous that they sold everything and came to Thailand.

Laura heard about a healer in town that said she would clear people's energies and set them on a fresh slate. She never really believed in things like that but wanted to go there to see what it was about. Thomas decided to go hiking so they would spend a couple of hours apart. It was good for couples to have some time apart anyway. She meandered through the streets, walking slowly, just taking in the sights. There were kids tossing a red ball in the air and screaming; there were flowers covering sidewalks; there were two old men sitting on a patio playing chess. The mood was calm, and things appeared hazy as if you were looking at them through fogged up glasses. There was no sense of urgency happening around here. It felt like a cool glass of lemonade on a hot day or a dip in a lukewarm pool on a cool day. She got to a little, white house that had a sign on the outside, "Come in and change."

When she walked inside, it was dim with faint blue lighting spreading everywhere. There was red and gold fabric on all the walls. It felt like being wrapped tightly in a blanket after having drank a bottle of wine with a very insulated and warm feel. The lady who approached her looked to be about fifty years old with short black hair and long silver earrings. She walked slowly as if she was thinking about every step before she took it.

"Hi, come in and sit down." The lady clearly knew English and must have decided that Laura needed to be spoken to in English.

"Ok, I just wanted to ask you what you do and how much it costs," Laura started to mumble thinking of all her questions.

"Please. Just stop thinking. Stop talking. Sit down." With that, the lady whose name she did not know sat in the chair opposite Laura with no table between them and just spent a minute looking at Laura. Laura started to wonder why she had walked in there. What was wrong with her? First going to New Zealand and having that injury over there and now she found herself in this room. For a moment, her heart started beating fast and she lost all belief in herself and her decisions. It felt uncomfortable to be in that room with this lady staring at her.

"Just sit. Don't think or talk." After about five minutes of this, the lady began to speak.

"What do you want?" Laura did not know how to answer that and thought she would come in here and the lady would do something magical that would clear all her energies whatever that meant. She thought it would be quick, and then she would leave.

"Uh, I'm not sure what you're talking about. I don't really want to think about that. I thought you..." Before she could finish, the lady asked her in a sterner voice what she wanted. Laura put her attorney hat on and decided she was going to deal with this situation directly even though it wasn't one she had ever been in before. Maybe this lady was on to something and knew something she didn't. She decided to be open-minded about it. Laura was not sure what she wanted at this point. Had she made a mistake marrying Thomas? Why was she attracted to Edward? These seemed like petty things to talk about with this lady. Laura got the feeling this lady wanted to know something much deeper. She decided not to care and to just tell this lady what was on her mind.

"I'm married, but I find myself interested in a man named Edward." The lady put her palms up in the air near Laura's heart and made a small sound like *roooooo*. She continued that for a few minutes.

"Edward is the one you should be with. Get a divorce as soon as you can." She turned some flute sounding type music on and told Laura to listen to it for ten minutes while standing and stretching her arms towards the sky. She said Laura could leave after that. She did not ask for payment or say anything else; she just left the room and shut the door. Laura walked out of the healer's building and felt dizzy. She did not know whether to take this seriously, but at the same time she felt like something real had happened in there. She was making so many uncharacteristic decisions lately. She barely recognized herself and her life anymore. It was thrilling in a way, but she felt confused about Thomas and Edward. What about through sickness and health? All these things had always been important to Laura, and she felt confused because she was thinking about getting divorced from Thomas to follow her heart and possibly be with Edward.

There was no guarantee that anything would work out with Edward or that it was the right thing to do, but she felt something strong pulling her towards him. Was this healer confirming what she already knew? She used to read a lot of self-development books, and many of them said that happy people were contributing to the world and the universe in a way that unhappy people were not. She felt very conflicted, like no decision would be a good one. She decided that she would talk to Thomas that evening. When she walked into their hotel room, Thomas was watching a Thai cooking show. Even though he didn't understand the Thai language, he still enjoyed watching those cooking shows.

"Hi, honey, what are they making?" asked Laura.

"I'm not really sure, but they certainly eat a lot of vegetables here!" Laura did not want to waste time with chit chat tonight. She wanted to get straight to the issue.

"Honey, I'm not sure where to start." Thomas pushed himself further up on the couch and looked like he was becoming alert. He had figured out by looking at Laura that it was something important.

"What?" he asked. Laura paused for a moment and then began to cry. Thomas was wondering whether she was sick or something horrible had happened like a death of someone or anything horrible like that.

"Honey, do you remember Edward?" asked Laura. Thomas felt a pang in his chest like he was being attacked by something. He felt like he already knew what she was going to say and remembered Edward and Laura looking so happy together after their walk.

"Yes," he said with his eyes looking down at the carpet.

"Ever since we met, I have been thinking about him almost non-stop. This is not like me. I love you; you know that, but maybe love is not enough. This is the first time in my life that I've experienced something like this. When I talk to Edward, I feel on top of the world, like I have no problems, and everything in my life is great." She felt bad saying this to her husband, but she wanted to tell him everything. She owed him that. After she said it, she started to think about how stupid what she was saying was. She didn't even know Edward very well. Was she some stupid schoolgirl? The two sat in silence for a good five minutes before Thomas spoke.

"I sensed something. I knew it," Thomas said matter-of-factly. Thomas got up and left the hotel room and did not come back until morning. After he left, Laura got into bed and cried for hours. She had just hurt the one person she loved more than anyone or anything in the world. She did not know how else she could have handled this and did not know what had come over her. Maybe it was common to have such feelings for someone, but there was no reason to tell Thomas about it or do anything about it. She felt very confused and bad about hurting Thomas. The look on his face when he left was one of complete despair.

As Laura laid in bed at 4 am, she thought about meeting Thomas in New Zealand. She had started something that felt like it was going to continue forever and then in what seemed like the blink of an eye, it had already ended. How did people end up in Thailand suddenly without a clear plan as to why they were there or where they were going? How did they suddenly tell their husband that they were interested in another man? When she married Thomas, she felt that they would be together until the end. All of what was happening was making life seem to be a lot less certain. Maybe certainty was just for kids or dumb people. She remembered his face in that tavern where they met. The way his eyes sparkled as he spoke to her and when he came to see her after her injury in New Zealand. When he opened the door of their hotel room at six-thirty in the morning, Thomas walked slowly towards her.

"Laura, I understand. I'm not mad at you. It's ok. I'm an engineer. We are scientific people at heart. I accept this. I'm going to go back to New Zealand. It's good that we sold everything in the US already. It will all be less complicated than you think. Maybe our time together was supposed to be limited from the beginning." Laura had nothing to say but just gave him a small kiss on the cheek. This was the same man she fell in love with – a man that was logical and calm and never made a big deal out of anything.

Two weeks later, Thomas was gone. Laura continued to stay in the hotel since things had changed so much since she got to Thailand. She and Thomas were thinking of buying a property there, but everything had changed. After Thomas left, Laura spent time on herself trying to make herself feel better. She did facials on herself and did her nails. She read books that she liked. She needed some time to do mindless things and see if relaxation brought her any clarity about all the things that had happened. She was grieving the loss of Thomas but what really helped her was seeing his face on the last day that he was in Thailand. He did not look bitter or angry. He looked like he had accepted the situation fully and even though it was shocking, he understood why Laura had said what she said.

He did not want to be in a relationship where the other person felt like they were just settling to be with him. On their last day together, he looked at her with respect and with love. He told her that he was very happy he met her in that tavern in New Zealand and that she had taught him things that would stay with him for the rest of his life. They parted as friends and knew they would always have a type of love for one another. Their goodbye was a testament to the fact that not everything in life involved jealousy or bad feelings even after a breakup or even a betrayal.

She had not seen Edward for weeks. It was time to call him and see how he was doing. He did not know all that had transpired between Laura and Thomas or the fact that Thomas was now gone. Laura talked to Thomas one time after he left, and he said he was settling back into his home country. He went to the pub where he met Laura early after returning and all the decorations were different, and Larry, his bartender friend, had moved and was no longer there. The changes in the pub were like a reflection of the changes in his life. His friends and family were happy to have him back and were cooking him healthy meals every week until he got back into a routine in New Zealand. He continued exercising, and his diabetes was better. Laura felt grateful that she had married someone as kind-hearted as Thomas who didn't even get mad at her for this.

Laura felt scared to pick up the phone and call Edward. She had come out of her marriage because of him, but what if he was gone or worse yet had no interest in speaking to her? She decided that there was nothing guaranteed in life, and there was no point thinking too much about it. If he was gone or had no desire to talk to her, that would have to be fine.

"Hello?" said Edward.

"Hi, Edward. It's Laura," she said as her pulse suddenly shot up.

"Well, hi there! How is everything? I'm about to go swim at the pool in town, do you want to come?"

"Sure!" said Laura excitedly. She was so happy that he wanted to see her too. Laura threw together a bag of swimming clothes and headed out. When she got to the pool, Edward was busy talking to three attractive women and sitting at a table sipping a yellow tropical drink. All the women had their gaze fixed on Edward. He was a very captivating man with light brown hair, green eyes, and a story for every minute. He was not fake though or trying to get attention. It was just his essence. Laura was sure all the women around him had some sort of interest in him, but she could also tell that Edward did not care and was just being friendly. Edward and Laura got into the pool and started doing breaststroke. He stayed by her side the whole time, and they started to float a bit and talk.

"So, you aren't planning to return to London any time soon?" asked Laura.

"Well, I don't think so. I always come here on a schedule, but this time I want to stretch things out a bit. I have a manager in London who can handle the shop while I'm gone."

"Edward, I'm just curious. Why haven't you gotten into another relationship after your ex-girlfriend?" asked Laura wanting to cut to the chase as usual.

"I want to have freedom."

"What do you mean by freedom? Like being able to go out with as many women as possible? Being able to travel? What?" asked Laura nervously.

"No, not really any of those things. Just a feeling in my heart. Most relationships don't represent that to me. It seems like an economic partnership a lot of times. I don't want that."

"Ok. Do you ever feel lonely though?" asked Laura. They continued to float and alternate with swimming. It was a beautiful day outside, not humid, and the pool was not very crowded. They served drinks at the side of the pool, and Laura could smell the coconut drinks even in the middle of the pool.

"I don't really feel lonely. When I was young, I wanted to learn how to be self-reliant and be able to handle most things and my emotions by myself. I started to learn about meditation and how to be creative so that I would never need anyone to entertain me. Over the years I've really perfected that I think. I love people, but I don't need them," said Edward. Laura thought about what Edward said. She was kind of the opposite and could not really imagine her life without people in it. She had recently started to think that she relied on her connection with people too much, but it just was who she had been all her life. Interestingly, she had started trying to learn to be more introspective recently so she could understand where Edward was coming from. She just wondered whether that meant a relationship with him would not be meaningful or even desired on his part.

"Oh, I see. That sounds really smart." Laura said while feeling her heart sink.

A cloud started to come over the sun and half of the sky turned a darker color.

"Where is Thomas?" asked Edward.

"Oh, that's a long story. He's no longer here. We have decided to end our marriage, and he returned to New Zealand." In her usual style, Laura just said things straight.

"What!? How did that come about?"

"It's really a long story. Let me talk to you about that later. Right now, I just want to focus on this beautiful day and our swimming. I'm sad about it; you don't get out of a marriage with no scars," said Laura.

"Ok, but what was the disconnect between the two of you?"

"We were just missing the sense of oneness that I wanted to feel. The sense that I could talk to him forever, and he would not get tired of it or not understand. The sense that we could always teach each other something," said Laura.

"Ok, those seem like pretty good reasons." Edward got worried about Laura, and he was not the worrying type. Now she was suddenly alone in Thailand, and he was wondering if she would be up to the task of re-creating her life alone at such a young age in a foreign county. Laura couldn't believe it herself, but at the same time had decided she was going to push her limits. The two swam for another thirty minutes and as slight drops of rain started coming down, they decided to leave. They swam another few minutes in the rain because the sound of it and the feeling of it on their faces was pleasurable as their bodies moved through the silky water.

"Do you want to come back with me to Elizabeth's house?" Without thinking, Laura said yes. After dinner, the three sat on the back porch and had tea and passion fruit. Elizabeth started to tell the story of a day in 6th grade when she met her best friend Shelley back in England. The two of them clicked right from the beginning and felt they had found the world in each other. They would go to festivals and eat cotton candy; they would practice piano together and sit and watch sitcoms together. Each day seemed so long back then, and each possibility seemed so endless. She did not know why she was remembering that time now, but maybe it was because she valued good relationships so much and sitting with Edward and Laura reminded her of that. She noticed from the time of Shelley to her present-day life how much difference having good relationships made in her life. She never needed too many, but the ones she had were so important to her that she always went out of her way to help her friends and family.

Laura and Edward sat on a swing with soft, light green cushions. They both felt like they were seated a little too close to each other on that swing, but at the same time it felt natural. Laura always felt good when she was in his presence. He made the room feel like there was a good party going on or there was a warm fireplace nearby. Laura always paid attention to people's energy and seemed to have no control over that habit of hers. Some people really had bad energy or were control freaks. Other people were just dark in their mind and still others were just self-centered jerks. She had become better over the years at identifying these things about people before getting too close to them.

The porch had potted plants all around it and little lamps to light the way and sitting there with Elizabeth and Edward was so soothing. Elizabeth was going to stay in Thailand another few days and then return to England. Laura wondered whether Edward was going to leave at the same time, and the thought of that gave her a mild chill. After a few more hours with Elizabeth and Edward, Laura went back to her hotel and hoped to get a good night of sleep.

Chapter Nineteen

Laura arranged to do some social work while she was in Thailand. She was going to go to a food kitchen that day and help prepare meals for poor people. She enjoyed cooking so this seemed like a good thing to do, and it suited her personality. When she got there, she noticed how precise everything was. Everyone was standing in a certain spot on the kitchen line and doing different tasks from chopping tomatoes to washing cilantro. She did not care which one she would end up doing since she just liked working with her hands; it made her feel present and stopped her overthinking. The lady next to her on the kitchen line looked to be about seventy years old, but maybe because of all the healthy food they ate in Thailand, she looked vibrant and did not have saggy skin or anything that made her look old. The only reason Laura thought she was about seventy years old was because of her grey hair and how her husband looked. Maybe the people in Thailand had less stress. Maybe it was something in their food, or maybe it was family or community support. People in Thailand had a sense of community and viewed others as friends and neighbors even when they didn't know them very well. It made sense that good community support would help people in every aspect of their lives including how they aged.

Laura was given the task of chopping cilantro. She had learned from a Julia Child cooking show a long time ago to roll herbs up and then start chopping them. The only thing she ever used cilantro for at home was a rice dish that her friend from law school had taught her. It gave such a good fragrance to white rice. She didn't have a lot of time during law school to cook but whenever she did cook, it reminded her of home and comfort. Law school wasn't full of all home cooking though! She remembered staying up until three in the morning to study on many nights and finishing an enormous bag of Reese's Pieces followed with huge amounts of Mountain Dew soda to help herself stay awake. She also remembered being exhausted during some tests but doing well on them. She continued chopping cilantro for four hours and did not really talk much to anyone there. Many people did not speak English anyway, and it seemed that people just wanted to be in their own little worlds while doing their tasks. Laura had learned that sometimes silence was really a beautiful thing. This was new knowledge because she had spent most of her life talking or distracting herself from things. At the end of her shift, the manager came and threw all of the cilantro she had chopped into a big, white bin and left. Laura wondered where that cilantro would go. What exotic Thai dish was that cilantro going to end up in? Well, the day was complete, and Laura had thoroughly enjoyed the process. Arriving back at her hotel, Laura felt like she had accomplished something good that day. Who knew some time ago back in Duck, North Carolina that she would be standing in a kitchen in Thailand chopping cilantro for hours in total silence? She could not have even imagined that then. Maybe anything was possible in life. As she sat down to take her shoes off, her phone rang.

"Laura? Hi, it's Edward." Laura brushed her bangs away from her eyes and tried to sound alert. She was tired from the day but wanted to give Edward all of her attention.

"Hi, Edward!" Laura said enthusiastically.

"I want to let you know that I'm leaving to head back to London tomorrow." Laura immediately decided she was not going to be sad about this. She was not a teenager, and she knew all along that Edward's life was in London not in Thailand. It would make no sense to be sad or to think anything of it despite all the feelings she had for him.

"Ok, well, I'm sad to see you go, but I understand that you need to leave." Laura fumbled for the right words to say. She did not want to act like she did not care at all, but at the same time she didn't know how to react.

"Laura, I will miss you," Edward blurted. The two of them paused not knowing what to say.

"Thanks for saying that. Of course, I will miss you too. Most men I've dealt with in my life could never say that even if they felt it. I appreciate you telling me your feelings," said Laura.

"I don't know, Laura. It just came out." The two paused on the phone for a little while longer.

"How long are you staying in Thailand?" asked Edward.

"I really don't know. I have no idea about tomorrow anymore and try not to worry about it. Most things are unknown, and it doesn't help to worry about it. You know I came here with Thomas initially, and we were going to buy a place here."

"Ya, but since that has changed what are you going to do now?" asked Edward with some worry in his voice.

"I think I'll stay here for a while longer and try to feel out what's the next best thing to do. Should I stay here permanently? I need time to think about that," said Laura.

"Ok, well, I plan on keeping in touch if it's ok with you Laura."

"Of course, it is," she said feeling very thankful that Edward had a desire to stay in touch. After all, she had broken up her marriage because of him.

The next day, Edward was gone, and Laura found herself lying down in a yellow hammock in the back yard of her hotel. She was thinking about the next project she could do in Thailand. Could one person really make a difference? It seemed that most of the time people were only spending their time on their own needs and desires. Although Thailand was a bustling country with a lot to offer, there were certainly pockets of poverty and people who wanted to get education especially in English but were unable to do so. Laura decided she would teach English and called around to find out which organizations she could work with. She found one with the name of a contact person listed as Aranya. When Laura called her, Aranya said that there was a group of twenty-something year olds that had gotten together at the local diner and put bulletins up saying they were looking for someone to teach them English. They did not have access to the internet or digital devices and were looking for local people to teach them. Aranya thought this was the perfect opportunity for Laura. Laura arranged it and was scheduled to start in three days.

They decided to hold the class in the same diner since it was inviting and spacious. Laura arrived at the diner and was nervous, but she found the group of ladies sitting in an empty section in a corner. They brought a lady with them who could speak English so that she could explain to the ladies what Laura was saying. The lady was not interested in teaching English, but she could be a translator for them. Teaching required a certain level of patience that she did not have. The lady's name was Mali, and she told Laura she would let her know if the ladies had any questions. Mali's English wasn't great, but she knew enough to be able to facilitate in this situation. Laura had created worksheets and planned out how she was going to conduct her class that day. They all looked so excited to finally be pursuing a dream they had. One of the ladies said her motivation for wanting to learn English was that one of her favorite shows was in English, and she was tired of watching it while reading the subtitles. Another lady said she wanted to move to the United States in the future for school. Another lady said she had family that had married into English-speaking families and wanted to learn to be able to speak with them.

It seemed like people in Thailand were more honored to do basic things that others in the world just took for granted. Many young people Laura knew over the years would never be so excited to come and learn a new language. Their level of appreciation for the lesson made Laura feel good and showed her what it meant to be grateful for things in life. The translator told Laura that one of the women wanted her to know that she liked her blouse. It was a linen red, white, and blue blouse that Laura wore whenever she wanted to remind herself of the United States. For a moment, Laura wondered whether she could offer to give her blouse to the woman. She had seen her mother do that when someone complimented a piece of her clothing. If it was a coat or something, her mother would often just take it off and say, *here, it's yours – I hope you wear it in good health!* Since this was a blouse, Laura couldn't just take it off and give it to the lady. Instead, she started thinking about whether she had anything like it that she could bring for the lady during the next class. Laura enjoyed seeing the women gain words in English and see how proud of themselves they were becoming. They were so eager to learn, polite, and kind to Laura. She really felt like she was making a difference in their lives as she taught that class. Following her heart, intuition, and passions was creating a life that Laura was proud of.

One evening, Laura realized that she should find somewhere to stay other than a hotel since she was staying in Thailand for this long. She would need to spend some time figuring out where else she could go. Suddenly, it occurred to her that Elizabeth's house was empty, and perhaps Elizabeth would rent it to her now that she was back in London. She called her, and Elizabeth was more than happy to do that. It was settled; Laura would move into Elizabeth's house for a while, continue to teach English to these women, and pay Elizabeth rent. After that, Laura would figure out what was next in her life. She wasn't quite sure whether she would be buying property in

Thailand now that Thomas was gone. She kept in close contact with her parents back in DC as well as her friend Rebecca in North Carolina. They were concerned about her, but at the same time, they were proud of the obstacles she was overcoming.

Laura moved into Elizabeth's house the next week. Everything looked the same as when they were all there together. It made her think even more of Edward than she already had been. It was like she could feel his presence in the house. His energy was the type that filled the room and apparently also the type that stayed in it after he was gone. As she thought of her time in the house with Elizabeth and Edward, she started to think about how much longer she was going to stay in Thailand. It was good that she had become comfortable with not always knowing her next move and had become comfortable with ambiguity. The only path she could have taken in order to make these changes was the path of risk. She recalled reading a philosophy book written by a famous, old philosopher that said there really was no security in life and constantly looking for it made a person feel more insecure. She wanted to teach herself how to live by these words fully over time.

The next couple of months flew by, and Laura had fallen into her routine of teaching, taking long walks, and cooking a lot of Thai food which included using a lot of coconut milk! The flavor was so smooth and delicious. This was the first time in her life she had so much time to be by herself and not be distracted by other people's demands. She had always been too sensitive to other people's needs and often did not get a chance to take good enough care of herself. It was as if she never even factored into the equation; maybe she really was as unique as most people told her she was. She loved teaching English to these Thai women, and she liked the routine she had created there.

One morning, as she was making oatmeal, Laura suddenly decided that after Thailand she would return to the United States. As she was pouring the milk into the oatmeal, she thought about her parents and their age. They would not be around forever, and she wanted to be in the same country as them. She was going to rent an apartment in San Diego. She had always heard about the wonderful weather there as well as all of the beautiful parks and streets. Some of the things she heard about San Diego weren't that great. She heard people were much more superficial than on the East Coast and didn't want to take the time out to get close to others. In the DC area where she grew up, people often thought about things deeply and intellectually. Friendships lasted a long time, and they tended to be close. She would have beaches and plenty of places to get exercise outdoors in San Diego amidst the flowers and the sun.

She did some searching, and it didn't take long before she found a good apartment in San Diego online. A few hours later, she had signed the lease and would arrive there on May 1st. The weather was good year-round there but particularly good in May. She was excited to be returning to the States to start a new and independent life. She missed Thomas sometimes, and they stayed in touch regularly just to update each other about their lives, but she never regretted their decision to divorce. Laura had started to think she was too independent to be constrained by a marriage to anyone. As well as she and Thomas got along, there seemed to be an element of you scratch my back and I'll scratch yours in the marital relationship. Laura wanted to be free and do things she wanted to do without keeping score about whose turn it was for this and that. If it was possible to be in a marital relationship without that keeping of score, then maybe she would try it one more time in the future.

Chapter Twenty

After her time in Thailand, Laura was a different person. She had become grateful for little things in life like running water and feeling healthy. People around the world had a lot less and often had things a lot harder than people in the United States. Even in such a thing as small as customer service, there often was a lot of it in the United States whereas in other places shopkeepers often didn't really care if a person wanted to return an item or just wasn't happy with the service. These were little things but also just the freedom between places was very different. Perspective was everything, and Laura learned that through her experience in Thailand.

Laura loved her new, little apartment in San Diego. It was in a building with a nice pool in the back and palm trees all around. There were many older people in her building, but there were some people her age as well. She wanted to talk to Edward, so she picked up her phone and called him.

"Edward? Hi, it's me."

"Well, hello darling! Great to hear from you. I didn't want to bother you quite yet since I knew you were leaving

Thailand and had the move to deal with. How did everything go?"

"All is well! I'm really liking my apartment and just need to finish decorating it a bit. I'm looking for an ocean and sun picture that I can hang in the dining room. Haven't found anything I like quite yet. Better yet, I should say I haven't found one I love quite yet. Why would I buy a picture that I only liked?" asked Laura.

"Nice! Maybe I can visit after you're settled." Edward thought Laura sounded happy with the move, and he was glad because he was worried about her.

"Why wait? Can you come next week?"

"Sure!" said Edward taking a quick glance at his work calendar. Laura hung up the phone with a flutter in her chest. Edward quickly agreed to come to San Diego to visit her. She would need to feel out their relationship and start to make some decisions about it. This was different than their coincidental time in Thailand. Laura wanted to know what the purpose of their relationship was, and she thought the only way to figure that out would be to see him and maybe even directly ask him. She was not one to mince words. She felt something palpable in her heart when she was around Edward or even when she was thinking of

Edward. Maybe it was just the infatuation of his British accent or the exotic nature of the time they had together in Thailand. Maybe things wouldn't feel the same this time when he came to San Diego. Maybe the fact that she was no longer with Thomas would ruin whatever attraction was between them before. She just couldn't be sure at this point, although in her heart she felt that the gravitational pull she felt between them before would still be there.

Laura's mom, Candace, decided to visit her from DC and see her new apartment just a few days later. The morning her mom was to arrive, Laura was not in the mood to clean up all the clothes she had thrown everywhere and the empty yogurt containers that were lying around. She used to be so spotless with everything inside her house, but these days she thought it was not good to be obsessive about things like that. Perhaps she had gone too far the other way though. Her mom was sixty-seven years old, and Laura knew that one day not too far in the future her mother would no longer be around. It was something she never had to think about before, but with time things became clearer.

As well as the two got along, Laura and her mother's personalities were vastly different. All her mom cared about was fashion and gourmet food which were both wonderful things, but sometimes her mother took things to an extreme. Laura was sure as soon as she came inside the apartment, she would complain about the food in the refrigerator even if it was an apple but not the right type of apple according to her mom. The next thing would be her mother would find a bread crumb on the dining table from an earlier meal and probably be bothered by it. With some determination, she put one foot in front of the other and got up to start cleaning up a little bit. She wanted to listen to some old-time music while she cleaned; cleaning always went faster when it was done to music. She turned on Rick Springfield and started running around with her Windex. At the end, she sprayed some lemon spray all throughout the apartment and everything looked and smelled good. She hoped her mother would be happy with this, but she knew that it still may not be enough for her mother. There was a knock at the door, and it was Candace. Laura opened the door, and the ladies happily embraced.

"Oh, Laura, you've managed to keep this place tidy." Candace felt like the place had a good feeling to it.

"Ya, mom, I try," said Laura hoping that would be the end of the critique. Laura asked her mom if she wanted a cup of black tea. Her mom accepted, and Laura began the process of making the tea. She would make it British style with milk and sugar.

"So now that you're all alone here, what are you going to do with yourself?" asked her mother. Candace could not imagine living the type of life Laura was living.

"I don't know mom. I was always so planned about everything. I'm tired of that. Let's see what the universe brings. Who the hell really knows what is around the corner." Laura started to feel herself getting tense because like the obsessive cleaning issues her mom had, she could also be too pushy sometimes. Candace looked disappointingly at Laura like she was wondering where she'd gone wrong in raising her. Candace was wondering what Laura was doing with her life just picking up and going to Thailand and then suddenly returning to the States without Thomas. To Candace it looked like her daughter was taking too many risks. After Laura's shower, they decided to go whale watching later in the day. They got ready and left and soon got to the location. There were people milling about everywhere with ice cream cones and nice reggae music playing somewhere in the area. It was a happy scene that made Laura think of her childhood when there seemed to be a lot of good everywhere she looked. Environments were important to Laura, and she had learned over the years that what worked for one person often did not work for another. That was also why Laura did not like it when people tried to impose their way of life on other people. It made no sense because just like flowers that all have a different look and different needs, people were that way too. They got on the sailboat and there was a couple next to them with a toddler. The woman was feeding the child and carrying the child while the father just walked around the deck and talked to other people. That woman looked very tired, and her husband really did not seem to care or notice.

"Well, this was a nice idea, Laura. I'm looking forward to what we're going to see in the ocean."

"Yeah, I thought you would like this mom."

"So, Laura, I know you get tired of my lectures and questions, but I'm wondering what you are going to do with your life now. You know, you are no longer very young, and time goes faster than you think. Don't you want to have kids? Aren't you worried about the future or finding another husband?" asked Candace.

"Mom, no! Not at all. I think differently now. There was a time when all those things were things I thought about and desired, but that is no longer true. I've had a lot of experiences that have shaped who I am now. I think it's important to have an inner life and be happy with little. I don't think everyone has to have kids. If you are in a loving relationship, and you both want them then fine; otherwise, it really isn't something everyone has to do." Laura got all her thoughts on this out in one fell swoop. She just wanted her mother to enjoy their time together instead of using the time as a chance to question Laura about her life.

"Laura, perhaps you are thinking kind of pie-in-the-sky right now. Things get harder after forty years of age. You better start thinking realistically about what you want your life to look like. You want to be alone for the rest of your life?" Candace thought that Laura was too idealistic and had no clue how hard life could suddenly get.

"Mom, none of us really have too much control over what happens in life. We can control some things and make certain choices but ultimately, we don't really have that much control and shouldn't make our life decisions based on fears. I want my life to be led by what I truly desire or find meaningful. I don't want it to be led by fears and preventing dreadful things." Candace looked at her daughter and started to worry. She did not want to pry but wasn't it a mother's duty to help steer her child? She realized that Laura was no longer a child but to a mom, her kids were always her children. Candace decided to let it go for now and just enjoy the day together. The sailboat captain pointed out towards the ocean where some whales were swimming by. Everyone peered in that direction, and Laura heard gasps and saw a lot of people taking pictures. This definitely was an interesting planet if nothing else. So many kinds of animals and species of everything. Focusing on things like that always renewed Laura's sense of optimism about life even in hard times. The water was gently rolling by; it was not a rough day in the water. The sun was partially covered by clouds so that it wouldn't be blinding or too warm. Candace looked like she was finally relaxed. The whales were in a group of three and poked their heads up a few times. What a different perspective the whales had on the world. It was a fun and relaxing day, but when they got back home, Candace looked upset. Laura started to wonder what was going on because that really was not her mom's style. She expected her mother to want to go home and have some tea then immediately head out to the boutiques to do some shopping or take a stroll in a botanical garden or something.

"Mom, what's wrong? You look upset." Candace was not sure if she really wanted to get into it with Laura at that moment. She had come just to help Laura make her new apartment feel like home and to spend some quality time with her daughter. She really did not want to talk about sad things or cause Laura to worry, but she knew eventually she would need to tell her that she had been diagnosed with aggressive breast cancer. She was not sure when would be the right time to do that, but she didn't think it was at that moment.

"Oh, honey, I'm fine. I mean there is something I do want to talk to you about later, but there is no need to go into it now."

"What do you mean? Are you and dad ok?"

"Yes, honey, don't worry. We are fine." Candace felt bad that she hadn't mentioned the cancer to Laura yet, but she wanted the visit to be positive and not sad. Laura decided to let it go and follow the words of all of the spiritual books she had read that said sometimes it's best to surrender things to the universe. There would be no point in reading those books if she never implemented their words in her life. When she was younger, she would have pressed more to find out what was going on, but Laura decided to let it go for now. It was time for Laura's mother to leave and go back to DC. They cooked together, went shopping, and watched movies. It was very relaxing, and Laura's apartment felt more like home after her mother had been there. Edward was to arrive in San Diego the next day, so Laura started her preparations for that. She felt very lucky that she had her mother and Edward in her life; it really made her feel good inside to know that she had people that cared about her.

Chapter Twenty-One

When Edward stepped off the plane, he looked so attractive in his dark jeans and light blue button-down shirt. His light brown hair was hanging a bit down the side of his face, and his green eyes twinkled as he approached. Laura felt like she was in a movie since everything around her seemed so picture perfect, and she felt overjoyed as he walked closer to her. She was a little nervous and hoped that he found her attractive as well.

"Hello!!" beamed Edward.

"Edward! I can't believe you're here!" The two hugged and held on for more than a moment. It felt great to be in his arms. She loved Thomas, but she never felt this way when she hugged Thomas. She wasn't trying to compare Edward to Thomas, but sometimes the comparisons just popped up in her mind.

"I'm so glad you came! I'm really excited about this time we will have together here. I think you're going to like San Diego." Laura was so excited that she could not stop talking. She felt like there was so much she needed to tell Edward and that she needed to say all of it right then. She felt like there was no other moment, no future, nothing to wait for, and she wanted to blurt everything out RIGHT THEN.

"Thanks so much for inviting me," said Edward looking at her in awe and thinking how beautiful she was. Laura had different ideas about what the time with Edward should be like. On the one hand, she knew Edward was an adventurous guy so going around town and seeing sights would appeal to him, but since he was only going to be in San Diego for a few days, a part of her wanted to spend the time in a more leisurely way so that the time would feel stretched out. She decided she would ask him his preference later.

Edward was excited to be with Laura and remembered the time they had in Thailand as one of the best experiences of his life. He was not sure why, but Laura stirred something in him. She made him feel alive, and she inspired him. He wanted to come to San Diego to see if he would feel that way again after being with her in Thailand. He did not really care about seeing San Diego too much, but he wasn't going to spoil the fun by telling Laura that. She could have been in the worst location in the world, and he still would have come. His flight had been delayed, and he was tired and not feeling his best. Seeing Laura waiting for him in the airport was already helping tone down the headache he had during the flight. When they got back to Laura's apartment, Laura showed Edward the room he would be staying in. She had made it nice and fresh with gold and silver pillows everywhere and a vase filled with fresh white lilies. She wanted him to feel comfortable and to be in beautiful surroundings.

"Hey, do you want to take a nap or something and when you're up to it, come down and I'll make you some coffee."

"Sure! That sounds great. See you soon," said Edward. Maybe Laura had sensed that he didn't feel great. Edward was happy to have some time alone just napping. After

Edward went to get some rest, Laura started watching a movie. It was about people who were getting divorced. The lady in the movie did not want to let her husband go. He had met someone else and told her he was in love with someone else and yet the woman did not want him to go. Laura felt that she would never be like the woman in the movie. If her husband did not want to be with her, she would walk out the door as if there were nothing but doors to walk out of. Maybe the woman had some reason though. She would wait and try to understand.

It started to lightly rain outside. Laura had always loved the sound of light rain on the windows. She would not want to have rain every day, but sometimes it was nice. She was glad that she and Edward were comfortable enough with each other that they did not feel they needed to entertain each other. They could just spend time together in a comfortable way. She didn't need too much jazz or pizzazz when it came to these things. Edward headed downstairs around three o'clock. Laura made a big pot of hazelnut coffee, and they sat together at the kitchen table. She had fresh whipped cream and put some on top of his coffee with a dash of cinnamon.

"How are things in London?" asked Laura.

"All is well. Business at the store is going well. I've been really busy. It will be nice to have some time off while I'm here," answered Edward.

"Ok, that sounds great. We can spend our time in a relaxed way if you want."

"Yes, that sounds really good. I've really been working hard at the store, and you know the pace in London is very fast. Hopefully, we can slow down a bit while we are together."

"That sounds good to me, too!" Laura loved how she and Edward tended to so easily agree on so many things.

"So, what happened with Thomas, Laura? Why did you guys separate?" Edward was very curious about this because his feelings for Laura were building each day. He needed to know what her situation was. He was afraid to ask the question, but there was no point in dodging it. The reason they separated was because of Edward, but Laura was not sure she should tell him that. It may have made him feel pressured to be in a relationship with her. It was a risk she had taken, but even if it did not work out between them, she wanted to be honest with Thomas. She was not sure how to explain all of it to Edward and was surprised that he asked her about it on the first day in San Diego. It made her feel good that he cared enough to ask so quickly.

"Well, I started not to feel connected to him so much and Edward, to be honest, you were part of the reason for that." She wanted to be open with him. She waited to see what Edward's reaction would be. Would he get scared and think she was an idiot? What if he felt nothing for her whatsoever, and Laura just imagined that there was some deep feeling between them before?

"Laura, I get it," said Edward. The two sat at the table and both looked down.

"Do you regret that you did that?" asked Edward.

"No. Let's go take a walk around the lake." Laura started to feel uncomfortable and wanted to stop talking about it. Edward agreed, and the two left the conversation right where it was.

There was a little theater in town that did Shakespeare plays. Laura liked it because it was so well-decorated inside, and they served exceptional wine and appetizers. She asked Edward if he wanted to go there the next day to watch Romeo and Juliet. Edward was interested in that, particularly since he was British, so they got tickets. Laura loved literature so much and had studied it in college. She would never forget those days, sitting under an old tree and reading one of the latest novels required by her literature courses. She didn't know then that those times would never happen again in the future. Of course, she continued to read books, but it was never the same as those days under those old trees on campus.

In those days, there was nothing much else on her mind but the words on the pages she was reading and romantic thoughts of a beautiful future ahead. Maybe it seemed like it did not make much practical difference in the world to some people, but Laura had always thought that without art, there was no point to science. She certainly would not want to be on Earth if it were not for art. Laura had a broad definition of what art was. Art was in cooking; art was in restaurants; art was at concerts; art was at museums; art was in the way a person dressed or put makeup on. Art was everywhere as far as Laura was concerned.

Since Laura was an extrovert, she did not always think too hard before making certain decisions. She read somewhere that introverts tended to process things more before acting. She liked this quality about herself but was also trying to think a little more before taking some actions.

In this spirit, she did not want to just have a fun time with Edward. She wanted to talk to him so much that she knew exactly what he thought and felt about every topic under the sun. By the time it was time for him to leave, Laura wanted to know him so well that she could make decisions about their relationship that were not based on nonsense. Well, that was if he felt the same way about that. Maybe she was making too many assumptions, but it did not seem so because he came to see her, and he understood what she meant when she said that part of the reason for her separation from Thomas was because of him. She would not assume anything and would wait for things to become clear.

The next day when they entered the theater, everyone was dressed nicely and milling about with a glass of wine. There were peach roses everywhere and men in black suits offering appetizers around the room. Laura saw tomato and mozzarella toasts and shrimp skewers. She wanted to have some wine since she had not had any in a long time so she would also need to eat something. She remembered one time in Montreal she drank some beer on an empty stomach and realized that was a mistake! She got the worst stomach pain she had ever had in her life and did not ever want to repeat that again. The thing that fixed the pain that day was drinking tons of water, glass after glass, until the pain just stopped. She wasn't sure why that worked, but it did.

"What a nice place!" said Edward as he looked around the theater.

"Ya, I hoped you would like it. I love to come here, watch a play, and talk to people."

"I'm really glad you brought me," said Edward. Edward felt excited to be with Laura and yet comfortable at the same time. Her blond, straight hair bounced around her face, and her blue eyes were always shining. She made him feel like everything was right in the world, and there was nothing but good out there. They ate some shrimp and had some white wine standing close to each other and talked about their surroundings. They joked about a guy in the corner that seemed to be looking for a date. He was staring at every pretty woman in the room, including Laura at times. He looked like he was scared to talk to anyone though.

When they sat down in the theater, Edward lightly touched Laura's hand. He was not sure if he should do that, but upon thinking about it, not doing it would have been more awkward. The two of them were so emotionally close already. She was glad that Edward had finally bothered to hold her hand. The actors did a great job in the play, and many times Laura lost complete track of time as she watched. She and Edward exchanged some comments as they watched, but they were too involved in watching the play to talk too much. Yet another thing they had in common! Watching movies together in the future would be no problem then.

After the show, the two walked around the outside of the theater where there were violinists playing and desserts being served. They had little key lime pie pieces and different fruit sorbets in small cups being served by waiters in black and white attire. The theater always did a great job of making the experience of the shows formal and beautiful. The audience was taken away from everything for those few hours enjoying shows and the beautiful grounds of the theater.

"Laura, thank you so much for inviting me here. I wasn't sure how to tell you this, but after our time in Thailand, I knew I needed to see you again."

"I am beyond glad that you're here. Edward, our time in Thailand was magical; you made me feel like the world was nothing but joy," said Laura as she moved closer to him. As the laughter of other theater guests surrounded them in the warm, night air, Edward gave her a slow and steady kiss. It was a perfect evening, and one Laura would remember for the rest of her life. In the morning, Laura wanted to see what Edward wanted to do with the remainder of his time in San Diego.

"So, you mentioned wanting to relax, right? Are you sure you aren't interested in seeing all of the sights?"

"Yes, I just want to relax. No need for too many schedules and running around. I came here to see you, Laura."

"How about we go to La Jolla Cove?" Laura thought a beach with pretty cliffs and snorkeling would be both relaxing and fun for the two of them.

"Sure, what's that?" asked Edward.

"It's a beach with cliffs and we can sit in the sun and talk."

"That sounds good to me!" They changed their clothes, grabbed some snacks and were out the door. As they settled into their little corner of the beach, Laura started to get upset thinking about the fact that Edward would be leaving the next day. She had already gotten so used to him. When her mom came to visit her in San Diego, it went a long way toward making her apartment feel like home, but having Edward there also had changed things. She did not want to be clingy, but she did not want him to go. Life was so much better with a good person by her side.

"Well, Laura, I'll be leaving tomorrow. What a funny set of circumstances that we met in Thailand, and now we are spending time together in San Diego." Edward had started thinking about his departure and wanted to know how Laura felt about their time together.

"I know. I don't know what to say," said Laura trying to hold back a tear. She wasn't sure what Edward was getting at. The water was moving slowly in a gentle dance on the shore. The sound was like a soft lullaby, and the two fell asleep in their chairs hand in hand. When they woke up, it was almost dark. There was no one else there, and the sky had turned grey with purple streaks going through it. Laura could not believe that they both fell asleep for that long on the beach. She woke up remembering the dream she had during her nap. She dreamt that she moved to Australia and became a nurse. It was a weird dream because nothing about her fit with the medical field. Maybe it had something to do with the article she read in the paper the other day talking about the nursing shortage practically everywhere. Laura was confused as to how an all-American girl had become so wrapped up in international experiences and dreams.

"Have you enjoyed your time here?" Laura needed to know how he felt. She was trying to decide what would happen in the future between them.

"I can't explain to you in words how much I've enjoyed my time with you. I wish it would never end, and I'm really not sure how I'm going to be able to get back on the plane tomorrow and head to London." Edward felt more peaceful during these days with Laura than he had in the last ten years. He was surprised to find himself having this many feelings for Laura so fast since he valued his freedom so much. Edward looked sad, yet like a child who was not going to cry in front of the other kids - no matter what. Laura wondered why all good things seemed to have time limits. Why couldn't Edward and her just be happy and not worry about him leaving tomorrow? Edward started to feel a little tight tension in his chest. He did not want to leave, but he knew he had to leave. They were both single people and probably neither of them were in a rush to get back into a relationship. They probably both needed solitude and were defensive about relationships after whatever unpleasant experiences they had. Edward remembered that Laura said nothing bad happened in her relationship with Thomas, but rather, they grew apart. Maybe that would make their chances a bit better if her marriage had not left her bitter. Edward's breakup had been similar, but Edward remembered that he and his ex-girlfriend really caused each other a lot of pain. At the end of their relationship, his ex-girlfriend had even told him that there was nothing unique about him and that he was boring. That comment stuck with him and still hurt. Regardless, Edward knew there was no need to think about all of that now and that he would shortly be on a plane out of San Diego. What mattered at that moment was making the most of the time he had with Laura.

Laura decided not to ruminate and debate their relationship in her mind. For now, all she had to do was get him to the airport tomorrow morning. She also was concerned that she was focusing on him too much. She had always prided herself on not fully revolving around a man and from the many things she had seen and heard, it was for good reason. Despite this, her feelings for Edward had taken over her mind, body, and heart completely.

When Laura returned from dropping Edward off at the airport, she fell onto the couch and went to sleep. The place felt like an empty hole without him there; she wanted the ground to open up and swallow her. She spent the night sleeping poorly and feeling sad. If it was true that emotions were always guiding people, then her emotions were trying to tell her something.

Chapter Twenty-Two

Laura's new job was not going to start until the next month, so she needed to think about what to do to occupy herself in the meantime. The sun was shining through her white curtains, and she felt happy that morning. She just needed to make some friends in San Diego because she was not like some people who were simply happy being with themselves all the time. She started to think about which places would make the most sense to meet new people. She was not interested in going to hip places anymore or even taverns like the one where she met Thomas. She was drawing a blank about where to go to meet new people. All she knew was that this was a priority of hers, so she needed to think about it and put some time into it. Could a chance encounter in a restaurant or a grocery store lead to a good friendship? Afterall, her friend, Sara, met one of her best friends at a dental cleaning in the waiting room! It was possible to meet new friends anywhere; she just had to keep her eyes open. Suddenly, she thought of Randy, the plumber. She remembered she still had his business card and decided to give him a call. The phone rang, and a man answered it.

"Hi Randy! It's Laura Townsend from Duck. I hope you remember me."

"Hi there, Laura! It's great to hear from you. How is everything?" Randy had no trouble remembering her and had thought of her many times.

"I'm doing all right, you know I went to Thailand for a while; I also got divorced, and now I live in San Diego. How are things in Duck?" asked Laura.

"Wow seems like you've been really busy! I'm sorry to hear of your divorce. We are doing ok. My daughter is growing up fast and has developed a serious interest in music. She spends all her extra time practicing the piano and hopes to go to Julliard one day. I can't believe my little girl has changed so much," said Randy.

"Wow, Randy, Congratulations!"

"Thanks, I'm really happy to see her full of passion for life," said Randy.

"How have you been Randy?"

"Doing ok, just the regular job as a plumber still and just starting to feel like I'm getting old, like I need to try some new things in my life. Not sure what or how, but it's a feeling I'm having these days."

"I know that feeling. I really think you should try to pursue it. It's what we all want to taste in some way at some point in our lives. So much of life is just duty; where is the freedom?"

"Ya, do you have any ideas?" asked Randy.

"Why don't you start a book club or join a travel club and meet new people? It's just little things to start," said Laura.

"I dunno, I don't think I have the personality for those things. I'm not really a people person."

"It's just a way to think about it, Randy."

"Ya, thanks! I will definitely think. I'm just feeling the age going by and have a sort of angst about it. I have to figure out what to do," said Randy as he watched the tennis game on tv. Laura paused for a moment unsure of what else to say to Randy. She was not even sure why she called him. She just wanted him to know that she had not forgotten about him. Relationships were always important to Laura - like the bread and butter of her life. Maybe she just needed some human interaction at that moment; she really was not sure why she had suddenly called Randy. Maybe it was the vibe he had when he was in her house in North Carolina; he had such a peaceful energy.

"Well, Randy, it was nice to hear your voice. Just keep my number, and call me if you ever feel like it," she said wanting to get off of the phone.

"Thanks, Laura! I certainly will." Randy wondered why Laura had called him but felt appreciative that some people did not forget others. They hung up the phone, and Laura was glad she called but also knew in her heart that she probably would never speak to Randy again. It seemed to be the way of life that people crossed paths very briefly most of the time. She wished that others were more like her and wondered about how others were doing. She had learned that most people didn't really care as much as she did and forgot people a lot faster. She needed to learn to be a little less sentimental or she would spend the rest of her life getting hurt. On the other hand, she believed in creating a softer and better world even if that meant risking her emotions sometimes.

Laura walked into Nuance Art Museum excited for her first day. What a change it was from the law firm she worked for before! There were skylights everywhere with painted murals all over the walls; one was of people very dressed up floating down a river with flowing, white hats; the other was of a prairie filled with blue flowers and rain; there was another mural of triangles running all over each other. She loved the environment and felt like she was being embraced by it as she walked around. She didn't feel separate from it or feel like she wanted to get away from it. She wanted to be with it and to contribute as much as she possibly could. It must have been a good sign that she felt happy just to be in the space. Her position was in fundraising so she would need to spend a lot of time on the phone talking to potential donors to the museum. It sounded great to her and much better than sitting in a law library talking to no one.

A lady named Thomasina joined her in the lobby and gave her the tour ending up in Laura's new office. It was small but nice with soft lighting and nature artwork all over the walls. The ladies chatted a bit, and then it was time for Laura to go through everything on her desk and acquaint herself with what she would need to do. Halfway through her coffee, a tall, dark-haired man wearing very high-end clothing walked into her office.

"Hi Laura, I'm Grant."

"Well, hello. I'm Laura… I'm sorry I don't know…" Before Laura had a chance to finish her sentence, Grant interrupted her.

"I know you don't know who I am; don't worry about it. I head the fundraising department, and they told me you would be starting today so I just wanted to introduce myself." Grant thought Laura looked very professional, but at the same time looked like she had a creative flair about her. He was expecting her to look more boring since she had a legal background. Laura realized this was her boss sitting in front of her and hoped that he would be a nice person.

"It's great to meet you. I'm excited to be starting work here. It's almost like a dream come true. I've always been creative but have never worked at a job that required creativity so I'm really excited," said Laura.

"The world would be a much better place if we all followed our passions," said Grant. He was happy to have an enthusiastic person in the role because he knew it wouldn't always be easy to fundraise for the art museum. Some wealthy people were very rude and would just hang up on people. The two chatted for a few more minutes, and then Grant headed out down the hallway to his office.

Laura learned that Grant had a background in art history and also had an MBA.

Laura spent some time looking through her emails and looking at the past list of donors to the museum. She would need to figure out how she wanted to approach past donors and how she would find new donors. The donors made a huge difference to the museum's operations. If the cause was not something she believed in, she would not be able to raise one dollar for it, so it was good that she was raising money for the Nuance Art Museum. Later in the afternoon, a lady from the HR Department named Brittany came into her office and introduced herself. The ladies chatted for a bit, and Brittany told her about a poetry reading that she was going to go to next week. She asked Laura if she had any interest in going with her. Laura immediately said yes, never having gone to one before and hoped it would be okay to just sit in the back and listen. She was not the type of person that would want to read poetry to a group of people, but she loved reading it or listening to it.

On Thursday night, it was time to get ready for the poetry reading. Laura and Brittany were going to meet there; it was a ten-minute drive from Laura's apartment at a little, cozy coffee shop on a corner surrounded by bushes that were lit up with different colored lights. Laura loved that the city of San Diego cared about how the streets and shops looked. People seemed to like to go to this coffee shop with friends and talk for hours or delve deeply into some academic work or a great novel. The poet in residence was a lady named Theresa. She was going to read a poem that she had written for this occasion, and the rest of the time people could discuss poetry or ask her questions about it. Theresa got on the stage and collected herself for a moment.

"You were there, your heart, your soul, all there, I felt you, I knew who you were, I knew you were mine, you were the light on the petal, you were the breeze through the window, you were the relief for my pain, you were the reason I worked and the reason I left, you were everything like the caterpillar's cocoon, until you disappeared." Theresa completed the poem then walked off the stage looking like reading the poem had stirred some emotions in herself. Laura thought it was brave of her to read such an emotional poem on stage to a group of strangers.

After the reading, Theresa came and sat next to Laura and Brittany. Laura had gotten to know Brittany a little bit at work and learned that she was divorced and had one daughter that was fifteen years old. Theresa sat down next to them with a cup of green tea.

"Thanks for coming to the reading! I was really nervous," said Theresa.

"You did a great job. I really was impressed with your courage. I'm not the type that can share poetry in that way in front of so many people," said Laura. Theresa looked like she appreciated Laura's comment. Theresa looked a bit unkempt, like someone who just did not have the patience to brush every hair or iron every shirt. She was wearing a light blue t-shirt with white pants and a long necklace with a yin yang sign on it.

"You know I just love words. Everything about them. The fact that we humans have produced them to communicate with each other is amazing when you think about it. I just wish words were respected more," said Theresa. Laura liked the topic Theresa was talking about. She often felt the same way but had never really expressed that to anyone. Laura was saddened by the fact that people were becoming more like robots. People always talked about all of the ways computers and technology had made things in life easier, but there wasn't enough talk about how they had affected things in negative ways as well. Theresa's comment about words and language made Laura reflect a moment about the aspects of life that were palpable like language.

Theresa talked to them about how she and her boyfriend broke up because he decided that Theresa was not successful enough for him. She did not have an MBA; she was not a lawyer or a doctor and suddenly, he decided that was what he wanted out of his life. She just was not good enough for him anymore. Theresa still had a certain sadness in her eyes about it. It was ridiculous how little loyalty there seemed to be in the world, but then again, Laura thought about her own situation and how she and Thomas divorced mainly because of her attraction toward Edward. It seemed different than Theresa's situation because Thomas also believed it was the right thing to do. Laura was not sure if that really made a difference or not in the whole matter. Was it worse that Theresa's boyfriend left her more heartbroken than she left Thomas? Laura believed it was never right to hurt someone's feelings if it could be avoided. Theresa seemed like a good person to get to know since she was bubbly and open. Laura had not seen many people that way in recent years; it seemed as if most people walked around very seriously like everything was a matter of the stock market and geopolitical analyses.

"Theresa, I have to get going soon. I'm kind of tired, but if you'd like, let's exchange numbers maybe we can meet for coffee sometime," said Laura. Laura knew she wanted to continue getting to know Theresa.

"That sounds great! I would love to meet for coffee. I've found that my girlfriends have been more important in my life than many people," said Theresa. The two exchanged phone numbers and right about 10 pm, Brittany and Laura left the poetry room.

Two days later, Laura's phone started ringing as she was washing the dishes.

"Hello?"

"Hey, Laura, it's Thomas." Laura stopped for a moment and felt surprised that Thomas had bothered to call her. They did not talk anymore except for a random email updating each other on their lives. Thomas had gotten remarried and had a young son. His wife's name was Margaret, and she was a fashion designer in New Zealand. She was creating designs and clothes out of the house while Thomas worked as an engineer in the city.

"How is everything?" asked Laura excitedly.

"Margaret, Timmy, and I are doing well! How are you?"

"I'm doing well. I left working in the law and now work in an art museum in San Diego. I'm really enjoying it and feel like I've finally found where I'm supposed to be. I love art. I always have. I just never could figure out how to be involved in it as a job."

"I'm happy for you! I could always see you in an artistic field. It's just so funny the paths we end up on in life. We have some control but not as much as we'd like to think. Maybe the best thing is to attempt a direction but always know that it's not all in your hands; let go and see what happens," said Thomas.

"I think you're right, Thomas." There was an awkward pause where neither of them knew what to say next. Thomas was glad that Laura had found her spot in life. She was so smart, and he knew that she would land somewhere fitting. He remembered all of her stories after work when she was working for the Baker law firm, and although the work was rewarding in its own way, he never saw a glimmer in her eye when she talked about it. She talked about it grimly and in a tired kind of way. That was not how she sounded during their phone call. Thomas was proud of her for having taken the risk to change and follow her intuition.

"So, are you heading to the States anytime soon?" asked Laura.

"I'm not really sure right now. Margaret does not like to travel too much with Timmy yet. He likes his routines and probably won't do well on any sort of long travel." Laura would have liked to see Thomas and his family. From what Thomas had told her, Margaret stayed in touch with her ex-husband and would have no problem coming to the States and seeing Laura. Laura thought about their time in North Carolina and Thailand and could not believe how quickly it had passed. Now Thomas was in New Zealand, and Laura was alone in San Diego with a completely different career. It was very likely that Margaret was a better wife for him. They had a son pretty quickly, and Laura was not completely sure about having kids at any point. Maybe it had all worked out for the best.

Laura did not feel like hanging up the phone quite yet because there would be no way to know when the two would talk again. At the same time, she really could not think of anything else to say to Thomas. Their paths had irretrievably split and gone in separate ways for good. It was like the time she called Randy the plumber just to see how he was doing. She had a feeling in her heart that she needed to talk to him that time but that she would never talk to him again. She got the same feeling right then as she and Thomas were about to close off their conversation.

"Well, thanks for calling me, Thomas. It's always great to hear your voice. I'm so happy for you and Margaret and the family you've created. I could always see you doing that."

"Thanks, Laura." There was a twinge of sadness in Thomas' voice like he also knew that they would never talk again. Thomas thought about how much he always admired Laura's strength, humor, and determination and while he loved Margaret more than anything on earth, he knew he would always have a soft spot in his heart for Laura. Margaret had so many qualities as a wife that he needed, but she didn't have the sharpness of intellect that Laura had. It did not matter to him though because he was fully committed to Margaret and planned to see her on his last day on Earth.

"Well, Thomas, I've gotta get going. I have an appointment at the hair salon in thirty minutes. I'm dyeing my hair red!" Laura was glad she had that appointment to go to since it would take her mind off the fact that she would probably never talk to Thomas again.

"Ok. I'm sure it will look great! It was nice talking to you, and just know, I'll always be thinking of you in some way. Call me if you ever need anything." Laura was surprised that Thomas said that. She never would have expected him to say he would always be thinking of her in some way. She knew a part of her would always do the same thing. It seemed their relationship and marriage had sparked like a fire that was suddenly drowned out by massive rains. With that, the two hung up the phone, and Laura got ready to leave for the salon.

Laura was pleased with the color her hair turned out; it looked like a red rose that had fallen into a vat of orange Jello. It was not quite red, and it was not quite orange. She had always wanted to try having red hair since she had known many spunky redheads in her life. It was good she was paying attention to herself and doing little things like getting her hair colored. Those little things always made her feel better and helped her to live her life more creatively.

Chapter Twenty-Three

The next week at the museum was going to be busy. Even though Laura was in the fundraising department, it was a small museum so many times people had to chip in with everything. They were having a tour of the museum; a group of adults were coming from Seattle and later in the week, a private event was being held there. There would be a lot of preparation and organizing to get ready for those two events. On top of it, Laura would need to continue with her fundraising work. The last donor she spoke to was an eighty-eight-year-old lady who grew up in San Diego and was part of the reason the museum was ever started in the first place. She had been an artist her whole life and came from a very well-to-do family with old money. They had created one of the first antibacterial soaps on the market. Her name was Savannah, and she would donate to the museum every year. This time when Laura talked to her, she decided to donate five hundred thousand dollars. With that donation, the museum intended to renovate large areas as well as to purchase better lighting systems. Securing that donation made Laura feel productive and like she was contributing something good to the world; those moments felt very rewarding, and she realized how important it was to feel she was contributing to the world in the way that best suited her through her work.

Laura's museum was a modern art museum which was her favorite type of art. She could find herself staring at an abstract piece of art for a long time and would be mesmerized by its potential meaning. Maybe physicists felt the same awe when they looked at the universe through telescopes. Laura felt that everyone needed something they loved beyond the people in their life, and she was very happy that she loved art so much. She spent a good amount of time in recent years challenging herself and getting to know herself better. She concluded that she would not be having kids. It would make any future relationship a lot simpler in many ways as well as more complicated if the guy wanted to have kids. She would not be providing kids to anyone. If that became a problem in a relationship, then she would just stay single. Afterall, she did enjoy her own company.

Laura decided to book a ticket to visit her parents in DC on a whim, and the plane was about to land. It was Fall in Bethesda, Maryland, and Laura had always loved the Fall season in the DC area. She decided to visit her parents at that time just to be around the crisp air, colorful leaves, apples, and pumpkins. Her mom and dad had good energy, and they were always excited about something that was going on in their lives. Even in their older years, they enjoyed many things and kept up with their social life. It was very nice to see this since Laura had seen so many older people who had given up on life. She was glad to see their marriage had that longevity and that they managed to stay happy and healthy this long. She decided to stop by some of her favorite spots in Bethesda including a coffee shop that sold Greek and Italian pastries that she loved. She would spend some time walking around and look through the bookstore as well before heading back to San Diego. The vibe was different in the DC area. People walked a lot faster than people in San Diego. They seemed to always be thinking about something. Maybe there was such a thing as thinking too much. Many trees were crimson, orange, and yellow, and when the light shone on them, they looked electric. She loved the Fall feeling that surrounded her and was happy to be able to spend some time with her parents.

When she opened the door to her parents' house, there was a fragrance of freshly baked pumpkin bread all around the house. Laura remembered how her mother always loved to bake when she was growing up; she probably did not do it as much anymore but did for Laura's arrival knowing how much Laura loved pumpkin bread. Suddenly, her mother burst into the front hallway and swept Laura up in a big hug and looked so overjoyed that her eyes were teary. Her mother was always into fashion and today was no exception; she was wearing a light blue satin shirt with a light white scarf wrapped around her neck and little diamond earrings. Her hair, as usual, was perfectly done, and she did not look her age. It felt good to be at home; it was so interesting how just standing in the front hallway of her parents' house brought back so many childhood memories like the time her best friend Kelley and she decided to make their own Halloween outfits but had sized them wrong and had nothing to wear on Halloween requiring a quick trip to the party store with her mom running behind them. Candace was happy that Laura looked healthy and good; it seemed that was the first thing mothers looked at. She worried about her daughter now that they were on different coasts and could not see each other as often. She also still worried that Laura was not married yet. It did not seem settled down to Candace just based on the generation she was from. What was Laura going to do for the rest of her life? Work at the museum and be alone? Candace could not understand it and was always happy that she had such a good life partner in her husband. She hoped that one day Laura would change her mind and find someone to settle down with, but by the looks of it so far, Laura had no strong interest after Thomas.

"I'm so glad you're here, darling! I have lots of ideas of what we can do while you're here," said her mother.

"Oh mom, you don't need to entertain me. I just want to see you and dad. I'm happy just sitting in the backyard really."

"Oh, no, your father and I would not have that. We don't get to see you enough anymore, and we want to make sure that this is a special time for all of us." Laura decided not to argue with her mother and just let her mother decide. She could not imagine what it was like to be a mom and to be excited to have a few days with a grown daughter. Laura was going to let her mom have her way and was glad her mother still had the energy and desire to do the things she talked about. Laura was not looking forward to the day when that would change.

"Laura, did you hear about what happened to Ashley?" asked her mom as she sliced some pumpkin bread. Laura had not thought about her cousin Ashley in many years and had almost forgotten about her. When her mother mentioned her name, Laura suddenly remembered all the monopoly games they played and all the days at the pool they spent together when they were young.

"What happened to her?" asked Laura.

"She started some sort of computer programming company; I'm not really sure what it is or what she does but she became remarkably successful and recently bought a house in the nicest part of Georgetown. I don't know how she could afford it there; that area is so expensive for a relatively young person!" said her mom.

"Wow, that's great. Ashley always liked math and science unlike me!" Laura giggled.

"Ya, it seems to be the 'in' thing these days, this computer programming stuff," her mom said. Candace wanted her daughter to be successful and enjoy the good things in life. It seemed to Candace that Laura was just taking too many risks and following too many untraditional paths. As she and Everett were getting older, she was worried about what would happen to Laura.

Laura and her mother decided to go to Creme Orchards that day. They would walk around and pick some apples and pumpkins. Laura was really looking forward to it. These were not things she did in California in her regular day-to-day life. She wondered why they called the place Creme Orchards. Maybe it was because at certain times of the year, visitors could pick strawberries and make strawberry shortcake right there with fresh whipped cream and shortbread. Laura really loved doing little things like making strawberry shortcake. One of her boyfriends before she married Thomas had the complete opposite personality. Nothing was good enough for him; he always wanted more, more, and more. She heard that later on in life he became very unhappy, gave everything up, and moved to Iceland. He was so uninspiring and almost stressful to be around. He would complain about every meal in a restaurant; he had no interest in talking to new people and showing a genuine interest in them; he always wanted to buy the most expensive shirt in any store just to say he could. He would never enjoy doing something as simple as making strawberry shortcake, and Laura was glad that he was no longer in her life.

When Laura and her mother arrived at Creme Orchards, there was a good-sized crowd of people already there. There were enough people there to make it feel lively, but not so many that it felt uncomfortable. They went to the area where there was apple picking. The apples looked crisp and juicy and had a great fragrance like fresh rain on sugared leaves. They picked two buckets worth of apples, paid for them, and put them in the car. They wanted to go back to the pumpkin orchard and pick a pumpkin or two there. The pumpkins were lying on the ground like specks of large confetti on a cake. It was beautiful looking at them and thinking about all the things that Earth produced. Laura used to buy fresh pumpkin, wash it, cut it in half, and bake it in the oven. Then, she would take the baked pumpkin and turn it into puree that she could use to make pie or soup. She had not done that in a while because her life had been busy with too many other things. Maybe she would do that with her mom on this trip to DC. After they each found a pumpkin they liked, they headed to the car and went home. They spent a lot of time listening to music in the car, and occasionally her mom would sing along like she did to Simon and Garfunkel years ago.

That night, Laura's father, Everett, came home after a day at the golf course. He had retired a couple of years ago and spent much of his time at the golf course. He looked like he had gotten some good sun and looked refreshed when he walked in the door. He spent the day there with Paul, his friend of thirty years. They always went out on weekends and got coffee or breakfast and played golf together very often. Men were not necessarily like women when they got together talking about all the emotional aspects of their lives, but their meetings were highlights of each of their days.

"Laura! I'm so glad you came for a visit!" said her father as he gave her a similar bear hug to the one she received from her mother earlier.

"Hi dad! You look good! You must have been out golfing, right?"

"Yes, of course. You know my schedule." Everett had always been a person who said what he felt genuinely in his heart. Many fathers were more stoic, but Laura had always appreciated how expressive and honest her father was.

"Ya, dad. It's great that you are staying active and keeping up with Paul." Paul's wife had died of brain cancer a few years back, and his kids lived in Oregon, so Paul did not get a chance to see them too often. Paul spent many holidays at Laura's parents' house and viewed them like family. Paul had a genius IQ and had created a device for car engines that Laura never understood. His intelligence sometimes caused him to have a cynical view of life, and he was not always comfortable talking to new people. He liked time alone with his books, music, and only a few special people that he felt very comfortable with.

Candace made meat loaf and potatoes for dinner, and they all sat down to eat. Laura told her mom about Theresa, the poet she met at the poetry night as well as Brittany, her friend from work. Her mother commented that most of her friends these days were artsy people and that maybe she should balance it out by talking to others as well. Laura never really viewed herself as a particularly creative person, but her life had taken her down that road. She told her mom that she enjoyed working at the museum; the patrons were great and were so happy when they were in the museum. The museum had a lot of followers and people who visited regularly. The crowd tended to be really educated about art, and they were fun people to interact with. As much as she enjoyed her job at the museum and was so grateful to have it, sometimes Laura thought about having a business of her own. She was not sure exactly what type of business it would be, but an artistic coffee shop sounded appealing to her. Sometimes she wondered whether Brittany and Theresa would be interested in starting something like that with her. Maybe next weekend she would give them a call and find out.

When Thomas opened his café in Duck, Laura was not involved with it, so she'd never learned about that business at that time.

The next day, Laura and Candace decided to make baked salmon with dill and vegetables. Her father was generally healthy but had started gaining some weight, and her mother wanted him to start to eat better. They got the pinkest, most organic wild salmon they could find at the local market and bought very fresh dill, broccoli, and cauliflower for the sides. Laura was a rather good cook, so she started the whole process by seasoning the salmon but first she washed and dried it. A pat of butter and into the oven it went. Right before it was almost done, she added the chopped dill to the top with a squeeze or two of fresh lime juice. The vegetables had roasted in a pan, and it was time to eat. It was an easy dinner to make but was delicious. The family sat at the dinner table Laura grew up at and were so happy to have the time together like the old days. Her parents wished Laura had stayed on the East Coast, but for whatever reason, she was happier in San Diego at least for the time being.

"Dad, I've been thinking about starting a coffee shop," said Laura as she took her first bite of salmon. Everett knew a good amount about business, and perhaps he would have some good ideas for her.

"Why, honey? I thought you were happy with your job at the museum."

"Absolutely, I love my job, but the idea of being self-employed and running an artistic coffee shop that gives people a beautiful place to come and relax with friends really appeals to me. I mean I know there are plenty of coffee shops around, but they are not all the same. I think I could create a unique one."

"Well, honey, you know there's a good amount of risk with any business. Are you prepared for all of that?" Everett wasn't sure that Laura was made for all that came with running a business.

"Ya, dad. That's the part I'm thinking about these days. All of that risk." The next day Laura called Theresa to see if she had any interest in opening a coffee shop with her. Theresa seemed like someone who was up for a challenge and for trying new things.

"Theresa, I have about five minutes sorry to call you in a rush, but I wanted to ask you something funny. Do you have any interest in being self-employed?" asked Laura.

"Uh, why? That's kind of a funny question out of nowhere!" Theresa was completely confused by the question.

"I know, but I try to do things right when I think of them. I thought about it and thought of you, so I figured it was best to call you fast and ask," said Laura.

"What kind of business are you talking about?"

"An artistic coffee shop."

"There are so many coffee shops, Laura. Why do you think a new one would be successful?"

"Because I will make it a place people want to come to and a place that people don't want to leave."

"Ok, let me think about it. I'll call you in a few days." Theresa felt uneasy and wasn't sure what she would end up telling Laura, but she would sit on it for a few days. With that, they hung up the phone, and Laura picked up the phone to call Brittany to ask her the same thing. After she hung up with Brittany, she already had one yes. Brittany was definitely interested. She loved art too and that is why she worked at the museum. During their first phone call on this, Brittany was already talking about decorating ideas. Laura hung up the phone feeling excited about this possibility. The next question would be where would they open this coffee shop? The West Coast? East Coast? Nebraska? She decided she had done enough for one day about it and that she would start thinking about it some more tomorrow.

Laura extended her visit with her parents, and Brittany and Theresa decided to come to DC to visit Laura and her parents; they would also use the time to look around the DC area for possible spots for the coffee shop. They stayed at Laura's parents' house since the house was large with plenty of room for everyone. When they arrived, Laura was rushing to get ready and come down the steps. She had not slept well the night before and did not feel great but nothing a splash of water on her face and a strong coffee could not help with. She ran down the stairs, and the ladies were sitting on the couch with her mother talking about the old show The Simpsons. An interesting topic of conversation for sure, but it was good that they seemed to be comfortable getting to know each other.

"Hi there! I'm glad you guys all had a chance to meet; well, Brittany and Theresa you've already met at the poetry reading, but this gives you more time together," said Laura.

"Yes, it's great to be here," said Brittany. Candace decided to show them around the house and talk about all the exotic places where she purchased a lot of the artwork and rugs that decorated the house. The ladies were not rolling their eyes, looking bored, or looking like they felt Candace was showing off. They seemed genuinely interested in the details Laura's mother was giving them about the different objects and where they came from. Laura's mother and father had traveled a lot and been to Turkey, Greece, Spain, and so many other places. They adorned every inch of their home with objects from those places. There was a medium-sized, silver statue of the Earth, moon, and sun like they were one object that they bought in Greece that always made Laura think when she looked at it. It was a physical reminder of where people found themselves in the universe. Whenever Laura looked at the statue, it reminded her not to take life too seriously and to keep a sense of wonder about everything.

"So, ladies, are all of you seriously thinking of opening a coffee shop together?" asked Candace.

"Yes, Laura called us and brought the idea up. Working with friends and creating something good for the world sounds fun," said Theresa.

"Well, I'm sure it's not quite as easy as that," answered Candace without a negative tone in her voice.

"Yes, that's true, but sometimes you have to try things in life when they appeal to you strongly," said Brittany. Laura wondered why her mother seemed negative about the idea. She should be proud that the three of them would be willing to take such a risk to follow a dream.

"Well, how will we ever know if we don't try?" asked Laura, turning towards her mother. They decided to start the next day at the local diner, have a bite to eat, and then go searching around town for areas that might be good for their coffee shop. None of them had decided that the DC area would be the place they would actually do this, but it made sense to look around since they were all there. Brittany and Theresa had never lived on the East Coast, and they were both curious about how it was different from the West Coast. They felt that people were a bit more serious, and the pace was much faster, but they were both open to possibly moving to the area. Laura was enjoying her life in San Diego, but there were things about the DC area that she really missed. Sometimes, Laura missed the beautiful four seasons despite the very humid summers. She missed Georgetown, all of the major offices in downtown DC, the beautiful wineries, and the parks. The area offered a lot although many people from California complained that it had too many rainy days. Laura thought that with so many areas having problems with drought and other natural disasters, some rain wasn't such a terrible thing.

Chapter Twenty-Four

The ladies walked out of the first commercial space thinking it was a definite no. That landlord would be awful. He kept complaining about the previous people that rented his space and just complained too much in general. The ladies were a bit discouraged but knew that every space and landlord would be different, and there was no reason to let him ruin their optimism and excitement. They walked around Bethesda for the rest of the day and visited an outdoor flea market that was there. Laura bought a scarf with a picture of the Eiffel Tower on it. One day she would make it to France.

    The next day, the ladies decided to take it easy and watch old movies. They got the popcorn and M&M's ready and sat in their pajamas. Their friendships were blossoming, and Laura really looked forward to working with a couple of ladies that were her close friends. Looking at commercial spaces had taken more of their energy than they expected it would. Each of them had started developing doubts about the coffee shop business during the stressful parts of looking at properties. There seemed to be a lot of barriers to being able to open a coffee shop. They would need to negotiate with the landlord, buy expensive equipment, pay for marketing, and find customers. They could also never be sure that they would even break even from the investment. It was scary to think of signing all of those loans. The ladies needed a day to not think about it and just be happy. Brains seemed to work better when they were happy and relaxed anyway. Laura had definitely tried both ways, and there was a big difference between a stressed brain's results and a relaxed brain's results.

"Hey, give me the popcorn!" said Brittany jokingly as if the ladies were hiding it from her.

"It doesn't have enough butter; it's not really very good," said Laura.

"I don't care. I just want to munch. It's calming munching on popcorn. Have you ever noticed that? That's a big part of the reason we all eat. It's definitely not just hunger and needing nutrients. There is such an emotional aspect to it too," said Brittany.

"Yes, agree," said Theresa. It was nice not having to think about complicated business details for this one day. When Laura was honest with herself looking at all of what it would take to open the coffee business was daunting. In her mind, she could imagine what the place would be like and all of the customers she would get to know there, but there were so many details and costs. She just was not sure if she had the guts and the financial risk-taking ability to do it. What if it was a total failure, and she ended up with a lot of debt? She never really looked at herself as a very entrepreneurial person. Maybe that sort of work was really for other people. At the same time, the idea of opening a coffee shop made her feel very excited.

Brittany and Theresa both stayed another two days and then had to get back to California. In another two days, Laura would be returning to San Diego as well and back to her job at the museum. She wanted to make the most of the rest of her time in DC with her parents. After the ladies left, Laura found herself in the backyard looking at the rose garden, and Edward popped into her mind. She missed him, but not as much as she thought she would. He was the cause of her divorce so she thought he would be taking up more space in her head than he was. Laura was not sure if that was because after being single for some time, she just did not need a relationship anymore or whether it was that the connection with Edward was not really as spectacular as she once thought. It was also possible she was repressing her feelings. Sometimes she just did not want to think about love.

Back in San Diego, Laura put her suitcase down and immediately opened a window in her apartment. The trip had been great, but it was time to get back to her routine. Places had a way of smelling funny when people were gone for a while and regular life was not going on inside them. Opening the windows would help with that dry smell in the apartment. She knew she would miss her parents after being with them for so long, but it was time to get back to her regular life. That thought made her ask herself what her main priorities were in her regular life. Maybe her mother was right all along wondering why Laura was in San Diego alone. She started to spiral in her mind and started thinking that maybe she was stupid for believing there was something special about Edward. Just for a moment, Laura felt sad and put her head down and cried. She did not know why other than she needed some clarity. Wracking her brains looking for it had not worked though so maybe she would need to try and give it some time.

Back at work, Grant walked into the hallway really excited about the new collection that would be on display in the museum that week; the artist was in his thirties and grew up on a farm. Everything he painted and created, including his sculptures, had something to do with farm life yet he managed to make them into modern art by the lines and shapes he used. There was a hay truck he created out of steel that had the sharpest lines Laura felt she had ever seen. It was clearly a hay truck, but it looked like a hay truck that flew around at laser speed in outer space before it landed at Nuance Museum. His work was good, and the paintings made a person feel like they were cooking with fresh eggs just out of chicken barns.

"Hey, Laura! I'm so excited about the Milner exhibit. It's so interesting to make modern art out of objects and ideas that come from growing up on a farm," said Grant.

"Ya, me too! I've never lived on or near a farm, but after looking at all of his work, I feel like I know quite a lot about that lifestyle now. I wonder what made him leave farm life to become an artist. I mean, I was a lawyer and now I'm in fundraising, so people definitely make changes in their lives," said Laura.

"Ya, maybe when he comes for opening night, we can ask him about how that transition came about," said Grant. With that, Grant started to walk away. Laura continued down the hall to grab some lunch at the cafeteria. They had a vegetarian lasagna on the menu that smelled so good as they were baking it. It was filled with zucchini, mushroom, and asparagus, and she felt like all of her blood labs were getting better each time she ate it. If Laura had not gone into art at the museum, she could see herself having become a chef also. She had so many interests when she thought about it and had heard that creative people often did. As a young adult, she loved playing piano, and one of her piano teachers said she was so good that she should try to become a concert pianist. That teacher was too serious though, and Laura liked music and the piano for the levity and freedom that it brought to life. That teacher turned her off to continuing her studies when she made it such a serious matter. The teacher was never smiling and did not make the lessons or the talk fun. The type of people she dealt with had a huge impact on Laura's decisions, and she was glad that she knew that about herself.

At work that day, Laura emailed many people regarding donations and made a few calls. One of the ladies she called was a lady by the name of Aloutra. She had never donated to the museum before but often came to events at the museum. Laura did not know whether she would be an average-sized donor or a person who could make a significant contribution to the museum but had noticed that when she came to events, she was dressed in what looked like extremely expensive clothes and had a royal air about her.

"Hello?" Laura felt herself get nervous for a moment when Aloutra picked up the phone. Most people were quite nice during these conversations, but it wasn't always that way.

"Yes, Mrs. Lina, this is Laura from the Nuance Museum."

"How can I help you?" Aloutra was not really in a good mood and wanted to get this conversation over with as fast as possible.

"I hope this is a suitable time; please let me know if it isn't. I wanted to talk to you a little bit about our museum and ask if you could perhaps contribute towards our efforts."

"Well, right now isn't really a wonderful time, but if it's not going to take long, go ahead."

"Ok. I'll try to be quick. Right now, we are trying to add staff to be able to host more and bigger events at the museum. Many corporations like holding events here, and we have people wanting to get married here. There are all kinds of events that we host, and we have found that we do not have enough staff to handle some of it," said Laura.

"Why did you call me?"

"Well, you registered with us, and we've seen you at many exhibitions so we thought you may like to contribute." Aloutra paused as if she did not like being contacted just because she had come to the museum for a couple of events. After a long and awkward pause, she started to speak.

"Ok. That's fine. I can donate one million dollars." Laura felt like she was going to pass out. She did not believe what she heard. ONE MILLION DOLLARS!? When Grant and the other members of the team heard about this, they would be in complete shock. Maybe they were used to these types of donations though. Laura was not sure what the museum would do with one million dollars, but she knew that there were always projects they could do to improve the museum. Maybe they would even add additions to the building with such a donation.

"Mrs. Lina, I can't believe you would like to make such a generous donation. Are you sure?"

"Yes, darling. I love coming there, and you guys have always done an excellent job at making the museum a beautiful and tranquil place to visit. We need beauty and tranquility in this world. It would be my pleasure to help you." Aloutra felt her mood get better as she continued talking to Laura. She was reminded of the museum and how many good moments she had there. She went there once after her mother's passing when she felt like the world had come to a complete end, and after spending an hour in the museum she left feeling as if life still had value. With that, the ladies finished their conversation, and Laura went happily dancing down the hall to let everyone know. She started to think about all of the positive changes they'd be able to make to the museum with Aloutra's donation.

It was Saturday morning, and Laura was going to make herself chocolate chip pancakes. The sun was shining through her white curtains and landed on the picture of the one red rose she had on her kitchen wall. It looked like a beautiful day outside. After breakfast, she would head out to the nursery and buy a couple of small plants for her apartment. They would freshen up the air and just make everything look much better. The pancakes smelled heavenly like a pie baking in the oven. After eating, she headed out to the nursery. There was a guy looking at some plants who looked like he knew a lot about plants. Laura was not sure why she thought that since he was just a customer, but she had a feeling about it. She decided to go ahead and approach him.

"Hi, I'm sorry to bother you. I'm here to buy a couple of minimal maintenance house plants, but I'm really not sure what to get. I was wondering if you had any pointers on that."

"Yes, of course. I can show you a few that I like if you're interested. These plants grow quickly, don't need a lot of water or sun and are generally hardy plants," said the man. Laura followed him down the aisle where he picked up two small, potted plants.

"Thanks! These look great. Thanks for showing them to me," said Laura.

"Sure. I hope you enjoy it." The man started to walk away and then turned back towards Laura.

"By the way, I think it's great that you felt comfortable just asking me that. People don't talk to each other enough these days. All the screens are really taking over too much," said the man.

"Yes, I agree with you. I miss that people-to-people connection. I guess there are people that are more comfortable without it, but I'm not one of them," said Laura. With that, the man walked away and disappeared into the distance.

When Laura got back to her apartment, she decided she would put one plant near the television and the other by the kitchen window. She decided to call Theresa to talk a little bit more about the coffee business.

"Hey, Theresa, how's everything?"

"Good! I was just getting ready to go for a hike. What's going on with you?"

"All is well. Just was thinking about our coffee shop idea. I read a little bit about it, and it looks like it would cost between $80,000 and $400,000 to create a sit-down coffee shop."

"Ya, I expected as much. Are you willing to take that kind of risk?"

"Well, the thing is I love the idea of creating a unique coffee shop where people can come to relax and chat. We could decorate it fully the way we want, and I'm sure over time we would get to know the customers, and you know me, I love talking to people so I think I really would enjoy that. It would be my way of contributing to the world and bringing people together. This world just needs more joy," said Laura.

"Ya, I know what you mean. Honestly, Laura I'm a little afraid of that kind of financial risk, but if we're doing it together it will be easier to handle everything and all of the details," said Theresa.

"Where do you think we should consider opening a location?" asked Laura.

"I mean, we're both in California but a part of me wants to try living somewhere new. Should we think about that a bit?" asked Theresa.

"Sure, let's talk to Brittany too and start to think of possible locations." Laura thought about the fact that it was interesting that she met Theresa at the poetry reading, and now they were talking about opening a coffee shop together. So many things in life seemed to be like that.

Chapter Twenty-Five

Laura read a bit about West Glacier, Montana. Somehow as she was bouncing ideas around about where unique locations would be to open a coffee shop, she realized she did not know anything about Montana. The city of West Glacier had Glacier National Park in it, and Laura thought she read somewhere that there was a lake there called Lake McDonald that was supposed to be beautiful. She saw that a person was trying to rent their log cabin home there. Perhaps she, Brittany, and Theresa could rent that house and start their coffee business there. She had always liked cold weather because it made her feel alive. It would certainly be vastly different and very cold at certain times, but the people there would need their hot coffee. It seemed like a once in a lifetime chance. If the ladies were open to such a unique and cold location, then maybe the decision would be West Glacier, Montana.

Laura figured out that they would not be able to run the coffee shop there year-round because of the weather so they would have it open during the warmer months and closed during the winters. That would mean they could either continue staying there when the business was closed or have another location where they also had a place to live.

They would need to make enough money while the coffee shop was open to carry all of them through the whole year. Laura wondered if that would be possible. She talked to Brittany who was on board even with West Glacier, Montana. They knew it was a very small town with barely any people in it but that could contribute to a successful business if they did a good job. After doing more research, they discovered the town had less than five hundred people in it! None of them had ever heard of or much less lived in a town that small. Despite that, there were a lot of yearly visitors to the national park there. They would know everyone in town, and customers would not have many other options for coffee shops. It could be designed like a home away from home for the locals and a beautiful place to sit and chat for tourists as well. If everything went well, they could even open another location in a different state.

Laura imagined it to be like living in a very secluded part of the world. She liked the idea of being away with nature, a few friends, and her thoughts. She wondered whether the three of them could really do all of what it was going to take to make this dream happen. Being trained as a lawyer, Laura never really thought of herself as the entrepreneurial type, but maybe she was overcomplicating it. What was business anyway? It was bringing some sort of benefit to people. It was not adversarial like law; it was more about creating things. She realized that one of the downsides of being an attorney was attorneys were trained to identify and avoid risks. That trait wasn't always helpful in life depending on what the situation was.

The week at the museum was very busy. There was a tour group of senior citizens that came from Vermont, and they had a lot of enthusiasm about art and a lot of questions. Laura found herself fielding a lot of questions regarding the different exhibits and sitting with them in the cafeteria just to socialize and discuss their lives. Some of the ladies she spoke to reminded her of Grace from North Carolina, her old neighbor. She missed Grace and wondered how she was doing. The visitors talked about how different exhibits reminded them of various times in their life like when they had a baby or when they got married. They agreed that good art was evocative of so many things and gave life meaning and value. Laura was not able to secure any more donors to the museum that week, but Grant was incredibly happy with all of her fundraising contributions so far. Laura had really made a difference to the museum with her efforts, and Grant was beyond happy that she was on their team. He saw how much Laura enjoyed talking to people and how much she cared about her job. Those were not easy traits to find in employees. Things at the museum had become so much better ever since Laura had started working there. Laura wondered sometimes how she was going to tell Grant that she was leaving her role if she and the ladies really did decide to open the coffee business. She figured she would do everything she could to get the museum on a good path before any of that happened so that if she left, the museum would be in good shape. She was a dedicated person and would feel bad if she left an employer with any problems. Instead of worrying about that, she decided to just focus on the moment which included a hot cup of coffee and a piece of caramel cheesecake.

The ladies made a video call that night and decided they were going to open the business in West Glacier, Montana. Laura felt fear and excitement and decided to just surrender to it all. She was not going to overthink this like the way she thought too much about her dress for her friend's wedding and then ended up going to the wedding in a dress that scratched her arms the entire time or the way she thought too much about what she was going to cook for a dinner party and then confused herself so much that she burned the roast.

Before they knew it, it was time to go to West Glacier. Laura had resigned from her job in San Diego and ended the lease on her apartment. When they landed in West Glacier, the ladies started driving straight to the house they rented. They signed a lease for six months and were happy the landlord was willing to let them sign a six-month lease. During this time, they would scout locations for the coffee shop and decide whether they were going to lease an existing space or try to buy a commercial location. Finding something existing that they liked would be the best way even if they had to do some renovations to the space.

"Hey, look at this shopping center," said Theresa. The ladies were in the car and looked to the left where Theresa was pointing. All the stores looked like little cabins rather than strip malls with something that almost looked like handwriting saying the name of the store. It was very quaint and different from what the girls were used to. One of those cabin-like buildings had a leasing sign in front of it. The ladies took down the telephone number and continued driving.

"Let's not stress over this. That spot looked great. Do we want to spend months and months agonizing about a space? I have a good feeling about that space we saw," said

Brittany. Laura wasn't quite so sure. She had a habit of needing to think hard before making some decisions although in recent years, she had really combatted that with her travels and decision-making. She didn't think that it was always good to make fast decisions because life was never so simple and doing so could lead to disasters, but she also knew that there were times in life when a person's instinct spoke to them clearly and strongly.

"Ya, it looked cute. Let's call them tomorrow," said Theresa. When the ladies got to the house, they were very pleasantly surprised with the beautiful stone walkway in front surrounded by flowers flowing over in every direction. The house had wonderful curb appeal and just invited a person to come inside. There was a fragrance of evergreens all over; the air smelled so fresh like pinecones with cinnamon on them. They took everything inside and looked around. The couches were all beige and filled with light blue pillows. There were beautiful light gold drapes throughout the house, and the kitchen was huge and bright with glass cabinets which showed some pretty pink plates inside. This would be a wonderful place to brainstorm, live, and work. Laura had realized that especially for creative pursuits, it really helped to be in an aesthetically pleasing environment that got the brain juices flowing.

It was May, and the temperature was 65 degrees which was Laura's favorite temperature. She never liked humidity and hoped this area would not have much of it. Brittany liked the house but felt a little nervous about the change they were all making in their lives. She had never done any of the things Laura had already done in her life like travel and change careers. The only thing they had in common was that they were both divorced. Brittany left her daughter with her ex-husband so that she could come to West Glacier. Her daughter was old enough that she was okay with having a change of pace and living with her father for a while.

Theresa had only positive feelings about the change and was a very adaptable person; she never thought there was much security in life and felt it was best to take risks and do creative things even if they didn't end up working out. They were all confronting their fears and working hard to make some dreams come true. The ladies ordered food since they had not gone to the grocery store yet and sat and started talking about their coffee business. Interestingly, there was a nearby Thai food restaurant which was funny since they expected the small town to only have American food. When the food arrived, they set out some paper plates that were in the kitchen cabinet and opened the wine they brought with them. They enjoyed eating together while bouncing around some business ideas. After dinner, Laura decided to make some phone calls and decided to call the number they had jotted down about the space for lease. Maybe someone would be available to pick up the phone that night.

"Hello? Hi, my name is Laura, and I saw a sign in front of your property saying the space is for lease."

"Well, yes, thanks for your call. We are currently looking for a tenant. What are you looking to do there?"

"We are extremely interested in creating a unique coffee shop in West Glacier. What will the monthly rent be?"

"Well, as you know, West Glacier is not a very populated area, so we are very reasonable with rents here. That space is 2600 square feet so certainly enough size, and we will rent it at a rate of one thousand dollars monthly," said the man.

"Oh ok, that's great. May I ask what type of business was there before?" asked Laura.

"Sure, it was a nail studio but that really wasn't a good business idea for this area because many women have no interest in doing their nails here. I'm not really sure why that tenant thought it would be a good business for this area."

"Ok, well what are the next steps?"

"We can arrange to meet next week if you like." Laura told the man that she would be interested in meeting, and with that, they hung up the phone. It was not long before the ladies decided that they were going to rent that space for one thousand dollars a month. They met with the man the next week, made the deposits, and signed all the paperwork. The thrill of acting on their dream was invigorating! They extended their house rental from six months to two years and were ready to get working hard on creating the beautiful coffee shop they imagined. They knew it would only support them six months out of the year so they decided to look for another house back in San Diego where they could go during West Glacier's colder months. They were all extremely excited and proud of themselves for all the changes they had already made in their lives.

It was a brisk Saturday, and Laura decided to go for a walk first thing in the morning. She loved the brisk air and silence. She got out of the house and saw several ducks waddling around the back yard. She wondered where the water was since as far as she knew, ducks were usually around water. She never considered herself a naturalist or someone who would know all of that information, but then again ducks flew so maybe they could really be anywhere. She took a moment to slow down and look at the birds for a minute or two. There were always so many beautiful things around if a person slowed down and took the time to look. Giving herself those few minutes with the ducks seemed to slow down her heart rate and breathing and give her a sense of calm.

After her walk, she went to local shops looking for decorative objects for the coffee shop. She found a beautiful blue and white vase that immediately caught her eye and did not hesitate to buy it. She learned over the years that when something fully and quickly captivated her, she should not hesitate. It had become one of her general life policies. She picked up a few other objects including some beige and brown coffee cups and fancy napkins and went home.

Chapter Twenty-Six

"Hello?" Laura was surprised to hear her phone ring at eight pm on a Tuesday night; she did not usually get calls at that time.

"Hi Laura! It's Edward." Laura felt frozen for a moment because she had not spoken to Edward since he visited her in San Diego. She was trying to forget about him because she no longer thought their relationship was going to go anywhere. He was back in London, and she was in West Glacier, Montana, and they no longer thought much about each other it seemed. Had she just misjudged the feelings between them? It did not matter anymore because she promised herself that she would no longer think of Edward. She just did not want to be lost in fantasy for no reason. Women needed to focus on so many other things like their dreams and independence. She did not want to sit around thinking of some guy who probably didn't care about her half as much as she cared about him.

"Hi Edward! How are you?" She noticed the excitement in her own voice.

"Things have been better, Laura. I just called to let you know of some bad news. I was diagnosed with stage three lung cancer. I'm really sorry to call you and tell you something so sad. I wasn't even sure if I should call." Laura did not know what to say or feel when Edward said that. He was a young guy! She was frozen in time and didn't believe what she heard.

"Edward... uh... what..."

"Laura, I'm sorry to call you with such sad news. I really don't want to bother you with it or make you worry. It just is what it is. I've accepted it. I'm not sad anymore. I just want to live my days in peace doing the things I like. I don't think we should see each other again, but I wouldn't have felt right if I hadn't contacted you to let you know what was going on. I've never even smoked in my life. They aren't quite sure how my treatment will turn out or how long I will live. Maybe I'll be ok. I don't think it's fair to a wonderful, young woman like yourself to be saddled thinking about a guy like me now," said Edward.

"Edward, I can't even believe it; of course, you should have called me. You sound like you have really come to terms with it. I just don't know what to say or think about this though." Laura was at a loss for words which was not typical for her. Obviously, their relationship had meant something to him too. For a moment, Laura felt like she was going to start crying, but she held it back. The two sat in silence for a moment on the phone.

"Laura, let's just say goodbye here and not be sad. I enjoyed all of the conversations and time with you, and I'm sure your face is one I will see before I say my final goodbye to this world if that's where this goes sooner rather than later. I always thought you and I would see each other again, but after this diagnosis, I don't think that is fair to you." Edward's voice trailed off and sounded weak. The first person Edward thought of when they gave him the diagnosis was Laura. He knew he was going to let her know because the feeling that was there between them was different and strong, and he could not go the rest of his life without communicating with her. Laura told him that she didn't agree with him that they should stop speaking because of his cancer diagnosis. With that, the two abruptly said goodbye, and Laura hung up the phone. Laura could not believe what she had just heard. She sat by herself on the couch and cried for twenty minutes. Soon, she was in a deep slumber.

It was Monday, and a lot of equipment was going to be installed at the coffee shop. Laura found herself thinking of Edward most of the time, but she decided that she needed to put a brave face on to get through the day. Hearing his voice on the phone brought back so many feelings. She thought of their time together in Thailand and just wanting to spend hundreds of hours talking to him and him only. She knew she had to try hard to focus on the day at the coffee shop. There were all sorts of things coming to the shop that day including a complicated water filtration system and many different models of espresso makers. The ladies had gotten loans for the equipment and decided to rent some of it and buy some of it.

Laura was the one staffing the shop while all the deliveries were being made. The once empty space was starting to fill up and take some sort of shape. They were still far from the final product, but even this stage of the process was showing their vision coming true.

"Well, I think it will take me a couple of hours to finish installing these pipes," said one of the men.

"Sure, I understand. Take your time, and please make sure to take some breaks," said Laura. The men were working so hard. Laura felt bad just standing there watching them. Laura headed to the front where she could talk to some people outside and get some fresh air. Brittany and Theresa had stayed home because they were working on marketing issues. They were trying to figure out what was going to make their coffee shop a unique place and what methods of advertisement they were going to use. They were also thinking about what snacks and types of coffee would be best. Since West Glacier was a small town, local ads would be the best thing although there were a lot of visitors to Glacier National Park. Maybe in the future they would add some international coffees and food items to the menu as well. That was something to think about another day though. The furniture was going to be delivered next week. The ladies had picked light brown couches and chairs with beige cushions. Laura wanted to have fresh flowers in the shop every day. They purchased a large oil painting of people in France sitting outside at a coffee shop on a pebbled street in fancy multi-colored hats and boutique clothing. That did not really fit the scene of West Glacier, but it had the best coffee shop feel to it.

Laura decided to get a book out of the car and sit outside the shop and read for a while. Reading was still one of her favorite hobbies. She was reading a book about a girl in the eighteen-hundreds who worked in her father's shoe repair shop and on her off-hours was writing a book on philosophy and spirit. In the philosophical book, the girl talked about the different people who came into the shoe shop having deep attachments to their shoes. They could not part with them and wanted them repaired rather than replaced. Their shoes had become part of their identity, and it wasn't just about the economics of it in a lot of situations. There was sentiment behind it, and the girl told the story of an elder lady who remembered that her damaged shoes were given to her as the final gift from her brother. She never wanted to throw the shoes away.

The girl also wrote about how much life and world was outside of her father's shoe repair shop and their local area. She wanted to experience it all but somehow knew that she could not. The girl felt that the universe was going to stop her from ever seeing past the shoe repair shop. Laura stopped reading and looked around the coffee shop. Things were starting to come together as more items were installed. It was not long before a few hours were over, and the men were leaving the shop. When Laura went back in, there was a large counter, a cash register, equipment needed to make the coffees, and a light already put in. It was a productive day. They decided to call the coffee shop Hot Ice and Rocks. The name was inspired by Glacier National Park. They put a picture of a hot, steaming cup of coffee next to the name so that people would not be confused as to what type of shop it was since the name was not too clear. They were hoping that the business decisions they made, the name of the store, the decorations, and everything else were good decisions and that people would come into their shop.

"Ladies, can you believe it!? Our coffee shop is opening today!" said Brittany as the ladies gathered in the store on opening day.

"Ya, this is crazy. I can't believe everything has come to fruition," said Theresa. Theresa was really looking forward to working in the shop, and she hoped she would get to know the customers and that some of them would be artistic people. Theresa was still writing poetry every week, and her favorite thing in the world was to sit with other artistic types. They turned on all of the lights, and Laura patiently placed little white roses on every table. They were ready for their first customer. They turned on light classical music in the background and went to work on getting machines and tables ready.

The view from the coffee shop was nice because there was a forest across the street filled with different colored bushes and flowers. The area was quiet and the perfect place to sit with a nice cup of coffee and think. Being there that day was a dream come true for all three of the ladies. They hoped to create a warm and welcoming place where the community could get together and talk about everything going on in their lives. The automation of the world had created some distances between people, and the ladies hoped that Hot Ice and Rocks would change that in just their little corner of the world. Two hours into the opening, a lady walked in with two toddlers.

"Hello! I've never seen this shop here before! We come here every year," said the lady.

"Yes, this is our opening day," said Laura. Laura got nervous and wasn't sure how to talk to this customer. She wanted to make a good impression on their first customer.

"Wow, how wonderful. I've often craved a good cup of coffee when we come here to visit but have had trouble finding one before," said the lady. Her kids were running around the shop and talking about needing to buy a Nintendo.

"Can you make a pistachio latte? I know it's not on your menu but just wondering."

"Sorry, we don't have the ingredients for that, but it sounds great so maybe we will add it to the menu at some point," said Laura.

"Ok then, I'll have a caramel latte." Brittany started working on preparing her drink while the kids decided to buy two blueberry muffins.

"Ok, well thanks for everything and for bringing a coffee shop to this area!" said the lady as she took her coffee and muffins. With that, the lady and her kids left the shop. The ladies gave each other a hug and could not believe they were coffee shop owners that just served their first customer. A smile came across Laura's heart and face as she shuffled to get ready for the next customer.

Chapter Twenty-Seven

"You know, I can't believe he actually told me to cook him dinner," said Theresa. The ladies were having dinner at home, and Theresa was telling them about a guy she met in the grocery store who was very charming and got her phone number in the dairy aisle. When he called her though, he suggested that Theresa cook dinner and have him come over. Theresa was disgusted by that suggestion for a first date and assumed he was just a chauvinistic pig for saying that.

"Ya, that is a very weird suggestion for a first date. First, why would you want to have him in your house for the first date?" asked Laura.

"Ya, he just must be a creepy guy although when I met him, he acted so elegant and refined," said Theresa.

"What are you going to do? Are you going to keep talking to him?" asked Brittany.

"No, life is short. I don't need to waste my time with him," said Theresa. Laura agreed with Theresa that if her intuition was telling her no about something, there was no reason to challenge it. She was proud of Theresa for being strong even though Theresa wanted to meet a guy.

That night, as Laura struggled to fall asleep all she could do was think of Edward; she thought of his smile and the way he spoke. She felt her heart jump, and she felt a kind of sadness she never knew could exist before. Even though they had not pursued a relationship, Edward had left a mark on her mind and heart that she knew would never go away. She could not believe the situation with his cancer and felt like she wanted to drown herself in ice cream, water, or sadness. She wondered whether she should call him and offer to go to London to visit him. She had no idea what to feel, think, or do. She and the girls were creating a life in West Glacier, and she had been trying to make herself forget about the relationship. If Edward had really loved her, wouldn't he have done something about it already? Wouldn't things have flowed in some way? Instead, he went back to London, and she went to Montana. Those were probably signs that it was not anything more than a passing infatuation like the millions of those that happen over time to everyone on the planet. She was trying to be sensible and not believe in these things, and yet when Edward called her about the cancer, she wanted to DIE. She knew she wasn't going to be one of those women that lingered around waiting for a man, but her time with Edward had changed her. She missed him in a way that made her feel like she wasn't really living unless he was somewhere around.

The ladies continued decorating the coffee shop and by the third week, they had already gotten to know the names of several customers. One was a lady named Rose who lived down the street and had twelve birds in her house. She said they made incredible companions, and the noise they made did not bother her. She felt humans had separated themselves from nature way too much, and she did not want to live like that. She never got married or had kids. She worked her entire life in the local grocery store and had a small house she lived in for all those years. When Laura asked her whether she ever had an interest to visit Paris, New Zealand, or anywhere else, she emphatically said no. She said the sky is blue everywhere and that she liked the predictability of her routine. She had no need to see the Louvre or anywhere else for that matter. Laura found her to be quite an interesting lady although Laura could not relate to her complete lack of curiosity regarding the world outside of West Glacier. Laura had noticed people like Rose had very active minds, so it wasn't easy for them to get bored. One of the reasons Laura wanted to open a coffee shop was to meet people like Rose.

Brittany met a guy in town who was a tour guide, and they started dating. She was incredibly happy with him because he always listened to her and showed interest no matter how much she rambled or talked about the trivial things of the day. Theresa started painting when she wasn't at the coffee shop. If her paintings turned out good, she would create a website and sell them online. Her paintings were still life pictures of fruits on tables and baskets of flowers. Laura suggested that she create more dynamic paintings as well, but it seemed Theresa only wanted to paint still life pictures. Laura was working hard at the coffee shop and spending every other spare minute thinking of Edward and his diagnosis. One evening, she decided to call him.

"Hello?" said a tentative, male voice. It sounded like Edward, but his voice was weak. Laura was not even sure if it was him.

"Edward?"

"Ya, hi Laura," Edward said somewhat relieved that she called.

"Hi." Laura didn't know what to say. The two just sat on the phone a minute while Laura thought about how quickly it would be okay to go straight into asking him questions about the cancer.

"Uh, Edward, how is everything? Are you..."

"Yes, I've started treatment," said Edward interrupting her. He didn't want her to feel uncomfortable.

"How are you feeling?" asked Laura.

"Better than I expected. Thanks for checking in. Laura, I don't know how to say this again, but now that I have this diagnosis, we're going to have to forget about each other." Laura stared at the clock on her wall and wanted everything to stop. She wanted those words to go back into Edward's mouth and never come out again. She wanted to throw something at the wall, the clock, the Earth, her own face.

"Edward, why do you say that? Edward, I don't know what to say. I love..." Laura felt an urgency and swell of emotion in herself. She was not going to hold back no matter what.

"Laura - stop! I don't want to hear these things. You are a young, beautiful, and healthy lady. I will not have you loving me or wasting your time with this. I would never do that to you. Laura, I'm going to go now. Goodbye." With that, Edward hung up the phone. Laura cried for the next hour in her bed and then fell asleep.

The next day at Hot Ice and Rocks was very busy. The ladies were all working and had hired a couple of staff too, but still they were having trouble serving everyone quickly enough. They had added a mozzarella, tomato, and basil sandwich to the menu, and people ordered it a lot. There was a hum in the coffee shop now, and the ladies figured out when their busiest times were. They felt that the risk they took in opening the shop was well worth it, and they each felt they were contributing their talents in different ways. Laura did a lot of business portions and accounting since she had a background as a lawyer. Theresa managed a lot of the events they held in the coffee shop, and Brittany focused on marketing, new products, and promotions.

They would not spare any effort needed to continue making the coffee shop a success.

There was a lady who lived in town that came several times a week to the shop just to sit with her computer and watch movies using her headphones. She seemed to enjoy watching movies at the coffee shop a lot more than at her home. Laura wondered why, but she did not want to pry. There was a difference between being friendly with customers and asking them questions when they just wanted to sit and relax. Still, Laura wondered why someone would like to watch a movie in a coffee shop on their computer instead of watching it at home. Certainly, there were many people who came in with a book or a friend, but the lady who watched movies there was something new. Maybe she was lonely and wanted to be around other people. In a world full of people, there were still too many lonely people.

Surprisingly, the ladies were not having trouble paying all of the expenses associated with the shop including the lease, rentals, product expenses, insurance, fees, payroll, and everything else that went into keeping the place running. Business had gone better than they expected for their first year. They did not expect to make any profit during their first year, but the shop was already turning a profit for the year. As the weather got colder, the ladies would close the shop and move to the house they rented in San Diego for the cold months. It would be harder to pay bills during the months that the coffee shop was not running, but perhaps each of them would find some sort of job in San Diego that would help with that. Laura's phone rang, and it was her mom.

"Honey, how is everything? When are you going to come visit us?" asked her mom.

"We are good! How are you and dad?" asked Laura.

"All is well here, darling. We just miss you and are wondering whether you are planning to come home for Thanksgiving."

"I'm not sure. We need to get back to San Diego during that time and set everything up there. This first year of moving back and forth between the two places will take some adjusting to, so I'm not sure if I can make it there this year," said Laura.

"Ok, honey. Maybe your dad and I will come visit you in San Diego then."

"That sounds great, mom!" Laura really wanted them to come. She enjoyed every minute with them, and she knew they were all just getting older. These times would not come back. Laura hung up the phone and decided to go to the grocery store to get ingredients to make chicken chili. Once she started cooking, she always enjoyed the creativity, the fragrances, the physicality of making something with her hands. It allowed her to get in touch with her senses and the ingredients of the Earth. It wasn't long before she had the chicken chili ready for everyone.

The ladies sat down and ate the smokey, woodsy flavored chili. They looked forward to dinners together when they could update each other even more than normal on their lives. Brittany's parents retired and decided to move to Jamaica. They were from the Midwest and stayed there their whole lives, so that was going to be a substantial change. Brittany did not want her parents leaving the States, but she wanted them to be happy. Brittany's daughter was okay living with her dad but called Brittany every day. She decided to go to medical school in the future and was thinking about what subjects she should focus on in school to prepare herself for that. Brittany mentioned that many doctors had studied biology or chemistry in college, and she did not think her daughter would like those subjects. She wondered if her daughter was just trying to impress everyone by saying she was going to go to medical school in the future. Brittany tried to keep her opinions to herself though because her daughter was at an age that she really did not want to hear it, and it was her life anyway.

Laura updated the ladies on her feelings about Edward and how she really did not know how to process the fact that he had cancer. She would think of him happily strolling with her in Thailand full of joy and words. The ladies knew the whole love story between Edward and Laura and always thought Laura should keep talking to him since it was so hard to find a connection like that. There was some sort of insecurity about love Laura developed, and she really wasn't sure why. Her breakup with Thomas was done as well as any breakup could be done with an affectionate and respectful parting. Perhaps it was because she started to think that the world wasn't reliable, and things could just fall apart so she was protecting herself in this way and trying to step back from the relationship with Edward.

It was only in her quiet moments when she felt the same pangs she felt for Edward in the past. When those moments came up, she felt confused and pushed the feelings away. Now that Edward gave her the news of his diagnosis, she was more confused than ever. She thought she had come to terms with their relationship never going anywhere, but when she heard his voice on the phone, all she wanted to do was jump over the ocean and be in London with him.

Chapter Twenty-Eight

One of Laura's customers was a lady named Patty who used to work as a lawyer. She worked in a big New York City law firm for many years before deciding that wasn't what she wanted to do with the rest of her life. She moved to West Glacier to work as a manager in a small furniture company. She saw the job ad and made an impulsive decision to apply, never expecting to hear back about it. When she got an interview and eventually was offered the job, she shocked herself by turning in her resignation at the law firm.

She had lived in West Glacier for two years and was dying for a good coffee shop to come into the little town. She loved the caramel pumpkin coffee at Hot Ice and Rocks and practically came in every day for it. Sometimes, Patty and Laura would sit together and have coffee and talk about their old days practicing law and other things. Patty was much more introverted than Laura so much of the time Laura talked, and Patty listened. Laura seemed to attract introverted friends, which was great, but she felt that she needed to find some extroverted friends as well so that she wouldn't feel she was always talking and perhaps burdening the listener.

Patty and Laura were becoming close friends, and they would invite each other over for dinners and lunches. Patty never married and was never sure about the concept of marriage like many others Laura knew. It was kind of sad because marriage could also be so wonderful. Patty enjoyed her job in management at the company and would give opinions on the aesthetic aspects of the furniture. She did not just do the books or other corporate type things in her job. Her favorite part of the job dealt with the aesthetics of furniture design. It was like a creative outlet for her, and she had learned over the years that creative people needed to have those. Otherwise, they felt like soda without carbonation.

The ladies decided to get a contractor to come out and install a gas fireplace at the coffee shop. It would make it so much cozier. They were not sure why they had not thought of it before but like so many ideas, they come when they come. So many problems could be solved with a hot cup of good coffee next to a warm fireplace since those moments of warmth and relaxation helped a person recollect their thoughts and come up with solutions. One afternoon, Laura decided to call Edward since he was the only part of her life she felt uncomfortable about. She needed to figure out what to do about it. Edward picked up the telephone and sounded a little sleepy.

"Edward?"

"Yes, hi Laura." Edward was upset that she was calling since he told her not to.

"Are you still going into the shop every day?" asked Laura.

"No, I stopped doing that a while back. I have people covering work for me for now. I'm looking forward to going back, but there is no way to know what the future is going to be with everything."

"Edward, just hear me out and listen. I want to come to London to visit you next month. It is more important to me than anything. You can't crush me by saying no. I need to come and see you. There is no other way. I have to see you, Edward." Laura started to cry and could not hold it back enough so that Edward would not hear it.

"Laura, honey, don't cry. Ok, you can come. Please stop crying." They talked a bit more about his treatment and how he was feeling, and then they said goodbye.

When Laura woke up the next morning, she felt a million times better knowing that she would be going to visit Edward in London the next month. Just being able to look at his face and give him a hug would go a very long way towards healing the pain in her heart. Obviously, nothing would completely heal it unless his cancer went away, but this would be better than nothing. As independent of a woman as Laura was, she knew that what made life worth living was connections like the one she had with Edward. She could not imagine life without him alive. She wanted him to be there even if they never pursued a relationship or ever saw each other again. He was a source of light and good. He always made the room feel better and brighter. He brought joy and education to those around him. He knew so much about so many things. She had never known anyone like Edward. She would go to London and see Edward and every day until then she would pray or just call out to the universe to help him recover as fast as possible.

She would only stay in London for four days because she did not want to impose on him plus the ladies needed her at the coffee shop. In those four days, she wanted to fix everything that was wrong. She wanted to make him fresh juices and salads and sit with him and meditate. If he felt up to it, they could go on nature walks together and listen to classical music. Music was like the sound of the universe in play, and Laura believed it had healing properties. She wanted to be there to help him and be with him in this time.

Time flew by as it tended to do, and Laura arrived at Heathrow Airport full of optimism and excitement that she would finally be seeing Edward. Edward had his friend Robert pick Laura up from the airport since he was a bit low on energy that day. Robert looked younger than Edward and seemed very energetic. He had texted Laura his picture so that it would be easy to spot each other in the airport. Robert ran up to Laura to help her carry her bags as she walked out of her gate. They chatted a bit, and she could see why Edward would be friends with him since he was gracious and funny.

"Edward was incredibly happy that you were coming. He didn't want to bother you with this, but I saw his face light up when he told me that you were coming to London," said Robert.

"I could not do anything but come here. I've been thinking about him for so long."

"I helped him prepare a room in his house for you, so you'll have everything you need there. He also cooked a lot of food already so that the two of you wouldn't need to worry too much about that. Edward is a great cook. You'll enjoy the dishes he's made for you," said Robert.

"I can't believe you guys went to all this trouble. I'm a pretty easy guest. I just want to see Edward. We could eat popcorn for dinner and sleep in sleeping bags, and I'd still be happy," said Laura. The drive to Edward's house was relaxing and comfortable with the two of them chatting all the way. Robert thought that Laura was a beautiful lady and one that Edward would be lucky to have as a girlfriend. He was not sure what the nature of their relationship was, but Edward told him that they had an exciting time in Thailand together. Edward also told Robert that he missed Laura but was not sure what to do about it. It was clear even to Robert that there was some sort of magical connection between them though.

Robert told her a little about himself. He was trying to start a robotics company and spent many hours working late. He thought that robotics would really change the world in a positive way. Laura told him that she saw all of the good about it but was concerned that humanity was slowly being taken away from life. Maybe there would be a way to incorporate all of that technology into life without removing everything from life that made life good for people.

When they pulled up to Edward's house, Laura was impressed with the simplicity of it. Everything in Europe was on a smaller scale than in the United States. Edward's house looked like a townhouse in the United States with a dark brick front and off-white shutters. It was quaint and cute. It looked like more than enough space without going overboard. When they walked up to the door, Edward was already there waiting for them. He looked great, and no one would know he was sick if he didn't tell them. His hair was shining, and he had a big smile on his face. Laura and Edward grabbed each other in the longest hug Laura ever remembered having in her life. Edward thanked Robert for picking Laura up, and Robert said goodbye and left.

    Edward had a fruit platter ready on the kitchen table, and it was an unusually sunny day in London, so the sunshine was flooding the house. Edward looked like before, perhaps a bit thinner, but otherwise she saw the same glimmer in his eyes. He must have been taking diligent care of himself. Edward believed in reiki and other energy healing modalities, and Laura wondered whether he had been doing that too. She had only gone to a reiki session once. She went before a very hard exam she had to take in law school, and she didn't feel up to the task. She felt depleted and no matter what she did to give herself energy like exercise, take vitamins, or drink more water, nothing was working. She booked a reiki session at the last minute the day before the exam to try to give herself an extra push of studying. Somewhat surprisingly, something had worked. She still wasn't sure what it was that had worked. She remembered liking the lady who did the reiki session because she was a good listener and gave good insights into things. Laura talked to her about a disagreement she had with one of her friends, and the lady listened with an open heart. Laura could tell that the lady was really paying attention and after Laura told her about the disagreement, the lady gave her some good advice on it. She said that it didn't seem to her that friend was someone Laura should be putting so much trust in. She pointed out why she thought that, and it made sense. Laura was surprised she hadn't paid attention to that before herself. It was through experiences like that one that Laura came to learn sometimes she needed other people in her life to point certain things out to her.

"Laura, it's lovely to see your beautiful face." Edward interrupted her thoughts while looking at her contemplatively.

"Thank you for letting me come. I've been thinking about you almost constantly, Edward." Edward reached out and put his hand on top of Laura's. His hand felt warm and soft like silk.

"You know how important it was to me to not bother you with this stuff. You know I didn't want to drag you here so you can see these problems and worry about me," said Edward.

"I know, Edward, but really, I had to come. You know how much you've impacted me as a person. I know we haven't spoken regularly recently but that was because we were confused. There is nowhere on Earth I would rather be than here with you now."

"Laura, what about the coffee shop and your life there? You said you were only going to stay four days. Can you stay longer now that you are here?" asked Edward.

"Everything is under control back at home. Nothing to worry about. I think four days is good because I don't want to tire you out. I am here as the person who fell in love with you in Thailand." Laura said that before thinking, and it felt good to have that out in the open air. Edward just smiled lovingly at her after she said that. They got up and went into the living room and fell upon a movie about a lady who quit her job as a line cook and became a deep-sea diver. The lady never saw herself as so risk taking, but one day she just jumped.

At ten o'clock, they decided it was time to go to sleep and each went into their room. Edward offered her some herbal tea before bed, but Laura just wanted to get into bed and sleep. She felt tired from the flight over and needed some quiet time to absorb everything that was going on around her. She easily fell into a deep sleep that night.

The next morning, Edward called her down to the kitchen to eat some ham and eggs. It smelled great in the house, and the pot of coffee Edward made smelled like nuts and vanilla.

"Hello there, pumpkin!" Edward said with a bright smile.

"Hi, did you sleep well?" asked Laura while feeling bad that he was doing so much work in the kitchen.

"Yes, I had dreams of climbing mountains in Nepal, and I think part of the time I was walking around waterfalls," said Edward.

"Well, that definitely is a good dream!" The two sat and ate breakfast and chatted some more.

"Edward, how often do you need to go to treatment?"

"Right now, I only need to go once a month. Since they removed the lump during surgery, they think a couple more rounds should take care of treatment for now. I'll have to do follow-ups for sure, and hopefully the cancer will stay in remission."

"Did you have anyone in your family with lung cancer?"

"Nope! Not a single person I know about, and I've never smoked," said Edward.

"Wow, life is so random and unpredictable sometimes."

They decided to spend the day at the local park walking and people watching. It did not usually take more to entertain Laura than some fresh air and the company of a good friend. As adventurous as Edward could be, he also had this quality about him. He did not always need a lot of stimulation to be happy. Edward looked at Laura walking alongside him and felt like he had everything he wanted in the world. He did not want to think ahead to when she would be returning to the States. He did not think of marriage much anymore and did not want to have kids, but there was something about Laura that still captivated him even after he told her that they should no longer talk. Edward was not sure what was drawing him so close to her emotionally. He just knew that if the cancer took his life and ended his time with Laura, he would feel anger towards the universe forever. At the same time, he wanted her to be free of him and his illness.

After strolling in the park, they decided to go back home and take it easy for a bit. Laura wanted to read some magazines on interior decorating, and Edward wanted to work on the little foot stool he was constructing out of wood. They went back home and worked on their own solitary activities. It was as if they were an old married couple that did not need to fill all silences with conversation. She looked at him sometimes when he wasn't looking and wanted to cry thinking of him not being on Earth.

The next few days were spent at restaurants, movie theaters, and living simply at home. Laura made him many organic salads and fresh juices, and every afternoon she would give him a whole-body massage. She wanted to support his health and his recovery. They talked a lot during her time there. They talked about their childhoods and the things they never got in their lives. Edward always wanted to get his MBA and was disappointed with himself that he never did it. Many of his friends had MBA degrees and would tell him that while they struggled to find jobs, he started his own business without an MBA and should be proud. Edward always had this nagging sense that he should have buckled down and gotten the MBA. Laura talked about how she wanted to spend more time with her parents. She knew they were getting older, and her life was so busy that it made it hard for her to see them as much as she wanted to. She told Edward about these feelings and loved how their conversations were always so fluid and enjoyable. One of the main reasons Laura loved Edward was because of how much she enjoyed talking to him; he was also a wonderful listener. This time in London was for them to be together sometimes in silence and sometimes in conversation, but it was not time for Laura to bring up the cancer too much.

One evening, they decided to make a pot roast with mashed potatoes for dinner. Laura walked to the grocery store, bought the ingredients, and got back home at about four o'clock. Everyone in Edward's neighborhood was so polite and well-dressed; Laura liked strolling around there. There were many streets that had beautiful stones on them, and there were gorgeous gardens and fountains everywhere. She wondered why there were not more fountains in the United States. The sound of the water was so calming, and the look of it inspired presence. She was really enjoying the new scenery and the time with Edward. She was so immersed in what she was doing that she didn't think about West Glacier and the coffee shop at all. It was as if none of that existed. It wasn't that she didn't love her life in West Glacier; it was that she was fully present where she was, which was a good thing and didn't always happen.

"Should we add garlic to the pot roast?" asked Edward.

"Yes, my aunt used to make a pot roast growing up that was filled with fresh garlic cloves, and I loved it!" said

Laura. Edward proceeded to put little slits into the pot roast while Laura cleaned up some garlic cloves.

"Laura, what was it about our time together in Thailand that meant the most to you?" Edward asked knowing they wouldn't have too much more time together, and he wanted to talk about some meaningful things while they could. Maybe there were things on Laura's mind that she wanted to get out also. Laura looked at Edward and wanted to spend a minute thinking about the answer to that and put down the garlic.

"I'm not sure how to put it into words, Edward. I guess what things like this come down to is how you feel in the company of someone."

"So how did you feel when we were around each other?" asked Edward.

"I felt like I was protected, and I felt like someone was with me that understood me well. I felt like we would never get bored talking to each other. What about you?" asked Laura.

"I also felt like I had a woman by my side that I could talk to about anything. I was very attracted to everything about you as well. You were with Thomas though, so I tried to keep all of those kinds of thoughts at bay," said Edward.

"Edward, I'm so glad we had that time together in Thailand. I still think of those times as some of my favorite memories." Laura wanted to say everything that was deep in her heart. Edward looked interested to know, and they could tell that this conversation meant something to them both. Laura had lived long enough to know that some moments only happened once, and she wanted to say what she had to say right then.

"Is it all just a memory?" asked Edward.

"Somehow, I don't think so," said Laura. They didn't know what else to say at that point. It felt like a book that would have a sequel but one that was unclear.

It was the morning that Laura was scheduled to fly back to West Glacier. She wasn't happy about that, but for some reason during the four days together, it had become apparent that this was not the end. She also felt like his cancer would be no problem, and he would be cured. She could not say why she thought or felt any of these things, but she felt them strongly. Robert was coming to pick her up and take her to the airport. He offered to do that so that Edward could go straight to a nap after Laura left. They hugged each other for a very long time in the kitchen, and then Robert knocked on the door.

Chapter Twenty-Nine

"Laura, why didn't you stay longer than four days?" asked Brittany. Laura was trying to find the soy milk for her next customer's coffee while Brittany looked at her as if she had two heads.

"I've heard that people who aren't feeling well do not want the added pressure of having to entertain people. I just wanted to show him support and have some time with him. I did not want to tire him out," said Laura.

The shop was busy that day, and the ladies were running around trying to give the customers everything they needed. It was loud in there that day, and the shop had the buzz of a business that had been around in the community for a very long time. It felt great to be in there and to make a difference in their customers' lives. Many people would tell them how happy they were that Hot Ice and Rocks was there. One customer that day told Laura that sometimes she wanted to be away from her husband to clear her mind, and she was so grateful to be able to come to Hot Ice and Rocks. Laura felt grateful that they were having a positive impact. That night, Theresa came home with a funny look on her face.

"Ladies, I don't know how to tell you this. I'm just going to come out and say it. I don't want to be part of the shop anymore. A friend asked me to move to San Diego and help her set up a photography studio. You guys know my first love has always been art. I said yes to her." Brittany and Laura looked at each other like they were not really hearing what they just heard. The ladies had uprooted their lives and made a commitment to this store. Laura felt anger for a moment and could not believe that Theresa was just going to leave the situation so suddenly. They needed all three hands on deck.

"Theresa, are you kidding? We all committed to this. How could you just decide to leave?" asked Laura angrily.

"I don't know what to say. I'm sorry." Theresa sort of felt bad about it, but she knew she wanted to go back to San Diego and was not going to have it any other way. The next day, Brittany and Laura talked about it and decided that they did not have to care. They would make it without Theresa. They could find someone else if necessary, and the shop was doing so well that it likely would not affect anything. The bigger problem was the sense of betrayal they felt. They had come to trust and rely a lot on each other and to see Theresa just walking off like that was disconcerting.

"We will be fine, Brittany. No biggie. She can go, and we don't even have to be mad at her. People change, and situations change. It's nothing that we have to take personally." Brittany agreed, and they were ready to say goodbye to Theresa when it was time for her to leave. They even decided that they would keep the friendship with her if she wanted to keep it as well.

Brittany and Laura decided that a suitable time of the year to close the coffee shop for the colder months would be November 1st. They considered October for a while but then decided against that because it would be better to produce income a bit longer than October each year. It was getting close to the time of year that they would need to start wrapping things up for the year. Theresa left a few days earlier and was really excited about the new life she was going to start back in San Diego. The ladies parted ways on good terms and said they would keep in touch.

"I'm going to miss our customers and serving coffee!" said Brittany.

"We'll be back in May. It will go by before you know it. Besides, now we get the change of going back to San Diego and enjoying everything beautiful there," said Laura. The house in San Diego was large, and they rented it fully furnished which made things a lot easier. The fact that the decorations were decent was a good thing also. They had a little backyard where Laura planned to plant some azaleas and rose bushes. Roses did not always thrive easily, but they were worth the effort. Neither of them had a job in San Diego but since they planned for that, they each had enough money to get through the next months while the coffee shop was closed. Laura talked to Edward regularly, and things continued to go well with his treatment. He sounded upbeat on the phone and ended each phone call by saying he missed her. Brittany joined a yoga studio and went to yoga every day and sometimes twice a day. She considered getting her yoga teacher certification so that she could possibly work as a yoga teacher while in San Diego. Laura was back to cooking a lot. She had time now, and Brittany loved her cooking, so it worked out well. Laura did the cooking, and Brittany did the dishes. They fell into a good living pattern and felt happy back in San Diego. One Saturday morning, she got a call from her mom.

"Laura?" said Candace.

"Ya, hi mom. How are you?"

"Good, your father and I decided to come visit you next week if that works for you."

"Sure mom, Brittany and I have an extra bedroom just for that purpose. Look forward to seeing you." Laura was glad she would be having some time with her parents but wondered whether there was something wrong just based on the way her mom's voice sounded when she said they were going to come next week. The next few days were spent hanging out with Brittany and getting adjusted to life in San Diego. Laura would occasionally talk to her customer Patty on the telephone since they were so used to seeing each other at the coffee shop. On the day her parents were to arrive, they decided to take an uber to Laura's house instead of asking Laura to come pick them up from the airport. When Laura answered the doorbell to let them in, she was surprised by how her mother looked. She had lost a lot of weight and was moving very slowly, which was not her usual way.

"Mom, ok, tell me now, what is wrong? You don't look well." Her mother looked towards the ground with a morose look on her face. Laura did not want to mince words after looking at her mom.

"Laura, dear, I have about four months to live," said her mother. Laura felt like she was in a nightmare and what she was hearing could not be true. She grabbed her mother and started crying uncontrollably.

"Mom, what are you... what... mom..." The tears continued coming down her face uncontrollably, and her father put his arms around her to try to calm her down.

"Laura, dear, don't cry. I've had a good life. I'm ready to go. I don't want to suffer any longer," said her mother.

"How long have you known this? What is wrong?" Laura felt like simultaneously banging her head on the wall while falling into a dark hole and dying right there. Laura could not collect her thoughts and in that moment felt like she would go mad. Her father sat down on the couch and put his head down. He stared blankly at the floor. They were not that old yet and were a very happily married couple. Everett did not know what he was going to do after Candace died. He wanted to die with her. They had been married for decades and did everything together. They were truly the definition of two people that turned into one after marriage. Her mother walked to the couch and sat down.

"Laura, you are going to have to accept this. It's aggressive breast cancer. There is nothing they can do. I'm ok with it now. I've had it for a little while but did not want to tell you about it until now. I'm at peace, Laura. Please don't cry." Laura left and went into the bathroom. She sat on the floor and prayed and yelled inside her mind while crying droplets of tears onto the floor. She stayed on that floor for a good thirty minutes before coming back out into the room with her parents.

Laura could not imagine life without her mom and wanted to fly away. She would not be able to deal with this. She felt a severe oppressive feeling in her chest and suddenly passed out.

When Laura woke up, she was in Kettering Hospital. She opened her eyes to see her parents seated next to her hospital bed and a nurse checking her blood pressure.

"Honey, you're ok. Your blood pressure must have dropped, and you fainted. Everything is stable now, and they are going to release you in about one hour," said her mother.

"Mom, what, I don't know, why..."

"Everything is fine sweetie, just close your eyes and get a little more rest." For just a moment, Laura felt like she was twelve years old with the flu, and her mother was taking care of her. Candace wondered whether she should not have told Laura about the cancer, but there was no way around it if she only had four months to live. When they got back to the house, Brittany had dinner ready for everyone. The house was filled with the smell of vegetarian stir fry when they walked in.

"Hi everyone, welcome back!" Brittany said. Brittany heard about what happened with Laura's mother and wanted to be sure that they had a relaxing evening at home. She knew how close Laura was to them and felt unbelievably bad that Laura not only had to go through this but also the situation with Edward's cancer. She would do whatever she could to make the night a good evening for everyone. They all sat down at the table and chatted about different things including missing working at the coffee shop and the town of West Glacier. They were so busy with the coffee shop so far that they had not had enough time to spend in the park and on Lake McDonald, but they decided that when they went back, they would spend a lot of time there. They heard there was a certain spot in Lake

MacDonald that was filled with different colored rocks that you could see through the water.

Everett was glad to be having a nice dinner with everyone and had learned to appreciate those moments because life was so unpredictable. He knew that despite his emotions, he needed to be strong for Candace and Laura at least on the outside. At night, he would often curl up in bed before Candace came up and silently cry to himself. Being in San Diego with Laura gave him some peace in his heart because he was not alone in the pain anymore. It was hard for him to keep this from Laura for so long, but Candace wanted it that way. Laura always had such good energy that she could turn any tough situation into a tolerable one. Everett always loved that about his daughter. She was always trying to improve things and help people. She cared about others often more than she cared about herself. He did not want to dump the stress of this on Laura, but he needed some of her emotional support to try and get through it. With Laura's help, he hoped to be able to focus on the good moments they still had and to not look far into the future. He also wanted to try to be grateful for as much as he possibly could.

After dinner, they decided to watch the old Karate Kid movie. They relaxed and immersed themselves into the story. It was one of those movies that really transported the audience, which was what they all needed. The main character kept trying to improve himself no matter what challenges came his way. He overcame his desire to quit, and he kept his eye on the goal. As Laura watched the movie, she hoped that she could have a tiny fraction of the character's determination during this new situation with her mom. As her parents got ready to leave and go back to DC, they decided that if Candace started to take a turn for the worse, they would call Laura and let her know. Laura planned to go ahead of that anyway but that was what they decided for any emergency situation. They all needed some time to themselves for a bit to absorb everything. Everyone felt better after Laura found out, and Laura planned to be as supportive as possible. After her parents left, Laura spent a lot of time meditating and taking walks. She was going to have to find a way to accept this situation. She started to listen to different spiritual teachers, and she even started praying. She was never raised religiously, but sometimes prayer made all the difference in the world. She spent many days crying as well and looking at old photo albums with pictures of her younger mother in them. She could not believe her mom had cancer and was going to die from it. The thought haunted her every night when she tried to go to sleep.

One evening, Brittany asked Laura to come to a yoga class. Laura liked yoga but preferred to do things like that at home and not in a class with a bunch of other people. She decided to be open-minded and to try it. When they got to the class, everyone was already lying down on their mats with their eyes closed with very relaxing music playing in the background. The teacher walked in and started giving directions. Laura felt stiff and as if she would not be able to keep up with the level of yoga these people were doing, but she pushed herself and slowly started to feel the tension leave her mind and body. The music was beautiful, and she was wondering if there was a way she could get a copy of it or listen to it sometimes at home. She enjoyed coming to the yoga class for one day, but Laura knew that she really enjoyed yoga more when she was at home doing it alone so that she could focus on the meditative aspects of it more.

After the class, the two went and grabbed sandwiches down the street and took a walk around the neighborhood lake. It had been an enjoyable day with a good friend, and it helped Laura feel a little bit calmer about her mom's situation. Laura started to think about what she was going to do during her time in San Diego, and she was at a loss for what things mattered to her after finding out about her mom. It was then she realized she wanted to tell Edward about her mother's diagnosis. She dialed his number and before long, they spent thirty minutes talking about it. Edward gave her a lot of strength about the situation and told her that he would be there for her throughout the whole thing. He said that he could even come from London to be with her if she needed him to at any time. After the day with Brittany and after speaking with Edward, she felt like she was not alone in dealing with her pain. Brittany suggested that they plan a party and invite all their friends and acquaintances for the next weekend. Brittany wanted Laura to feel alive again and to be around people in a fun environment. She had never seen Laura with the mood she developed after finding out about her mom. Laura reluctantly agreed knowing that it was a good idea.

Brittany knew a lot of people in the San Diego area since she grew up there and was planning to invite most of them to the party. Laura had only lived in San Diego for a brief time so most of the people that would be coming to the party would be Brittany's friends or family. Laura enjoyed meeting new people, so she looked forward to meeting all those people. Having to plan the party gave her something to distract her mind, since she could not stop thinking about her mother's illness for very long. They decided to make the theme of the party ski slopes in Switzerland. They would decorate with skis, hot chocolate mugs, evergreen trees, snow, and silver glitter everywhere. The house was a good house for entertaining because it had a lot of open space and a big deck where people could mingle and look at the trees and birds in the back yard. They would cater the event, but Laura decided she would try her hand at baking a few pecan pies as well as making some pumpkin cheesecake. She had made cheesecake before, and it came out so good that she always remembered how much better home baked items could be. Laura wanted to put together a nice, festive outfit to wear to the event. She used to love mixing and matching outfits and jewelry when she was younger but had fallen out of that routine in recent years. She planned to go to the local boutique and find items; she wasn't sure whether they were called boutiques because they were expensive or because they were stand-alone stores that were usually well-decorated inside.

On the evening of the party, people started ringing the doorbell at six-thirty with bottles of wine and beautiful flowers as music played inside the house. Brittany and Laura were both dressed beautifully and had their hair done in the salon. Laura had found a silver, sleeveless dress that had pieces of gold fabric falling off the sides of the dress. Every time she moved, the gold fabric would go swaying behind her. Brittany's sisters and parents arrived early and seemed to be genuinely nice people. They were friendly and looked like humble people who didn't even dress up much for the party. Many of Brittany's older friends and current friends also came, and Laura was happy to get a chance to get to know Brittany even better by getting to know the important people in her life.

Laura only invited Kelley, who was a patron of the museum and had become friends with Laura at that time. She arrived early on as well and brought a huge chocolate cake. Kelley was single and worked as an architect downtown. She loved building designs and created a lot of beautiful home plans in her career as an architect. She did not always talk much and looked a bit nervous to be coming to the party only knowing Laura, but Laura was glad that she made the effort to come. People ate phyllo with spinach and little skewers of chicken while walking around and mingling. The only drink that was available was champagne because the ladies thought it was light and festive. Most people had a glass of champagne in their hands, and there was a lot of laughter and music all around. There were several people dancing on the makeshift dance floor as well. People looked comfortable and relaxed and not like they had come to the party out of a sense of obligation. Laura decided to try to enjoy the party as much as she could and not be like a typical host that only cleaned things up or worried about what food was missing. She walked around and introduced herself to many different people and had conversations ranging from astrophysics to family medicine, to how to improve one's reading comprehension. She felt glad to be at the party, especially since so much of her life recently had just been about work or worry. When the party was over, Laura and Brittany happily looked at each other.

"Brittany, thanks for suggesting we have this party. I really had a wonderful time, and this was the first time in a long time that I did not think about anything except where I was. The food was delicious, and I loved meeting so many of your friends and family," said Laura. Brittany gave Laura a hug and said that the party was all that she had hoped it would be, and she loved seeing Laura happy again. Laura felt very grateful to have a friend like her.

If the doctors were right, and Laura's mother only had four months left to live, Laura would be in San Diego at that time. She really did not know what to think of that situation and decided she would need to let it go for now and just talk to her mother every day. She decided to give her mom a call to figure out when the next best time would be for her to go to DC to visit. Her mother told her that she could come anytime she wanted. Laura decided to go the next week. When she arrived, her mother immediately told her that they could not spend each day worrying about when her time would come and that she just wanted to enjoy her moments. She did not want to think about what was coming or think anything about illness at all. Laura obliged and during the whole trip to DC, they never once talked about her illness. Instead, they played scrabble, they watched movies, they went to restaurants and even made crafts. It was a peaceful and beautiful time with her mother and father.

Back in San Diego, Laura spent one morning strongly missing Edward. She felt like there was a void in her when she was not in some form of contact with him. She decided to email him and see how he was doing. They exchanged some emails and at the end of it, they decided that they both needed to see each other again. Edward was going to come to West Glacier when Laura went back there in May. Brittany was more than okay with Edward staying with them in their house in West Glacier. Edward said he would stay for a good amount of time since he had someone running the shop in London, and his treatment was going well. He only had to go to one more session of therapy before he would be done and then would only need to go back periodically for checkups. Laura made the plans with Edward for May, but she made sure not to think about the future at all given her mother's situation. She was living in a weird kind of twilight zone.

    Brittany kept herself busy with teaching yoga and going out with her friends. She missed the coffee shop but because she knew so many people in San Diego, she was enjoying her days. They occasionally talked to Theresa, and she was doing well working with her friend on the photography studio. The ladies maintained their connection with Theresa, but the feeling was not the same ever since Theresa suddenly left them and the business. It seemed just like the other day that Laura met Theresa at the poetry reading, and now they were almost fully disconnected. Laura thought about how unpredictable life could be and how fast time passed, and it made her think that it probably didn't make sense to get too upset or angry about anything.

Chapter Thirty

Brittany and Laura arrived back at the West Glacier house, and the weather was warm with birds singing outside. Back to the coffee shop business! They were both excited to be back and got cookie dough in the grocery store to bake cookies as soon as they got back in. The fragrance of the baking cookies would be a nice welcome back to the house. They already ordered all of their products for the shop and were ready to get back to daily work there. From the sounds of the activity on their social media account for Hot Ice and Rocks, the customers were eagerly awaiting their return. The shop gave everyone a haven away from stress and negative thoughts it seemed like. Sometimes people needed to get away from their regular home environment and be in pretty surroundings with other people. It was so much fun seeing happy tourists come into the shop too. The risks in opening the shop had worked out, and it was certain that was not always the case for everyone.

Laura and Brittany got back into the routine of the shop and their evening routines of exercise, dinner, and relaxing. They missed Theresa a bit since the last time they were there Theresa was also there, but they accepted the change. It did not seem that they would need to replace Theresa because the seasonal staff they had was exceeding expectations. Laura had to get ready for Edward to arrive in two days. She was going to spend time with him at Lake McDonald. They would get some kayaks and go. Laura loved how West Glacier had such a wide variety of plant species. There were ferns, wildflowers, mushrooms, grasses, lichens, mosses, and liverworts. She loved spending time walking around in nature and slowly looking at everything. She was looking forward to Edward coming and sharing the surroundings with him. She hoped that he would be feeling well and would have the energy to do that. He had always been an adventurous guy so she thought he would be able to do that, but she was going to follow whatever energy level he had. She had never gone kayaking on Lake McDonald and was glad that the first time she would do it, she would be with Edward.

Edward arrived a few days later. The weather was a beautiful sixty-five degrees, and it was a bright, sunny day. She picked him up at Glacier Park Airport, and as usual, he was looking sprightly and happy. Maybe he was cured of it forever. For a moment, she thought of her mom who was still doing well even though it was May, and her heart sort of skipped a beat hoping it would remain that way. The family decided to put away all ideas of how much longer she had to live and just keep doing healthy things and having good times together. They were not going to think of dates and times at all anymore. Her mother was living her life in DC and still had a good amount of energy for her hobbies and friends. Laura came to some sort of peace about the situation. As she walked through the airport with Edward, they talked about her mom and also about how happy they were to be together again.

When they arrived back at the house, Edward mentioned how beautifully they had decorated it. He loved modern art, like Laura, and he spent a few minutes looking at her light fixtures and paintings. Laura had a set of light blue geometric vases on a table by a window in the dining room, and Edward spent five minutes just looking at them and rearranging them.

"Laura, your place is lovely. I would expect nothing less from you." Laura was happy that Edward liked their decorations and felt like if they ever bought a place together, it would not be hard to agree on furniture and decor. Hopefully, that would expand to their other decisions in life too like what to do for the day or what to eat for dinner.

"I'm so glad you are finally here! I've been waiting to go kayaking on Lake McDonald so that I could go with you," said Laura.

"That's great. When should we go?"

"Well, if you aren't too tired, the weather looks great today. What do you think?"

"Sure, let's go." They drove there and rented a red kayak. As they set out on the kayak, the mountains surrounding the lake looked like a beautiful fortress that protected them from everything. It felt like being in a sandbox as a kid when nothing else existed outside of that sandbox. The sounds and air around Lake McDonald were almost magical. There was no one there that day, so Laura and Edward had the whole place to themselves. Edward looked fully at peace and incredibly happy to be there with Laura. They rowed a bit out into the middle of the lake or what looked like the middle of the lake. They saw a bald eagle and a loon pretty early into the trip. It was so calming to just be around animals, water, and air. This felt like paradise to Laura to be on a beautiful lake with Edward who at this point seemed like he was the love of her life. They looked at the beautiful birds and clouds and listened to the sounds of the water. Laura didn't know what she had done to deserve such a beautiful day, but she was very happy where she was. Edward started speaking after being quiet for a while.

"Thanks for inviting me, Laura. I've missed you a lot. I love London and my life there, but recently it's becoming clear to me that I may have stronger feelings for you than those things. You know that when I first got diagnosed with cancer, I was planning to never talk to you again because I did not see that as fair. I'm not sure what I think now. I feel like I'm getting better and that maybe this won't be as big of a problem as I thought." Laura stopped for a minute before responding because she really wanted to take in what Edward said.

"Thank you for saying that. I think about you almost every day even when I don't want to think about you." Laura was glad that Edward was starting to see past his cancer diagnosis and was willing to keep his relationship with her. They continued to row and look around at their environment. The sun was shining brightly, and the few clouds that were in the sky were beautifully shaped like artwork. They decided to stop rowing for a few minutes and just sit on the kayak and talk. Laura brought some watermelon, cheese, and a thermos with hot tea in it. They enjoyed eating, letting the watermelon juice fall down their chins and then started talking about their relationship. Laura told him that she was relieved that he realized his cancer diagnosis did not have to stop their relationship, and she told him how calm and happy he made her feel.

"Edward, I don't want to talk about this much, but are you really feeling well? Do you think you're in full remission?"

"Yes. Fully. I feel great. There is something I want to talk to you about. I don't know if this is the right time, but I want to ask you if you are ready to settle down in your life in some way." Without even having to think for one moment, Laura said yes. Yes, yes, yes! She did not know if that was a marriage proposal or just a general question, but she didn't care. She wanted to be with Edward with every part of her being. There was no doubt; there were no questions. Edward wrapped his arms around her as they sat on the kayak looking above.

They decided to talk on the phone after Edward got back to London to figure everything else out. Laura was going to be working in the coffee shop for quite some time, but they decided he would sell his business and home in London and buy a place in Annapolis, Maryland. He had distant relatives there and liked the description of the area. The Chesapeake Bay was there, and it was also near Washington, D.C. Annapolis would also be close to Laura's hometown so it would be perfect for both of them. Brittany was okay with keeping the San Diego house rental on her own for the time when the coffee shop was closed down; Laura would be going to Annapolis with Edward during those months in the future.

Laura got the phone call on June fourteenth. Her mother had passed. Her father kept his cool on the phone as he relayed the information to her and let her know that it was sudden. He would have let Laura know ahead if anyone had known it was going to happen. Neither of them wanted to get into the details, and Laura told her dad that she loved him and that everything would be okay. The next several months would be sad and long like a dark winter in the arctic pole.

Chapter Thirty-One

The months after her mother's passing, Laura spent all her time not at work mostly in solitude. She wanted to be silent and have as little stimulation as possible. She wanted to make a connection with the spiritual world where maybe her mother was. She spent a lot of time doing that after her mother's passing, and it was the only time she felt a little calm about it. She supported her father through it as well. Her father was trying to decide if he wanted to sell the house and move to an apartment in a different state. The memories he had with Candace in the house were too much for him to handle. Laura promised him that she would help him figure it all out.

It was November first again and time to close the coffee shop. Edward was already settled in Annapolis and waiting for Laura to arrive. He bought a one-story house in a nice neighborhood with a bunch of neighbors that all knew each other well. He wasn't going to decide on much furniture or decorations until Laura got there. He had never lived in the States before and was excited to start a new way of life. They would make new friends there, and he hoped be able to throw many parties. He loved the excitement of getting a lot of people together just to have a good time. Wasn't life supposed to be a celebration? Laura wrapped up everything in West Glacier and stepped off her flight with a renewed spirit, ready to embark on the next chapter of her life. So many times, endings signaled new beginnings, and Laura pictured all the various stages of her life as she walked away from her gate. There wasn't too much reason to get permanently sad over things since life had shown her that it was constantly changing anyway. The past several months after her mom's passing had been very miserable, but she finally started coming to terms with it. Her father fell into a depression after her mother's passing and wasn't quite getting better yet. She understood it and thought it would help him to move out of the house where he spent all those years with Candace. She knew how environments affected people positively or negatively. If he decided to move, she would be right there to help him along with the whole process.

Chapter Thirty-Two

When Laura pulled up to the Annapolis house, there were two gold balloons flying on the mailbox with a sign that said, *honey, welcome home.* As Laura looked at the balloons dancing in the air, she felt a tremendous sense of lightness as if she was one of those balloons flying in the air. She had been down a long and windy path for many years which had somehow led her here. She felt that the person she was meant to spend her entire life with was waiting for her inside the white house with green shutters, and the thought of that sent a good chill up her spine. Even though she always focused on work and tasks, in the end, it was her heart that led the way. All the risks and doubts finally made sense as she walked up the driveway towards the glass, open door.

When she walked inside, Edward was in the kitchen making lunch. He looked up and felt more joy than he recalled ever feeling as Laura entered the house. His whole life he had worked hard, been responsible, helped people, and hoped that one day he would have the love of his life by his side. It had never happened until the moment Laura walked through that door. He almost became paralyzed with joy as Laura continued walking towards the kitchen. He could not believe that his main dream in life had finally come true. He wondered in those few seconds what the next years would be like with them together. He wondered what he had done so right in life that he was given Laura somehow by the universe. He wondered whether he would always have her and for how long. When she reached him by the kitchen island, they embraced while Laura told him how much she liked the house he picked.

"Honey, I've missed your face so much," said Laura as she grabbed his cheek and kissed it.

"You don't know how much I've been waiting for this day," said Edward. The house had some furnishings so there were places to sit, but it was still pretty empty. There was a bed in the house, and Edward put up a few pictures. One of the pictures was of them in West Glacier walking around the lake; he had that picture enlarged and framed, and it was on the wall near the entryway. He did not want to decorate before Laura got there, but he also did not want the walls to look too sparse when she came.

"Honey, my cancer is better. You never know with cancer, but I hope it doesn't come back. Let's make the most of each day together. This is our life. No one knows what will happen tomorrow, but we know we are together here now," said Edward.

"I'm so lucky to have you in my life. I'm so glad that I went to Thailand, and I'm glad that there was the civil strife at our hotel or else I would have never met you. So many things look bad at the beginning, but sometimes those bad things lead us to good places," said Laura. Edward looked at her full of love and told her that he was thankful every day that she went to Thailand with Thomas. They spent the rest of the afternoon unpacking Laura's things and talking about their future.

The next day, they spent some time reading the paper together and started talking about jobs and finances. Laura was going to continue working at the coffee shop in West Glacier, and Edward would get involved with the shop as well. He had enough money from selling everything in London that they would not need to produce a huge income, but the two of them would work together at the coffee shop and try to grow that business even more. Maybe they would start shipping their products or open another location. When the coffee shop was closed during the cold months, they would return to Annapolis. Laura liked the idea of having so much time in the wilderness of West Glacier but also having time in the sophistication of Annapolis. She could not believe this was her life. It seemed thousands of miles away from where she started in Duck, North Carolina, alone and worried about starting her job at the Baker Law Firm. She was almost scared that somehow all of the wonderful things in her life would not last or maybe that life always messed things up.

The risks she took paid off, even though she knew there were many people who took risks that ended badly. She didn't feel that she had many regrets. She made the final decision not to have kids, and it felt good to be sure about so many things. She didn't feel it was a mistake to leave the practice of law because she didn't believe in argument anymore. She didn't regret the divorce with Thomas because they both felt that it needed to happen, and neither had bad feelings towards the other because of it. She also didn't regret her time with Thomas because it was her first significant relationship, and he showed her what it means to love someone. Not that anything in life was perfect or that her life was perfect, but she felt at peace with all of it. She wondered how long that would last. Would things get a lot harder as she aged?

Laura wanted not to think too far ahead anymore. She didn't want to be afraid about what was coming next in life. It seemed most people spent most of their lives in that sort of tailspin like a jumpy squirrel constantly looking around in fear. There had to be a better way to live life.

Chapter Thirty-Three

On Saturday morning, Laura got a call from Rebecca. They stayed in touch during all the changes that happened in each other's lives but had not seen each other recently. Rebecca got married and lived in New Hampshire. Her husband worked for the local plumber in town, and she was thinking about having a baby. She was conflicted about it because she knew from having seen her friends that it would completely change her life. She also wanted to have a career and wasn't sure if it would be possible to juggle both of those desires as well as she would want to. The ladies talked, and Rebecca told her about all the things that were going on. Rebecca told her that it seemed many women were not having babies anymore, but she knew it could be the most rewarding experience of a person's life; she could play a role in creating a good person for the future generation.

Laura listened and told Rebecca that she would really need to search deep down inside of herself to make the decision. This was not something to be taken lightly, and if she decided to become a parent, it would control at least the next twenty years of her life. Rebecca was working as a freelance writer while trying to figure out if she was going to take the plunge into becoming a parent. She saw so many of her female friends who had kids have to do all of the work alone. She wasn't sure how Eric would turn out to be with all of that, but she agreed with Laura that the decision would require deep soul searching. The ladies lived pretty close to each other with Rebecca in New Hampshire and Laura in Maryland. They talked about making plans to get together sometime, and before they got off the phone, Laura thanked her for getting the idea into her head to take the trip alone to New Zealand. That one decision completely changed her life for the better.

Annapolis, Maryland didn't get too cold during the winter months. It was just enough to feel the brisk air and sense the change in seasons but not so much that it was dreadful being outside. Laura really liked that about the area. Plus, there were lots of educated people with interesting degrees and backgrounds. On any given day, she could run into a lawyer, a physicist, a medical doctor, a fisherman, and many other types of people. Her life felt settled in a good way, but Laura started to feel like she didn't know what else would be happening for her anymore. She knew what the basic facts of her life were at this stage but was a little worried that she was losing some enthusiasm about the future. The most important thing to her was Edward, and she knew that with him by her side, most other things didn't matter too much anyway. When she was younger, it seemed like a long path ahead that she could do many things with, but at her current age, Laura felt a little listless and unsure of how to think of any future. She wanted to continue having an adventurous life with Edward. His cancer was still in remission, and their life together was everything they hoped it would be. They had interesting conversations, times in silence together, and a companionship that seemed to transcend time.

Laura wondered if she had done enough with her life since it seemed that time was running out. Professionally, she had tried different things and managed to become a business owner as well. In her personal life, she found a loving partner. She had met people from so many different walks of life. She wasn't sure what was left to do but felt that she needed to know how she would spend the rest of her life with Edward. She marveled at how different thoughts and feelings were at her current age as compared to how she was in her early twenties. It was like two completely different existences. Edward said he was happy at this point in his life having a more routine life and not looking for too much excitement anymore. Laura enjoyed that too, but she didn't want to stop there; the problem was she wasn't sure yet about how the rest would be. It would depend on her physical health as she aged as well as how her feelings about life changed over time.

Edward and Laura decided to get a dog. She had a friend from law school that had a Pomeranian dog, and she thought it was a cute dog. They decided to go with that and got a Pomeranian from a local rescue facility. They named her Skittles. She was a very mild-natured and friendly dog. It was nice to have her there when they came home; she was a great companion, and they would make sure that Skittles had a good day every day. The process of having Skittles gave Laura and Edward a chance to raise something together. It would not be a baby, but this was close in some ways. Skittles seemed to know when they were happy or when they were sad. She was an intelligent dog, and they were glad they decided to get her.

The couple would take Skittles for a walk every morning and often also every afternoon. They would walk through the trails behind their house and let Skittles walk freely for a bit. She looked so happy in those woods taking in all the sights and smells. Laura and Edward would spend the time talking about the day and things that were sometimes upsetting them. Laura always felt better after having time talking with Edward; this part of their relationship reminded her of her walks with Thomas. After their conversations, she felt like every problem had a solution, and there was no reason to worry. She wished that everyone had a person like Edward and felt that the reason there was so much sadness in the world was because most people did not have such a person in their life.

Chapter Thirty-Four

Laura's father was still dealing with the grief of her mother passing. Laura obviously still felt it too but because her father spent almost all of his adult life with Candace and was older now, he was having a harder time adjusting to the change. She wondered what she could do to help him. Her dad was seventy-six so there didn't seem to be much point in him dating. She wondered what changes he could make in his life to help him adjust to his new situation. He joined a book club and that seemed to be a highlight of his week. Hopefully, he would remain active and with people because that always made a difference for people. All she knew was that she would be there at any time her father needed her; so much had happened so quickly.

Edward wanted to add a sunroom to their house. They could use that space to meditate and just sit and look outside through the glass doors at the trees in the backyard. He would need to find a reliable contractor and figure out how much it would cost. He had the vision of it perfectly in his mind, but since he'd never done a big renovation before, he didn't know how much it would cost. Laura loved the idea of having a sunroom in the house. She was sure she would use it a lot. She thought about ways to decorate it and decided white, lavender, and blue colors would be nice. She always wanted to have one room that was decorated just in those colors. Edward found a guy named Rick who built sunrooms for the last twenty years. He was a personable guy, and Edward felt he could trust him. Instead of spending more time looking around for more people, Edward decided to go with him on gut instinct. They scheduled the work to begin in one week, and Rick said he could have the whole thing done within a month. It would be the perfect spot to read, have coffee, and meditate. Laura and Edward already had a very peaceful and loving home, and this addition would quite literally add to that.

Edward was looking forward to having a cozy winter with Laura in their first winter together in the new house. He missed London sometimes, but with the world being just one big place where everything was connected to everything else, he didn't really feel too far away from home. Every night before he closed his eyes, he would say a little prayer to the moon and hope that his cancer would stay in remission. He hoped to be able to live at least thirty more years with Laura. He wasn't sure how they would spend that time yet, but he wanted their time together to go for as long as it possibly could.

Laura told Edward that she was thinking about opening a healing center in town for the time they were in Annapolis. She felt like people were all so scattered these days and needed a space to absorb things, talk to other like-minded people, and face the spiritual questions in life. The lease amounts were high in the area, and Laura was not sure whether she could take that much financial risk, especially given they already had the coffee shop in West Glacier. She was getting older and not sure if she would have what it took to make a second business succeed. It seemed every other day businesses popped up and then closed. She decided to let the idea kind of bake in the back of her mind for now.

They decided to go to Georgetown and walk around the Washington Harbor area. That area was always full of happy looking people, beautiful restaurants and shops, and water. She always felt uplifted after taking a walk there. She felt the need to be dressed up when going there because people cared about their appearance there. It was filled with a lot of professional and sometimes influential people from the DC area. In recent years, Laura much preferred casual and comfortable clothes to getting fully dressed up with every hair in place. Women spent so much time on that. Often, when walking around the Washington Harbor area, she would see these beautiful women walking alongside a guy that looked like a slob. She wondered why women did not realize that they were doing all that work and spending all of that time on their looks really for no reason. The only way Laura could justify that in her mind was if the ladies were mainly doing it for themselves and felt better about themselves when dressed up like that.

There was a lady that looked to be in her early twenties sitting on the steps at the edge of the water just sadly looking down at her feet. She was the only one in the area that looked to be unhappy. She had red hair and was wearing all black clothes. She looked like she just wanted to fall into the water and be done with everything. Laura wondered what it was that could have a person looking that sad. She thought about approaching the lady and talking to her. For a moment, she wondered whether that would be rude. Before she knew what she was doing, she went and sat down next to her.

"Uh, hi," said Laura fumbling to figure out what to say next. The lady looked up and looked annoyed that her thoughts were being interrupted.

"Hi," said the lady flatly.

"Um, I was just wondering if you knew what time it was," asked Laura. The girl looked through her as if she could tell that Laura was just trying to start a conversation with her for no reason. Laura felt so uncomfortable she almost jumped up and walked away but then decided to stay where she was.

"I'm sorry, I don't know the time," said the lady.

"Um, sorry, I don't mean to bother you, but you look so sad. I couldn't help but come and sit next to you. Just wondering if there is anything I can do," asked Laura. The girl looked at her skeptically for a minute and then started to speak.

"I'm tired of everything. I'm tired of all of the violence in the world. I am tired," said the girl. Laura asked her what her name was. The girl said her name was Marie. Laura was glad that the girl was willing to at least talk to her. Edward went and sat at an outdoor restaurant and ordered a beer. He knew Laura wanted to go talk to that girl and was having a nice time just sitting outside while she did that. Laura tried to think about what would be best to do next. Marie looked like she really needed someone to talk to. Her pain was palpable all in the air around her. Laura decided to give her phone number, and the girl could decide to call her in the future.

"I know how you feel. The world has definitely gotten too violent. I feel it too, but remember life always has cycles and things improve as much as sometimes they get worse. We all have to cope with it and keep hope," said Laura. The girl looked at her and seemed to be listening but at the same time seemed like she did not believe those things anymore.

"I want to give you my number. Maybe we can become friends. If you ever want to meet for coffee or lunch, let me know. I would love to get to know you better," Laura said.

"Ok, I'll take your number," said Marie. Marie thought the lady looked genuine, so she went against her initial thought of saying no thank you. Laura pulled out a coffee shop business card that had her cell phone number on it and gave it to Marie.

"Well, I hope you have a good rest of your day here. Try to keep seeing the beautiful parts of life, and by the way, my name is Laura." Laura never asked for Marie's phone number, but she certainly hoped that she would hear from her. Laura always felt that if more people took a non-selfish interest in other people that it would make for a better world.

Edward and Laura spent the rest of the day shopping in Georgetown and had a nice lunch at the French bistro. They also visited the cupcake shop that had the best cupcakes Laura ever tasted. Her favorite cupcake there was called molten lava, and when a person bit into that cupcake, loads of warm fudge would seep out of it. She had to get a box of them every time she came to Georgetown, and they would make for wonderful moments with her coffee at home.

The next day, Laura got a call from a number she did not recognize. She picked it up to hear Marie's voice.

"Hi, it's Marie. I wanted to call you."

"Hi there, Marie! So glad to hear your voice. Thanks for calling me." Laura was glad that Marie did not waste time in calling her.

"You know, I just wanted to say thank you for reaching out to me when I was sitting outside yesterday. It showed me that there are still people who care about others in this world," said Marie.

"Of course! It was a pleasure to meet you. You are a young lady and have so many years ahead of you. I hope you start getting excited about your life and try to follow your dreams even if that means taking some risk. That's a better way of living than just following a path that is not meant for you," said Laura. Marie felt good talking to Laura. She wondered why a stranger would care enough to even approach her, and it affirmed to her that not everyone was really so greedy. Marie had thought about what she wanted to say to Laura when they spoke.

"I'm just tired of women working so hard and seeming to get nowhere or being so busy that they are exhausted every day. I look around, and it doesn't seem men live the same sort of lifestyle. I am tired of watching it. I'm tired of seeing women hit a glass ceiling and have a harder time being able to advance their careers. I'm tired of seeing women spend so much time dressing themselves up so a man will think they are attractive. I am tired," said Marie.

"I have felt your feelings so many times in my life, Marie. You are not alone, and I hope you always remember that. Don't give up hope. Things often change in life, and you always have choices in life," said Laura.

"Thank you, Laura," said Marie. The ladies talked a bit more about what Marie was thinking about, and then Laura told her that she had been thinking about possibly opening a healing center in the Annapolis area. She told her that she hadn't ironed out all of the details yet, but that maybe Marie could also get involved with that. She wanted to focus on the problems and stressors people had in their lives as well as the sorts of things Marie was talking about. Marie told her that it sounded interesting and that they should stay in touch about it. They decided they would keep in touch and that Marie would call her whenever she felt like talking or going out for a cup of coffee. Laura hung up the phone glad that she bothered to approach Marie at Georgetown Harbor. It had made a difference.

Chapter Thirty-Five

That evening, Edward and Laura were invited to Edward's friend's house for dinner. They were going to have a casual barbeque and eat in their screened in, heated porch. They hired people to do the barbecuing so that they could spend more time with their guests. When they arrived, Edward's friend, Todd, was standing at the front door. They greeted each other and went inside. Todd's wife, Eleanor, was an excellent decorator, and the house felt palatial only because of the way it was decorated. There were satin drapes and fluffy round carpets everywhere. There were oil paintings of meadows and a big grand piano in the middle of the room. The kitchen was sparkling white with gold trim and huge skylights above. There was a huge chandelier in the kitchen that was copper that gave out the most serene, yellow light. It was a great place to cook and had copper-colored pots and pans perfectly lined up on shelves. Eleanor told them that she had a vision for how she wanted the house decorated, and all of the ideas came to her quickly. She was a creative person, opposite of her husband, so they both used their different skills in constructing a full life. Todd was an IT executive and liked everything to have an order. He had an extensive music collection, and he kept all of his old records in the library organized by title. He loved having his space away from everything where he could just go and listen to his music in peace. He didn't need a lot of interaction with others, so he needed that space away. It made Eleanor feel lonely sometimes, but she made several close friends over the years and would always spend time with them when she felt lonely. The couples went to the kitchen table where there was already an elaborate spread of olives, cheeses, and wines. Laura looked forward to seeing people she liked talking to, and Eleanor and Todd were some of the people she enjoyed spending time with, so she was happy to be there.

"Edward, how have you been feeling?" asked Todd.

"Well, great. Thanks. No signs of the cancer returning right now."

"That's great. We should all think about going on a cruise somewhere sometime," said Eleanor. The four of them agreed that would be a good thing to do. The staff brought in some grilled chicken and shrimp and set it on the table. There were already a lot of roasted vegetables on the table. It smelled heavenly and was great because Laura was trying to eat more of a high protein diet. After dinner, they went into the living room and sat down with some champagne, brie cheese, and crackers.

"You know, I've been thinking about opening a healing center. I'm not sure what it would be other than a space where people could get to know each other and problem solve with one another as well as have a spiritual space of some sort," said Laura.

"Interesting. I wonder what that could be. Do you have the energy for all of that?" asked Eleanor.

"I'm not sure. I feel like I'm hesitating somehow. Maybe the idea needs to percolate for a while longer because I'm not clear right now what it would be or how I would go about creating it. I think I need to wait for some sort of intuition for it," said Laura. Todd told them about how he read somewhere that when the timing was right for something, a person would know. He said to not rush things so much and just give things some time. Laura thought his advice made sense and decided to follow that as much as she could. Laura dressed up that night and felt her shoe pushing on her right toe. She wore those shoes because they looked good but feeling the pain in her foot made her think it was silly that she was more concerned with the looks of them than her foot! The couples continued talking and laughing, and it was a great night with good friends.

In what felt like the blink of an eye, it was the end of April and time to get ready to go back to West Glacier. It was a rainy day in Annapolis, and the couple needed to go get some supplies for the shop. They would go to the neighborhood mall and pick up the things and maybe have lunch. Edward was looking forward to getting to know how the shop operated and getting more involved with the business there. Brittany was happy that Edward would consider becoming involved with it. She had no issues with having him join, especially since Theresa was gone. Edward thought he would be good at the bookkeeping portion since he already knew about that from his shop in London. He hoped to contribute from day one and was so pleased to be working with the love of his life.

Chapter Thirty-Six

When they arrived at the house in West Glacier, Brittany was already there and had made Italian sub sandwiches for everyone. Brittany was such a thoughtful person and showed that she cared about other people. She told them that she had missed the coffee shop during the off-season and all the customers. At first, Edward was a little put off by how deserted the area was being used to London and the DC area, but he decided to have a good attitude about it and open his mind to everything. Otherwise, he thought he may get depressed in such a sparsely populated area. Then again, with Laura by his side, there was little risk for anything like that.

The next morning, the line at the coffee shop was long. Edward, Brittany, and Laura were manning the registers and making the coffee, but they weren't getting through the people fast enough and some started to look annoyed. Their seasonal staff hadn't arrived yet, so Laura wondered whether they would need to hire another person before that. Their first customer was wearing a shirt covered in purple orchids and had a scarf around her neck that had lights on it. That was the first time Laura had seen anything like that. There were some unique people who lived in the West Glacier area. You would never see anything like that in the DC area or at least it would be unlikely.

"Give me the best thing you have," said the lady as she walked up to the counter. She didn't say anything else like whether she meant coffee or a snack. Laura asked her what she meant, and the lady just repeated the same thing. Laura kind of laughed inside wondering what this lady wanted. She went towards the caramel cheesecakes they had and made the lady a simple vanilla latte.

"Here you go," said Laura handing her the cheesecake and latte.

"Hey, why don't you make this on the house just to be different for today?" asked the lady. Laura decided really quickly that she would. What the hell. The lady smiled and left, and Laura told the customers behind her that she could not do that for everyone that day.

The months went by quickly, and the three of them fell into a good routine of work and evenings. Laura would mainly do the cooking, although Edward didn't want all of that responsibility just on her shoulders so he would often offer to do it. Edward was a good cook and enjoyed doing it. They would take turns washing the dishes, and there were no squabbles or resentments about things like that. Brittany often did most of their grocery shopping so the three of them had a good system going.

Laura's father decided to take a big risk and go skydiving with a friend of his. At his age, Laura was concerned that it wasn't a good idea, but for some reason her father was really interested in doing it. He said that he needed something exciting in his life and at seventy-six there wasn't too much exciting anymore. Laura was proud that he was so courageous and decided not to bother him about it. He had developed COPD which was strange since he never smoked. He would get winded when he walked for too long, but he still wanted to try skydiving. He had gotten to the point in life after Candace's passing that he didn't care anymore about some things.

Laura called Marie to talk to her about the healing center she was thinking about opening. Marie lived in Northern Virginia, and if they did anything like this it would be in the DC area. Laura told her that she was in West Glacier but wanted to chat with her about the healing center. Marie sounded interested to hear more about it since she was getting tired of her job as a cosmetologist. She liked the artistic aspect of her job, but she felt like she could make a bigger contribution to the world through a different avenue. Laura got the feeling that Marie liked talking about the potential of a healing center and when she talked to Laura about it, her voice sounded hopeful and happy. They talked about meeting for coffee when Laura got back to the DC area to talk about it more. Laura felt good that she made a little difference in Marie's life already with one simple gesture. There was no reason for someone so young to be tired of life so much already.

Some guy Brittany met at the coffee shop was constantly texting her and would not stop. She liked talking to him after she and her last boyfriend broke up, but this guy had become very annoying and would not stop texting her. She asked him several times to stop and told him that she wasn't interested in a relationship, but the guy would not listen. She told Edward and Laura about it, and they were all trying to figure out what the next best step was. He had a fiancé in the past who broke up with him before the wedding, and he never recovered from that. Brittany felt bad for him and kept a friendship with him but decided later that he didn't fit with her more than that. He could not take the rejection and would not leave her alone. She wasn't scared of him, but she found his constant contact annoying, and he just wasn't getting the message. He'd call and ask her what she was doing that day. It was an odd situation, and one Brittany didn't need in her life. She did not want men taking her time and energy for no reason. If she had known this when she was younger, she would not have married her ex-husband. He took all her time and energy and turned out to be a selfish jerk.

    Laura didn't feel well on Tuesday morning and had to tell Brittany and Edward that she wouldn't be able to go to the coffee shop that day. She was getting a sharp pain in her right side. She hoped it wasn't appendicitis or something. Her mother had that as a young person, and she said it was really painful. This pain didn't feel unbearable so maybe it was nothing. She got into bed with a good novel and read a little before drifting to sleep. She had a very vivid dream about walking on a beach alone for miles and seeing no one. She felt like she was the only person on the entire planet and would be forever. It was a dream that made her feel like she was hanging above the Earth looking down on it and that there was only water, trees, and her spirit. The dream made her feel the entire human existence she had always known really did not exist. She felt free until she woke up. She spent the day slowly walking around the house trying to get some chores done. It was the worst she had felt as far back as she could remember, and she hoped it would go away without needing to go and see a doctor.

In the afternoon, she made herself some tea and laid down for a few minutes. The pain in her right side was subsiding but was still there. She worried for a moment about something being seriously wrong. She just didn't want to think about it though. She didn't like going to doctors and generally took good care of herself. She went on walks almost daily and ate a lot of vegetables. She always lived a healthy lifestyle, but she knew that wasn't the whole story. Genes were a big thing too, and anything could happen to anyone no matter how well they took care of themselves. Knowing that, Laura always tried to make the best of moments because there never really was too much guarantee. A few days later, Laura still was not feeling normal. The pain wasn't as bad as at the beginning, but she did not feel like herself. She and Edward decided to return to Annapolis very early that year just in case it turned out there was something seriously wrong. Brittany was fine with that and knew several people in town that could fill in at the coffee shop.

Chapter Thirty-Seven

Laura was happy to arrive back home in Annapolis. If she continued to not feel well, all her doctors were in the area and that would make it easy to be seen and get any treatment. Their new sunroom was already completed, and Laura decided it was the perfect day to go in there and lie down on the couch with a blanket. The pain in her side was still there despite taking pain medication. Luckily, it was a sunny day, and there were birds chirping outside. That environment helped her deal with the pain. She needed to be still and quiet both mentally and physically. The sunroom was such a soothing space. Edward was smart for deciding to add it to their house. That day, she felt old. Her body somehow did not feel the same, and she was concerned about it. It was like the difference between the feeling of a dry swimsuit before jumping into the ocean and the wet, heavy one after walking out. She decided she would go to the internist the next day.

After some tests, the doctor told her that the pain in her side was a hernia but that her labs showed that she had become anemic. They could not figure out why because the typical reasons for anemia did not apply to her. They asked her to come back in a few months and to take some iron pills for a while. Laura started doing that but still didn't feel like herself. She tried not to bring others down by talking about it too much. She never liked to complain and felt like that didn't do anything to improve situations or solve problems. At the same time, she had learned that keeping everything bottled inside wasn't a great option either. She would need to find a balance between the two.

Edward and Laura asked Brittany if she would be okay hiring a temporary employee for the summer so that they could go to Spain. When they left West Glacier, they weren't sure if they would be gone for the whole coffee shop season or not, but upon thinking of it, they wanted to go to Spain and see if it would help Laura get better. Laura had never been there, and maybe a trip there would be just what she needed to get some of her energy back. Brittany was fine with it and loved how they had this kind of relationship because Laura and Edward always accommodated her too. They had created a great working relationship which allowed all of them to thrive and enjoy their lives to the fullest.

Laura started planning the trip to Spain. Things took her longer than they normally would because she was at about sixty-five percent capacity compared to her normal self. Edward had been there when he was much younger, but he didn't remember too much about the country. Laura decided they would stick to Barcelona and focus on art and architecture rather than try to see the whole country in a short time. There was the Sagrada Familia Church that looked like a beautiful building to see there, and Laura started getting excited about going abroad again.

They had a lot of Gaudi buildings in Barcelona and modernist designs that Laura was excited to see, and they had beaches. It sounded like the perfect place to go for a break. She decided to splurge on the accommodation and found a house with an ocean view in La Pineda, Barcelona. The pictures were so attractive; she wished they could be there already.

When they got to the Barcelona rental house around the beginning of June, everything was in order. Whoever had prepared the home for them had done an excellent job, and there was the fragrance of lemons wafting throughout the house. The door leading out to the deck was cracked a little open, and a nice breeze greeted them as they walked into the kitchen. Laura felt all her muscles instantly relax, and a smile came to her face. It was seventy-eight degrees that day, so warm but not stifling. After unpacking, they went to take a long walk on the beach.

They went outside to find little groups of people walking along the beach, and some were barbecuing and drinking beer right there. There were sounds of kids playing and people telling jokes and laughing. This was a world away from the busy streets of DC or London. Laura felt herself relax, and her mind turned from stress to positive and joyful thoughts. Laura felt lucky that she could normally make herself relax without needing any sort of trip, but this time, she felt it would be helpful to go to Barcelona to help her relax. She wasn't one of those people that always had to escape to relax. They walked along the beach as Edward told her how happy he was that they came; he was deeply worried about Laura and was hoping that this trip would take away whatever medical problem was brewing inside of her. He did not tell her how worried he was, but he felt it every day since her pain started.

The sun was starting to go down and created an orange shimmer all around them. There were streaks of purple in the sky and a lot of chubby clouds just wafting above them. They decided to walk slowly and since they were barefoot, they could feel the sand under their feet. They saw a sign for a restaurant that specialized in gazpacho and dishes with shrimp. Laura knew a little Spanish and that was really helping during the trip. They decided to go there for dinner but decided not to plan everything else out. They were living one moment at a time and at a slow pace which was very refreshing. The dinner was mouthwateringly good. They were having a great time even though Laura's anemia made her feel weak at times. She got used to taking breaks in between activities to shore up energy for the next thing.

After dinner, they walked a little more on the beach. A couple approached them and asked if they spoke Spanish. Laura said she did but that they were better with English. The man knew how to speak English and told them that he noticed how gently they seemed to be walking on the beach as if in some sort of daydream. He said he felt like stopping to talk to them because he was tired of seeing people rush around. He asked them where they were visiting from and other such questions. At the end of the chat, he wished them well and thanked them for coming to Barcelona. Edward thought it was good how comfortable the man was with just coming straight up to them and talking to them. The place felt cozy, friendly, and full of love. They decided to go visit the Sagrada Familia Church. When they arrived, Laura thought it looked like a chocolate ice cream cone that had tipped over on a warm day. As expected, the halls inside were beautiful and had a natural feeling to them while at the same time, they looked surreal. There were patrons there with their eyes closed in silent prayer as well as many tourists that walked around talking and laughing.

Laura decided to sit there with them and close her eyes for a moment. Although she had no religious belief, she believed in energy and spirit. She wanted to take some time, with Edward by her side, sitting there in silent contemplation. The lady next to her smiled at her and said, *que consigas lo que quieres*. Laura just smiled back not knowing what that meant. Later, Laura looked up the phrase and found out the lady wished for her to get what she wanted.

Back at their hotel, Laura decided to take a bath. She filled the bath with vanilla fragrance and put candles on. Edward decided to do a little work for the coffee shop on his computer. They would not spend a lot of their time on work while they were in Barcelona, but Edward had a need to be at least a little productive each day. He had a hard time relaxing sometimes and felt that he needed to get some things done. Laura used a loofah to scrape all the dead skin off of her body. She had heard of Turkish baths where at least in the past, people did that for the guests. She couldn't imagine what it would be like to go to a public bath. She would not feel comfortable with that, but the idea of exfoliating dead skin felt like renewal to her.

The next day, they decided to go see some of Barcelona's main attractions, which were Gaudi buildings. They went to the Casa Mila, a white building that looked nothing like anything she had ever seen. It looked like it did not have borders like one thing ran into the other, and everything was part of something else. Gaudi designed this building to look like it just naturally sprung up from the ground in a flexible and loose way. There were no strict lines as if everything was just a shade of grey in the world. Laura was having a great time in Barcelona with Edward. There were a few moments where she didn't feel great, but she didn't want to get Edward worried about it, so she tried to keep it to herself. She started to think that maybe keeping silent wasn't the best thing to do like the typical woman that always suppressed her pain and emotion. Maybe it was better to tell Edward that she didn't feel great when she didn't. It would be okay for him to take care of her a little bit. She always felt uncomfortable doing things like that and was used to being the one that took care of others. There was nothing wrong with being nurturing; it only became a problem when women didn't realize they needed a little nurturing themselves.

"I'm having a great time, Edward. How about you?" asked Laura. They were slowly walking around the grounds outside of the Casa Mila.

"This has been wonderful. Gaudi was so talented."

"Ya, I gotta say though, lately I don't have the energy I used to have sometimes. I hope it's nothing too serious," said Laura.

"Ya, I know what you mean. I've felt that a little bit too with the years but not really too much. Honey, you know we have to find out what's going on with you medically over some time," said Edward.

"Yeah. I'm hoping it will all just go away. Sometimes if you feel like it, you can go out on your own, and I'll just read a book in the hotel. I don't want to hold you back when I'm feeling a bit tired." Laura said this, and it was hard for her to say. She was used to pushing herself no matter how she felt, and this was probably the first time in her life she had said something other than that.

"Sure, that makes sense. Don't push yourself too hard," said Edward. What a simple thing. She wasn't sure why she spent most of her life just holding things like that inside. They were going to go to the Gothic Quarter during their trip as well as to Park Guell. The park was a combination of beautiful gardens intertwined with artistic buildings where they could stroll and do some people watching. The Gothic Quarter had medieval buildings and labyrinth like walks through tall walls. There was an old Roman wall there, and it seemed it would be a good place to think of history and all of the times and people that had passed. Laura was going to make sure to go to these sites with Edward, but she decided that she would spend time in the spa alone as well as just in her bed watching an old movie. She didn't need to feel bad about that. She saw so many women, especially mothers, over the years never give themselves the chance to just read a book or relax since they were always working on what someone else wanted. She spent many years of her life living that way, and maybe her body was finally saying that she had to stop.

The next day was stormy and the clouds outside of the hotel window looked dark and angry. She had no desire to go out in them. They decided to watch a movie together and since her back hurt, Edward gave her a massage. They watched a movie about life in India. It showed how people adapted to the crowded spaces and worked together to overcome the obstacles that came with living in such a populated country. They kept their spirituality and seemed to always see the positive side of things and the joy that was available in life. It seemed to be a life filled with a lot of rituals and ceremony. It was a relaxing day spent in Barcelona without the pressure of having to run to sightsee the whole time.

They went to dinner that night at a restaurant called Fluye. The name meant flows. Laura wondered why they called it that but heard that everyone in town loved the place. The entire restaurant was decorated with blue walls and white chandeliers. The light was dim, and everyone who worked there was wearing white. When they sat at their table, the server approached and told them that they had a vegetarian special that evening. They started talking to her about Barcelona, and she told them the best thing to do would be to have dinner in a family's house. She said they would really get a feel for Barcelona and the cuisine if they did that. Edward and Laura weren't sure how they would do that, but it was great to get suggestions from their server. Her name was Sofia. She had long, straight blond hair and brown eyes. She had a few moles on her face; one mole was above her lip and the other next to her eyebrow. They were big moles, and it was interesting that she had not removed them. They gave her face a distinct look, but in a way, they were obstructive to her face as well. She didn't seem to care. As she brought their meals, they continued talking with her, and she told them more about her life in Barcelona. She was thirty-two and never married. She never went to college and just hated everything academic. She talked about how short life was and how she thought it was funny that so many people spent so many years in school when life was already so short. She wondered whether it was just to impress others. She wondered why society was set up that way. She noted that certainly different professions and skills were important in life, and everyone helped everyone else with their skills, but she felt that humans had made life too complicated and too much about impressing others. She never followed that path and was not ashamed that she was a server. She got to talk to people every day and to be around food. She loved both of those things. She lived with her friend in an apartment in town.

Her friend was a journalist and wrote stories for the local paper. They had a simple life that they enjoyed, and they knew all their neighbors. In fact, they would cook for their neighbors, and their neighbors would do the same in return. She liked hearing about Laura and Edward's lives in Maryland and in West Glacier. She had never been to the United States but hoped to go one day. She heard that life there was fast paced, and she didn't think she would like that. She told them that they had smaller and less fancy homes and cars, but they all generally seemed to be happy in Barcelona. Sofia brought out their Crème Brule, and Laura dug in immediately. It had always been her favorite dessert. She remembered making it when Rebecca came over to her house in North Carolina for dinner. She couldn't believe she had not had Crème Brule since then.

"Honey, you look lost in thought," said Edward as Laura continued to enjoy her Crème Brule.

"Oh, no, I was just thinking a bit about what Sofia was saying. What an outgoing personality she has!"

"Ya, I liked talking to her too. In this digital world, it's good that some people still take time to talk to others," said Edward. They wrapped up their meal and said goodbye to Sofia. They walked into the balmy night, arm in arm, and walked back to their hotel feeling relaxed and fully in the moment. They went to bed that night thinking of what they would do during their last days in Barcelona. In the morning, they were headed to Park Guell. When they got there, they saw ducks in ponds and people everywhere. It was tranquil yet full of energy with all of the people there strolling, joggers, and people eating ice cream and sitting on benches. Laura fell in love with it immediately.

"Wow, can we stay here forever?" asked Laura with a big smile.

"Ya, maybe we should!" There were palm trees everywhere, and Gaudi had designed all kinds of eastern and western type buildings all throughout the park. It was a park filled with stone paths and bridges, alongside flowers and modernistic, abstract buildings. The park layout was so different from what typical life looked like that it took Edward and Laura out of their regular mindsets. It was a park that basically said just look around at all of the beauty and forget everything else. It was a park that Laura never wanted to leave. Maybe she would spend some time later reading more about the artist, Gaudi. His work was all over Barcelona and made the area look like some sort of fantasy utopia.

As they were walking, Laura got that same pain in her right side again. This time she couldn't shake it off; it was sharper than any time she felt it before, and suddenly, she felt herself fall over. She hit the ground with a thud, and everything went black.

Chapter Thirty-Eight

When she woke up, Laura was in the hospital in Barcelona. Edward was peering over her when she opened her eyes, and he looked beyond distraught. All the lines on his face were magnified, and his lips were downturned as if he could no longer lift them up.

"Laura, I'm so glad you opened your eyes. You haven't done that since we got here." Laura heard him but didn't have the energy to answer. She felt lightheaded almost as if her brain wasn't working properly like her brain cells were swimming in a fishbowl filled with Jello. She could not understand what was happening to her, but she knew she had never felt like this before. She understood that she was in the hospital with Edward in Barcelona, and she even remembered falling over in the park, but everything else was confusing. It was hard for her to perceive everything in the room and to think linear thoughts. She just wanted to sleep, but she was worried about Edward after seeing the expression on his face. Obviously, something had happened to her, but she did not even want to know what it was. She felt like her body weighed five hundred pounds and like her nerves and muscles no longer had the will or energy to move any of her parts. She felt confused and could not understand why this happened in the park. Edward told her that the doctors noted her anemia and saw that her blood cells looked different, but they weren't sure why. She understood him when he said all of that.

Edward told her that he loved her and tried to look calm despite feeling like his whole world was spinning out of control. He knew he had to be strong for her, and he knew that soon he would have to uplift his own spirits to bring her some sort of peace in the moment. He did not want Laura worrying about him. They would wait until the next day when the doctor was scheduled to come in and do rounds to see if they had figured out more. Edward would spend the night in the same room with Laura on a pull-out couch they had in the room. Unfortunately, when the doctor came the next morning, he did not have more information for them on Laura's condition. They were not able to figure it out. He said that she would need to follow-up with a hematologist and that her blood cells looked very weird. They were going to make her stable and then release her. As Laura listened to the doctor, she thought about how she had lived her life so far. She wasn't that old yet but look at what happened to her so unexpectedly. She was glad that she always paid a lot of attention to her most important relationships. She was never one that was operating out of ego or a need for some sense of power. She cared about her friends and family and always nurtured her relationships. She was glad she had spent her life that way. Her life could easily have ended during this incident. She would feel a lot worse if she had spent her life living according to someone else's values. If she had to die now, she was ready. She did not want to die, but it was out of her hands, and if it was her time, she was ready. She only worried about her father and Edward; how would they get through her passing?

When they released Laura from the hospital, Edward had already purchased tickets to return to the United States the same day. They agreed that despite this happening on the trip, their time there was magical and something neither of them would forget. Edward loved how the whole city was based on and surrounded by art. The food was great, and the people were warm. Hopefully they would get a chance to come back there one day.

Back in Annapolis, Laura had already gone to the hematologist and her internist to follow-up on all of what happened. The news was not good. The hematologist said that for some reason her blood cells were not behaving normally and after all the tests they did, they could not find the reason why. He was concerned that perhaps she had picked up some kind of infection at some point that her body had not managed to fight off that was wreaking havoc on her blood cells. They seemed to fluctuate so it was also hard to predict whether they would get better or continue to drastically get worse. The doctor's only advice was to keep monitoring it, but he told her that since the condition was rare, he could not guarantee that she would have a good outcome. Laura and Edward took in the news and decided to be stoic about it. Laura believed in the quote about the last thing people had a choice over was their reaction to things that happened in life. When there was nothing else a person could control, they could still control their reaction.

Laura felt like her body was not the same. She was surprised that she needed to deal with something like this but then reminded herself of all the kids all over the world that were sick from the beginning or hungry from the beginning. She did not want to be negative about the situation. Edward felt devastated when he heard that the doctors could not predict what would happen to Laura, but he was never going to show that to Laura. They let Brittany know about everything that was going on, and a part of Laura wanted to stop working at the coffee shop. She felt in her bones that it was time to take things slower. She wondered whether that would be okay with Brittany. She could sell her share of the business to Brittany. After asking her about that, Brittany was happy to continue the coffee shop without them and to purchase Laura's interest in it. She said she would get her new boyfriend involved in it, but that she would miss them and that there would always be a place for them at the coffee shop. Brittany was completely understanding about the situation and felt a little daunted by the fact that she would be running the coffee shop initially alone, but she had lived long enough to know that life was never predictable. Laura felt grateful that she had gone into the coffee shop business with Brittany since Brittany had always been so reliable and understanding. They decided they would talk later to figure out all the other details. Laura was grateful to have such a person in her life and knew that it was not common. Brittany also told her that she wanted to see her as soon as they could make it work out.

Laura knew she needed to adjust her normal behavior to the changes that had happened. She could not be as active as she used to be and found that she tired a lot more easily. Instead of pushing herself through the pain as she had always done before, she decided to honor her body and take breaks when she needed them. Everything seemed to progressively get worse when she didn't do that. She had good days and bad days and knew that she would need to adjust to all of it. She wasn't sure what the rest of her life with Edward would look like, but for the time being, Edward was doing all the cooking and cleaning and would bring her a cup of herbal tea every night after dinner. He would stare in her eyes and tell her he loved her and that everything was going to be okay. Laura decided not to tell her father about her condition because it would worry him too much.

Chapter Thirty-Nine

It was a partly cloudy day in Annapolis, and Laura could hear that there was a strong breeze outside. It was a Saturday morning, and there were the sounds of lawn mowers outside and birds chirping. Laura decided to start making a vision board. She needed some sort of help figuring out what the rest of her life would look like. She wrote down inspiring phrases and put inspiring pictures on it. One of the phrases said, *your most important relationship is with yourself.* One of the pictures she put on her vision board was a picture of two people in love walking down a path in a forest. She didn't want to be done with life and dreams yet. She still wanted to have goals and things to look forward to, but the problem was that her body seemed to be breaking down.

As she sat creating the board, she thought of the healing center she considered creating with Marie. That would be too big of an undertaking now given how her body felt. She would need to let Marie know, and maybe Marie would find a way to follow that path since she sounded very interested when Laura talked to her about it. Without doing something major like that, Laura wasn't sure what else to include on her vision board, which wasn't how she had always been. Life certainly had different stages though, and a person changed with each stage.

"Honey, you fell asleep!" said Edward. Laura must have fallen asleep on the couch as she was working on her vision board. She opened her eyes realizing how odd it was for her to sleep during the day.

"Yes, that was weird but definitely refreshing." Edward brought her the medication the hematologist prescribed for her. He was taking care of her almost all the time since they got this news. Laura could never have predicted any of this.

When they printed their Barcelona pictures, Laura arranged them in a beautiful, silver photo album her mother gave her a long time ago. She didn't want all her pictures to be digital. She liked flipping through photo albums and touching the picture itself. She took the time to look at each picture in detail. She wished there was a city like Barcelona in the United States. In one of the pictures, Laura and Edward stood hand in hand by a fountain with the sun shining down on their hair with wide smiles on their faces as a passerby whose name was Carlos took their picture. She remembered that moment very clearly. Right before the picture was taken, Edward told her that without her in his life, he would not want to live.

"Honey, it's funny. I always wanted to focus on being independent and not a typical woman from the past that revolved around a man. It seemed to me that women had come far from those days. In the end, though, the most important thing in my life is you. I think you feel the same way though, right?" asked Laura. If Edward felt the same way, then it wasn't just the woman who was revolving around the man. They were revolving around each other, and that was different.

Edward told her that of course it was the same for him. Laura felt bad for all the women in the world who were revolving around a man and trusting him with their whole lives when it wasn't reciprocated the way it was with Edward. Many times, she felt most women were in that situation. She saw so many of them in life and when she was practicing as a divorce attorney. She was grateful that she had Edward and hoped that all women would find someone like him or be brave enough to stay alone.

Chapter Forty

Despite all the struggles and change, Laura felt free in her heart. She fulfilled her life's dreams. She risked; she loved; she went through her own illness and the illness of many important people around her. She made changes even when she was scared to make them. She enjoyed her life and even if she died tomorrow, she would not have any feeling of regret. This spiritual type of freedom encircled her heart and seemed that it would protect her from whatever else life would bring. She didn't know how else to think of it because it wasn't total freedom; there was no such thing. She saw past all the basics of life after her experiences and was sure that wasn't something a person could just wake up one day and do. It took a lot of different experiences, many of them bad, to get to that point. Maybe if she ever opened the healing center with Marie, they could focus on that topic. How much better it would be if more people in the world sensed this internal freedom regardless of their circumstances.

She was grateful for all of her experiences and very glad that she had not remained in Duck, North Carolina, not having risked enough in life. She would have been a stifled person without all the experiences that gave her the strength and wisdom she developed. She didn't know what would happen tomorrow or what would happen to her health, but she felt a peace inside that was from knowing she was connected to everything around her. She felt peace because she lived a passionate life surrounded by people who loved and uplifted her.

On Sunday morning, Laura and Edward went to a yoga class in town then got on a boat and went into the Chesapeake Bay. They relaxed their bodies at the yoga studio, and it was time to relax their minds. Maybe they would make it to Gilpin's Waterfalls later that day. The waterfalls were a reminder of the beginning of everything and of canyoning in New Zealand; those falls ultimately plunged her into something totally new. She went down the twisty road of life led by her heart and her bravery, and it brought her to this beautiful place. As the boat breezed through the Bay, there were no more thoughts – just love, freedom, air, and water.

Made in the USA
Middletown, DE
14 February 2025